S0-CPF-856

The Hong Kong Affair

The Gordons

DOVER HILL PRESS SAN FRANCISCO

All of the characters in this novel are fictitious, and any resemblance to actual persons, living or dead, is purely coincidental.

Cover by the noted artist, Jerold Bishop

ISBN: 0-9643324-3-4
Library of Congress Catalog Card Number: 98-73558

Printed in the United States of America
First Edition

By The Gordons

DOVER HILL PRESS

THE HONG KONG AFFAIR
UNDERCOVER CAT (THAT DARN CAT)
FAMILY UP IN THE AIR

DOUBLEDAY

RACE FOR THE GOLDEN TIDE
NIGHT AFTER THE WEDDING
ORDEAL
CATNAPPED!
THAT DARN CAT (reissue of UNDERCOVER CAT)
THE INFORMANT
THE TUMULT AND THE JOY
NIGHT BEFORE THE WEDDING
UNDERCOVER CAT PROWLS AGAIN
POWER PLAY
UNDERCOVER CAT
MENACE
OPERATION TERROR
TIGER ON MY BACK
CAPTIVE
THE BIG FRAME
THE CASE OF THE TALKING BUG
CASEFILE: FBI
CAMPAIGN TRAIN
FBI STORY
MAKE HASTE TO LIVE
THE LITTLE MAN WHO WASN'T THERE

For precious friends...

Doby and Dr. Bill Hillenbrand
Ruby and Hugh James
Cynthia and Matthew Rattay

Chapter 1

The crumpled, coffee stained letter was written on that kind of thin, sleazy paper designed to save on airmail postage. The postmark was a smear that could barely be made out to read Hong Kong. It began: "Dear Gringo, By the time you read this I will be dead."

Tall and thin, Dave Anderson had been racing through the morning mail. His fingers now stopped in a still-life frame. He recognized the scrawling penmanship, which overlapped one line with another until the words were scrambled, as that of Mac Dunleavy. He could never forget that writing, no more than he could forget the best friend of his life.

There had been the time when they would sit evenings in a hash house, exhausted after hectic, grueling and often frustrating hours of working murder and gang warfare cases for the *Los Angeles Times*. Mac would slouch in a favorite booth, a big, strapping man with a smile that could con everyone from secretaries to felons, a smile that belied a computerized brain and a machiavellian mind. He would down shot after shot of vodka. Across from him would sit Dave with a cup of coffee growing cold, alert eyes bright, missing nothing.

They were a strange couple who disagreed on everything from womanizing to abortion. With long hair, a heavy black beard and rumpled clothing, Mac looked like a panhandling bum. Dave was clean-shaven, his hair cut in the style of the day, his trousers pressed. Mac was a chain smoker. Dave had never started. Mac couldn't speak a sentence without using obscenities. Dave thought they were the language of the lazy who couldn't be bothered finding the apt word.

Once they discussed how they possibly could be friends. Mac had found a newspaper story about a psychiatrist who had analyzed the attraction of opposites. Mac took glee in reading it. "He says you want to be like me. You want to swear and look lousy and sleep around but you're afraid to because of what people will think. So you run around with me and get a vicarious thrill out of it."

Dave thought that over. "Could be."

Mac laughed. "Nothing to brag about."

That had been years ago. Dave had gone from the police beat to become one of the *Times*' most respected foreign correspondents, the kind of journalist who wrote those long in-depth pieces that no one had time to read except retirees, and even they had no interest in Namibia or Eritrea. Yet the *Times* built a reputation for foreign coverage that in time rivaled and sometimes outdistanced its New York namesake. Dave had been shot down covering the civil war in Angola, barely escaped the Khmer Rouge in northern Cambodia, and was slashed across the back of his neck by a boatman on the Mekong River as he fled Laos.

He rose in the esteem of his *Times*' editors and wangled a promotion for Mac to foreign correspondent. Sometimes they wouldn't see each other for months but when both were in town, they would get together for dinner. Mac would bring his current girlfriend, always a different one. They were never floozies, one just out of law school, another a bank teller, and others a college professor, a nurse, a realtor. They all had his philosophy of immediacy. Never love. Love was frightening, love was possessive. Enjoy the passion of a weekend. The next Friday night, pick up another nymph, another stud. They had only two gods, career and lust, and which took priority varied with the time of the week.

Dave would bring his fiancee, Laurie. Mac would say, "How long you going to sleep together before you figure you got it right and get married?"

Dave would cover smoothly. "Don't pay any attention to him, Laurie. He's a slob and always will be."

Laurie would sit bright-eyed, amused. "It's fun to watch the animals perform. What a crazy world."

The truth was, they had never been intimate. They came from homes where parents were loved and their attitudes about morals and ethics respected.

God, what a life they would have had if she had only lived. On a dark night, a drunk driver...and dreams neatly stacked exploded into shards that in time even his shocked memory could barely piece together.

Maybe it was Laurie's death. Maybe he was burned out after six years in the field. There were several maybes that were pushing him one gloomy day in June, the most miserable month in Los Angeles, when he tendered his resignation. He was restless and weary of taking assignments in the backwoods of the world. Since his high school years, he had been stubbornly independent. He wanted to be on his own. Plus, he could see himself years down the road, growing old and being displaced by younger talent. With some exceptions, journalism was a young person's game. The new ones would tolerate, even respect an old geezer but "please don't get in our way."

However, all of this was not the decisive factor. For years he had dreamed of setting up a global news service — World Coverage — which would concentrate on what goes on behind the scenes of a major news break.

The *Times* offered more money, more vacation time, and up to a point his choice of stories to cover. As usual, his editor brought flattery into play. He told him he was "brilliant," one of the best newsmen the *Times* had ever had.

But what would happen when his health broke, as it did for many correspondents, brought on by eating strange foods, going without sleep for days on end, working in floods and hurricanes and disease-ridden countries, standing firm with bureaucrats who set up road blocks to keep him from the story, taking the heat when angry politicians descended on him, risking his life in riots and guerrilla warfare, drinking too much to blot out the horror scenes, calling a girl friend or a wife from 10,000 miles away to wish her a "Merry Christmas."

Another factor was weary disillusionment. While he was working his guts out to verify facts about a story, the competition was quoting "well informed sources advised today..." These "sources" could be hunches on the part of a correspondent or a publicity release from a government agency or spokesperson. Television news was more of a culprit than print.

And then there were the handouts, the publicity stories offered correspondents by the hundreds. The news set-up in every major capital was such that the journalists were dependent on these releases, even though many served as propaganda for a person or cause. A good reporter, if he had the time — and that was the crux, there was never sufficient time — would wade through them and then verify the facts. Often, you found the competition, with damning disregard for ethics, running with a half-baked story.

The truth was that the thousands of publicity and public relations people the world over wrote a good part of every day's news, from page one through the financial and sports sections. One could go through a newspaper or news broadcast and easily pick out the "planted" stories. Journalism, he believed, had fallen to a low valley, and television was the harlot, more so than print.

By coincidence, Mac left at the same time. He was offered an executive position, with double salary, by a large insurance company. He hadn't anticipated he would suffer a traumatic shock. He was required to shave, cut his hair, and remove his turquoise earring. He felt naked. "I've never been so humiliated in my life. This is the end of the independent spirit and signifies the collapse of civilization."

In time he rose to vice-president and then later quietly slipped away to Hong Kong amid rumors of a financial scandal.

"...By the time you read this I will be dead."

Dead of what? Cancer...suicide...murder...?

Dave raced through the letter, not stopping to unscramble words. There was mention of a girl by the name of Ming Toy, a wife, selling a sampan. But no clue about why Mac thought he would be dead. He couldn't be much more than 38. He took care of his body with the Biblical fervor of looking after a temple. Not that he would know about such scripture.

At the tap on the door, Dave looked up, annoyed. Marge came in, his secretary at World Coverage, a little on the heavy side at 52 who went about sniffing out diets with all the diligence of a bloodhound on a possum trail. The difference was that she never found the possum.

He had had his choice of two secretaries, one in her late twenties who could have modeled for a magazine cover, and Marge who could have passed for a mud wrestler. He chose Marge because she knew the business and could guide him through the shoals. He could depend on her. Instinctively he knew she would be fiercely loyal. And she was so efficient that if he asked for the name of a client in the checkered brown jacket who had come in a week ago she would come up instantly with the name, company and address.

Dave said, "Give me 10 minutes, Marge, please." She nodded in understanding and left. She knew him better than he knew himself and he knew that. Once he had heard her briefing a new secretary at her desk just outside his office. The door was ajar.

"He's not what he seems. He'll ask you to do something and say there's no hurry but don't you believe him. He wants everything done yesterday."

The girl broke in. "I heard he was a soldier of fortune."

"No, a foreign correspondent. A big difference although he's got a couple of scars to prove going after a story can be scary. Oh, yes, be business-like. Don't be cute or flirtatious even if you don't mean anything by it.

"All in all, he's a neat guy. I wouldn't work for anyone else. He's thoughtful and courteous and I don't know how many times he's helped someone around here that's sick or has a family problem. He thinks it's a crying shame we have anyone in this country who doesn't have food and a place to sleep, and that it's about time we kept some of those billions home that we hand out all over the world."

Dave went back to the start of the letter which was scrawled on both sides of one sheet.

"I want to ask a big favor of you, Gringo." The nickname, Gringo, came from the time a General in Mexico City, irate over a *Times* story, called Dave a Gringo. Mac never let him forget.

"I am leaving you a sampan I own. I have a girl, Ming Toy, who runs it to ferry tourists around the harbor. That is not her name but she uses it since tourists can remember it better than her Chinese name.

"I am sending you some money and hope you can come to Hong Kong and sell the sampan. It is not a law but ancient Chinese custom says the girl goes with the sampan. Would you see that the next owner keeps Ming Toy on? She has been good to me and I want her taken care of.

"My wife, Heather, can look after herself. She is very capable. If you come, you might want to talk with her. She can tell you about me. I'm not the same Mac you knew but who is as the years go by? We had some great times together, didn't we, old friend? I wish we could go back.

"You are the greatest, Gringo, the greatest. Maybe we will see each other some day on the other side."

He signed "Mac" as though it were an effort. He had started off with bold, regular strokes that gradually dwindled, like a pen about to go dry.

Finished, Dave sat numb. How many years had it been since he had seen Mac? Mac had never returned from Hong Kong and the gossip was that if he did, he would be indicted. Dave didn't care. Mac was his friend, no matter what.

And Ming Toy? He had never known Mac to look after a girlfriend once their affair was over. He assumed she was a girlfriend although it would seem odd that, if so, he would suggest Dave talk with his wife. Perhaps Heather didn't mind. He had known wives who didn't. Once the marriage was blown, the wife might prefer to stay on the payroll, so to speak, and ignore her husband's concubines — even content that she didn't have to continue sexual relations with a man she detested.

The sampan part intrigued Dave. He remembered once in Hong Kong years ago visiting a sampan harbor across from Kowloon. People lived and died on the little boats. They were homes to many thousands who cooked their meals and slept on them, even in typhoons. He wondered what kind of a financial arrangement Mac had had with Ming Toy.

The money arrived the next day. Five one thousand dollar bills, wrapped in a thin sheet of paper and enclosed in a regular airmail envelope. Quickly, he stuffed the bills in his pocket. He felt guilty of money laundering.

More money followed, in $5,000 segments, always in an airmail envelope. One was marked for the foundation for children Dave had set up in Laurie's name. Throughout the years, Mac had gone out of his way to help kids, usually those in the ghettos. Dave was touched that in a time like this, when he was dying, Mac would remember Laurie.

The amount climbed to $60,000. He had no idea what to do with it. He feared the money had come from drug running, smuggling, prostitution or worse, and that Interpol or a hit man might be tracing it. He grew paranoid. On the street he would stop suddenly and glance back to see if he could surprise someone following him.

He would ask Marge to book him to Hong Kong. He didn't like at all the idea of taking off to sell a sampan and find a girl a new job, if the new owner did not want her.

But for Mac he would go anywhere any time. Mac had saved his life once. He owed Mac one.

Chapter 2

Dave remembered vividly that horrifying night in Cambodia some years ago.

He and Mac, on different assignments, had met in Bangkok. At the time, little news was coming out of Cambodia. At least three guerrilla armies were fighting for power with their own private armies, supported by China, Vietnam and other nations. Most of the war was away from the big cities and out in the countryside and the jungles. All parties reported military victories but no one knew for a certainty what was happening. Yet the great powers, especially the United States and France, were vitally interested. Even though Cambodia was a small nation geographically, it bordered on Thailand and might be a threat one day to that country, and all of Southeast Asia, if a belligerent government came to power in Phnom Penh, the capital.

The Khmer Rouge was the worst of the warring armies. From 1975 to 1978 they had ruled Cambodia and put to death an estimated one million of their own people through torture, execution and forced labor in an attempt to reconstruct their society along radical lines. It was murder on a mass scale second only to the Nazi death camps or the Kurds killed by Saddam Hussein in Iraq. Bodies and skeletons were stacked like crates on "the killing fields."

For several days Dave and Mac talked about entering Cambodia from Thailand at that point where the Khmer Rouge dominated. The possibility that it would be a dangerous mission did come up but was quickly discounted. If they obtained advance permission then it was to be assumed that there would be no difficulties. They had followed this procedure in other parts of the world. Like other guerrilla forces, the Khmer Rouge would consider that any news coverage, even if unfavorable, would help bring their cause to the notice of statesmen and financiers.

Eventually Dave made contact with the Khmer Rouge through a bar in Bangkok. One hot, muggy day they entered Cambodia from the Thai side, walking across the border north of Poipet, near the old road to Siem Reap, site of the Angkor Wat ruins which thousands of Americans and others had visited in another era.

They slept on the ground that night. They heard people moving about them over a narrow, rocky trail. Night birds screeched as if to threaten punishment if they didn't move on. Twice they heard a shot and once the piercing cries of a woman.

Mac slept soundly but Dave shifted his body incessantly over the hard ground. He worked out in his mind the exact moves they would make the next day, in accord with a plan outlined by a contact inside the Khmer Rouge, a plan sketched out on paper and delivered to them at the bar.

He thought of Laurie and the accident. All over in minutes. You get up in the morning and all was well. You climbed into a car, not knowing by evening time you would no longer be here. There was no appeal before Death, no delays to discuss the hows and whys.

The next morning they persuaded a farmer to take them on an ancient wide-bodied truck literally wired together, to a village where they would meet a liaison from the Khmer Rouge.

For hours they sat, as instructed, under a big palm tree in a village that had known much history and misery. A 14-year-old girl stopped to talk with them, to put her sparse English to work. She wore a plain white blouse and a dark skirt, the uniform of a high school student. She was in sandals, and the tan on her legs stood in for hosiery. She had that spontaneous vivaciousness that could win anyone's heart.

"I Thai," she said right off. "Cambodian no."

They asked where they could spend the night.

"My house. Mother take pleasure if come you. Got go now. Late for school. Come back after school. Bring food."

She went off to school.

By four o'clock that afternoon they realized the liaison was not coming. For the last few hours, they had talked with people who were courteous but cautious. As with most dictatorships or countries in turmoil, the citizens were too fearful of punishment to be frank. Dave thought to himself how few Americans appreciated freedom to talk, to express their views.

As the heat of the sun waned with the coming of nightfall, the sidewalks and streets filled up. Little groups gathered here and there. The talking, whatever it was about, was heated. Men shouted at each other.

Dave noticed a little later there were no women or children about, only heavily-armed men who sneaked glances their way.

The two were growing ever more apprehensive when the 14-year-old came running up, breathing heavily and her hair askew.

"They kill you! Hunt you soon! Say you spy for Prince Sihanouk."

Immediately they were both on their feet. Prince Norodom Sihanouk was an American favorite and an arch enemy of the Khmer Rouge.

"How do we get out of here?" Dave kept a tight grip on himself. He had a reputation for never panicking.

"You swim?" she asked.

They nodded.

"Follow me." She headed for the jungle, not too far away. She walked at a steady pace until they were swallowed up, then she broke as fast as the heavy growth would permit. As they tried to keep up with her, they heard a volley of shots.

She paused, listening. "They come. Must take path."

She veered to the right and they were caught up in a mass of vines that tugged at their feet, trying to lasso them, vines that they had to hit hard to break through, vines that stung their faces. This was her country and she traveled the trail with ease. Born to concrete sidewalks, Dave and Mac continued stumbling and weaving. Dave's heart was pounding. He could hear it. His breathing was that of an Olympic runner.

There was a cloying, sweet-odored stench that blanketed and soaked up the heavy sweat that covered them. The trail was so narrow that the growth scratched and stabbed their bodies, and threatened to box them in. Overhead birds screamed at them. Once a few feet away they spotted a big cat. "No worry," she called back. "No like people. No taste good."

That stopped Mac. "Thank God for gourmet cats."

The trail dropped fast and a couple of times their shoes skidded and they went down as if k-oed by a boxer. The girl never looked back. She knew from the scuff of the soles they were not far behind.

They came to a picture postcard river, the width of a coliseum. Across the river was Thailand. They heard men behind them shouting orders as they broke through the jungle growth.

The jungle ended about a hundred feet from the water, sheered off evenly as far as they could see by a mighty knife. The three were now in a mud slough that sucked at their shoes and threatened to pull them under. They lifted one foot at a time, their speed reduced to a crawl. They headed for a lone, massively built tree with a trunk so thick no one could put his arms about it, and which spread its limbs far out over the water.

The girl said, "Must go. They kill me if see me help you."

Dave grabbed her to offer a $50 US bill. "Thank you, no." Dave insisted but she was adamant. "Me Christian. Do one good deed each day."

And she was gone.

"Damn!" Mac said. "She's right. You know that, she's right."

Dave took a quick look at Mac. It was so unlike him. Years later, whenever Dave thought of her, he wished some day he would have a daughter like her. They would never see each other again, and that was sad, but so like life. You have a flash encounter with someone you could love or adore and that's it, only a memory that grows faint with time.

Shortly after they took refuge behind the tree trunk, the first bullets splattered about them. Then three armed men emerged cautiously from the jungle trail they had just come over.

"We've got to make a stand," Mac said. "They'll pick us off if we take to the water. You got a gun?"

Dave shook his head in the negative. Mac continued, "I'll hold them at bay." He had a .38 Colt in hand.

Dave dropped his clothes to his shorts, then took the .38 and reloaded the chamber while Mac shed his trousers, shirt and shoes. Instantly, they were attacked by mosquitoes the size of bees.

If the enemy were at all professional, they would know how many weapons the two had and how much ammunition. If Dave and Mac fired sparingly, the killers across the way would figure they were low on ammo. Then the hunters would bide their time until the two either made a run for the jungle or took to water. Either way, a sharpshooter could put them away.

Dave's first shot scored, wounding a man who was hastily carried off by two others back into the jungle.

In the few glances Dave had, he noted the assassins wore gray workman's shirts and dark trousers. They looked like peasants which they might be. Somewhere, though, there was a mastermind plotting the strategy and procuring the hardware.

Next, Dave saw four men appear at the jungle's edge, barely concealed by the growth. On command, they put down a barrage of firepower. Several shots hit the tree.

Dave held his fire until he saw a pinpoint flash of light or determined by the sound where the gunmen were standing. He was so harassed by the mosquitoes he could scarcely hold the gun steady.

Mac said, "We've got to move. We don't have the ammo to hold out." He estimated they had about 60 rounds.

Dave handed Mac the .38, reloaded again. Mac got off a couple of shots but there was no reaction. He had missed.

Then, in flashes of seconds, Mac saw a man only a few feet away from Dave. He had a weapon dead set on Dave. He had slipped up the beach on their blind side.

As the man squeezed the trigger, Mac hurled himself on Dave, felling him. The shot the assassin aimed for Dave tore into Mac's shoulder. In the same second, Mac fired, hitting the gunman at close range in the chest. The killer dropped quietly without a word.

Mac turned him over. He was only 17 or 18.

Mac exploded. "Damn 'em!"

Fire again crossed over from the jungle. They were going to wear them down. On his feet again, Dave asked, "Where did they hit you?" Blood was spilling from Mac's shirt.

"Just a flesh wound," Mac said. "No problem."

"I'm going for the water. You move down river a mile and I'll get a helicopter to pick you up at sunrise."

"The hell you will."

Dave looked across the river, a raging torrent. "You can't make it."

"The hell I can't!"

Dave produced a hand grenade, pulled the cord, and with a mighty heave hurled it into the jungle at that point where several shots had come from. "That'll slow the bastards down."

The result across the way was panic, screams, barking dogs, yelling, and a barrage of fire power.

Mac headed for the river. Dave grabbed him. "No, Mac! No."

"Get your hands off me!" He slipped into the water and was lost from view. Blood trailed him on the water's surface. Dave followed, both swimming under water until they had to surface to gulp for air, then plunged down out of sight. The river was flowing fast and they had to struggle to stay a direct course.

They were about half way to the other side when the attackers advanced to the water line. They got off several bursts of automatic fire but were short by a few feet. Mac's wound was telling on his strength. He was floundering, gasping for air, and a burst of blood stained the surface around him a dull red. Dave, too, was gulping for air and his strokes were short and lacked punch.

"Come on," Mac yelled. "We're about there."

On the other shore, they dropped exhausted and never moved. A boy with a ratty looking dog came along, saw them, and dashed away yelling. No doubt sounding an alarm about an invasion.

By a half hour later they were sitting up, and shortly afterwards stumbled across a refugee camp. A nurse bathed Mac's wound, treated it with neurogene, and gave him several antibiotic capsules. "Sorry, we don't have many. Maybe these will do you until you get to a doctor."

The nurse told them about a village 20 miles distant where they might find food and clothing.

On the way, Dave said, "If it hadn't been for you, I'd be dead."

Mac shook his head hard. "Too much...shooting...people dying..."

Dave said, "Make love, not war.

Mac could barely talk. "You got it, baby."

That was five years ago.

Chapter 3

The morning after the letter arrived from Hong Kong, a depressing drizzle fell over Century City from a sprinkling system barely turned on. It was the first rain of the fall in Los Angeles and cars careened around on the freeways in the oil coating that had accumulated during the dry, hot summer.

"Mornin', Mr. Anderson," said the attendant as Dave pulled into a dark, foreboding, subterranean parking area. "Looks like we're in for it. A million dollar rain."

Dave nodded. "How's the son?"

"Got a job yesterday and getting married tonight. Told him to take it easy and get a little dough ahead but the kids these days, they want the works, car, TV, refrigerator, without working for it. Not like in my day."

Dave smiled. There was some truth to that although each generation echoed, "Not like in my day."

Marge was waiting in his office to brief him on reports that had come in during the night. World Coverage offered a weekly newsletter to many thousands at $500 per year plus $300 an hour for handling special requests, and there seemed to be a steady stream of them.

In some ways the coverage was the same as that of a news service. The focus, however, was different. The subscribers fell into three principal groups: (1) arms merchants and their money men who wanted to know about the credit and stability of their customers, (2) rebel and independence movements that were interested in a rundown on the geographical area in which they were either operating or planned to, and (3) legitimate businesses worldwide that requested detailed analyses of everything about a certain nation or area. The corporate clients in this category included IBM, General Motors, Mitsubishi, Hitachi, the oil and pharmaceutical companies, and other international businesses.

Dave had 17 top journalists at key points around the world filing dispatches reporting the news behind the news that seldom got a play in the daily press or the network evening shows. The television pictures of tanks rolling by or guerrilla gunfire in the mountains rarely answered the question: Where are they getting the money? Who is supporting this coup, and what do the backers stand to gain? On another front, who are the thousands of propagandists and lobbyists who are working the streets and alleys of Washington, D.C., London, Paris, Tokyo, Beijing, and other capitals, and who pays their bills?

Such coverage had cost more than he had anticipated. As fast as the money came in, World Coverage gobbled it up. There were times when all the money he had was the cash in his wallet. He would have to put the trip to Hong Kong on his American Express card. Yet despite financial problems, he retained his enthusiasm.

He was in his shirt sleeves. A tie and dark jacket hung nearby, in case a client called. His half-circle, oak desk was dotted with curios from his foreign correspondent years: a carved ebony elephant from the King of Thailand; brass "dogs" from a Chinese statesman; a spread-eagle Kachina from Hopi country in Arizona; a prayer wheel from Tibet. Alongside one wall near him was a long, low teakwood "chest" on which sat a luxuriant philodendron. He had bought the "chest" in Bangkok only to learn later that it was a coffin. Not until then did he understand the woodmaker's final remarks. "Not right for you. You much too long." Marge was constantly after him to get rid of it.

Now, slouched back in a huge leather chair that threatened to engulf even his tall frame, he asked Marge about her teenage daughter who had undergone surgery.

After two years, Marge was still uncomfortable with any delay. She wanted to brief him and get on with the day. "She's much better. She was thrilled with the flowers you sent her. First time she's had flowers."

She ran that sentence immediately into another. She referred to a fax. "General Kamil in Cairo wants an update on the Sudan. Chances of a coup in Khartoum, how strong is the support of the public for the rebel army in the South, the inflation rate..."

Dave interrupted her. "Get Rashid on the phone for me. We'll put him on the next plane out of Beirut for Khartoum, and afterwards I'll talk with the General."

She continued, "A bank in Istanbul is asking about the Kurds in Iraq and where they're getting their money. The bank wants a study of Kurds under age 30 to find out how many are serving in a guerrilla force, and how many more might be recruited."

He ran a hand through his dark, full hair. The Middle East was a problem, too many countries, too many ethnic groups, too many passions inherited from centuries before. "Perhaps Vladamir in

Moscow..." He scratched that one. "A Russian might be looked on with suspicion. I tell you what, an American might be best. What's Stevenson doing?"

"She's in Sri Lanka...in Colombo."

"That can wait. Forward a copy of the fax. Tell her while she's doing it to cover all of Kurdistan."

"That's a rough assignment for a woman," Marge said. "They're a chauvinistic people."

"Stevenson can handle it." Eight months ago he had hired Ramie Stevenson, twenty-five, a graduate cum laude from the Annenberg School of Communications at the University of Southern California in Los Angeles. She was the kind of woman World Coverage needed, very deceptive, with a quiet, soft-spoken approach, the look of an angel, slender, blonde, attractive, but with a rough, tough mind that hung in there, boring away, getting to the core of any subject she tackled. She would find Kurdistan a problem, he knew, since it was split up geographically, part in Iran, USSR, Turkey and Syria as well as Iraq.

And so it went for an hour. A few orders were simple. A U.S. senator asked for a rundown on Belize in Central America. Probably for a scuba diving trip under the guise of a fact-finding mission. A New York public relations firm asked for a current report on the Sorbs, a "nation" in the middle ages, now a people between the Elbe and Saal rivers in Germany. Dave recalled that one of his correspondents had traced the financing of the Sorb movement to a millionaire Texan, a Sorb himself, who dreamed of some day somehow restoring the country and becoming its George Washington.

Finished, Dave paced about, a caged bear. He could no more sit still than a three-year-old. "Would you phone Thomas Cook Travel Agency in Hong Kong and ask how you go about selling a sampan and how long it might take. First, though, see if you can track down a woman in Hong Kong by the name of Heather Dunleavy. Mrs. Mac Dunleavy. Get her address and phone number."

"What does Mac stand for?"

He had no idea. Years ago Mac had dodged the question.

"Hello." The voice was low, non-committal.

"Mrs. Dunleavy. Mac Dunleavy?"

"Yes."

"I'm Dave Anderson. Your husband may have told you about me. We were close friends for many years."

"He told me."

He hesitated. The voice was not hostile but flat. After all, she was in grief.

"He wrote me...asked me to come to Hong Kong."

"I know."

He wanted to hang up. Anyone that unresponsive. "Was he ill for a long time?"

"He never complained."

"When did he pass on?"

There was a long pause. "I don't remember."

"I understand."

"When will you be coming?"

"Friday evening. Your time."

"Please..."

"Yes?"

"Talk to me first. There is a problem."

"Of course."

"As soon as you arrive?"

"I'm due in about 5 p.m. your time. I'll check into the Regent Hotel, freshen up, and if all goes well, be at your home between 8 and 9."

"Don't bring anyone."

"I won't. God bless."

"He hasn't been any help."

"Who?"

"God." The phone clicked.

He sat replaying the tape. When you had lost a loved one, you didn't react normally. You were a robot going about the daily ritual scarcely knowing what you were doing. He should know that.

Still...

He was being too critical. Laurie had told him, "Look, Dave, don't go around analyzing everyone, what they say, their body language."

Still, when someone died, the exact day and hour were forever impressed in the memory.

He recalled vividly the night he lost his mother, his hand clasped to hers in the hospital, no relative around, his father having died two years before. A kindly nurse came and put her arms around him and told him it was time to leave. He walked sobbing all the way home, a mile, to an empty house. Later an aunt came and told him his love for his mother was an "obsession" and he'd have to get over it. He walked out, never to speak to her again.

The next month he was graduated from Tucson, Arizona, high school, tenth in his class. He worked his way through the University of Arizona as a waiter at the Varsity Inn, a hamburger joint. He was pledged to a fraternity but that lasted only until he discovered that a pledge was a serf.

That was the beginning of a lifelong rebellion against the establishment, a strange rebellion. He believed in the Constitution and the political system but he resented that same system for stacking the cards against the little people, from the IRS to a confusing, complex bureaucracy of red tape that often slammed the door on justice.

He tried out for the football team and at the first practice was flattened. They carried him off on a stretcher. The next week he was back and in his junior year was quarter-backing the team. He became a folk hero when he passed 70 yards in the last 10 seconds to defeat the University of Southern California. He was equally the scholar. In his senior year he was awarded the School of Journalism's highest honor.

On graduation he had two job offers, that of an assistant manager at a supermarket and as a reporter at *The Daily Citizen.* He took the reporter job. From the time he was 12 and sold an article for $20 to Parade magazine, he was determined to get into writing if there was all of that big money around.

At *The Citizen* he encountered a city editor who resented computers for the simple reason he couldn't do much shouting across the newsroom when he was editing a print-out of a story. The second day, he did yell at him, "Hey, kid, a female is a woman, not a lady. How the hell would you know if she's a lady?"

He worked a year without a promotion, then wrote a letter to the publisher of the Los Angeles Times, advising him he would be arriving Monday morning to go to work for him. That approach had worked before for a friend, Mark Finley, who was to become one of the greats in journalism.

With only $10 on him, Dave walked into the publisher's office.

"He knows you're coming to work here?" the bright, young receptionist asked.

"Yes, ma'am, he does." That was the truth. Dave had written him.

She picked up the intercom, then a visitor came out of the publisher's office and Dave walked in with the receptionist screaming after him.

"I'm here to go to work for the greatest newspaper in America...," he said, raising his voice, "and I'm one of the best reporters you'll ever have."

The receptionist was still ordering him out. The publisher sat stonyeyed, glaring at him. "You've got a gall."

Dave agreed. "I wouldn't call it that, sir. I would say I have initiative and I'll get stories for you that no one else could."

The publisher relaxed slowly, then laughed. "Phone Joe," he told the receptionist, "and tell him I'm sending a brash kid down and he can kick his butt or do anything he wants but I think the kid has something."

Dave Anderson was on his way.

Over the intercom, Marge said, "The South China Post on five. Bill

Lee."

Dave pushed five. "Dave Anderson."

"Bill Lee here. We heard you were coming to Hong Kong and my editor has assigned me to interview you."

Dave felt his way. "I'm a newspaperman like you, Mr. Lee, and newspaper people are not newsworthy."

"You are. I was one of your admirers when you were stationed in Bangkok for *The Times*."

"Why don't we forget the interview," Dave said, "but get together for a drink or something?"

"When will you be arriving, Mr. Anderson? I could meet you at the airport."

An inner alarm sounded. "I haven't finalized my plans yet."

"Where will you be staying?"

"Something has just come up that I have to attend to. Could I call you back in say 15 minutes? If you'll give me your number..."

The phone went dead.

Questions raced about. How did anyone know he was Hong Kong bound? Only Marge knew—and Mac's wife. Why would anyone want the time of his arrival or where he was staying?

A short time later, Marge came in. She had a wicked smile. "I called Thomas Cook and talked with a nice young Chinese about the sampan. He was obviously very amused and said he didn't know anything about sampans, that he preferred Lexus cars, but he would find out what he could. He called back and reported that there is no market for second-hand sampans and it might take you considerable time to sell one, if ever."

Dave returned her smile. "That's the opinion of a Lexus guy who wouldn't know a sampan from a rowboat. I don't think a sampan's going to be much of a problem. The problem will be getting someone to take on Ming Toy."

Maybe not so much of a problem. Chances were that she was petite, slender, well curved, and a sex bomb that exploded on command.

Mac would not have had any other kind of a girlfriend.

Chapter 4

Dave Anderson settled down for the 14-hour plus trip which would include four movies, two dinners, two breakfasts and one snack. That should keep the cattle contented, he thought. As for himself, he badly needed sleep. But air travel had advanced to the point where the flight attendant came around frequently with newspapers or drinks or forms to fill out. The attendants, too, had changed. At one time they had been young, slender, smiling. Now, though, the airlines transported entire mobs, including drunks, trouble-makers, countless families with screaming children, and an occasional hijacker. So most lines, especially those flying overseas, employed mature women who could handle emergencies. On this trip, he noted one who looked as if she had been a bouncer. Another could go trick or treating at Halloween without wearing a mask.

Aside from Ming Toy, Mac's wife was on his mind. Had Mac settled down? Dave had had another flamboyant friend whom — when the showdown came and he had to choose a mate for life — tossed aside the playgirl for a staid, intelligent, clever woman, who would help him in his climb up the ladder, one who would know what to say at a company meeting, and not say.

He welcomed the excuse to visit Hong Kong. These days he seldom got out into the field. The work of supervising 17 correspondents kept him desk bound in Los Angeles, and he did not like it. He was not a desk man.

For many, Hong Kong's status was confusing. He had written this note for World Coverage's next newsletter:

> FYI: Hong Kong (pop. 5.7 million) was a British Crown Colony, founded in 1842. Turned over to mainland China (the People's Republic of China), July 1, 1997. The Tiananmen tragedy took place in Beijing, the capital of Mainland China, 1300 miles north of Hong Kong.

Especially did he want to learn on this trip what the man in the street really thought about the takeover by mainland China. Millions of words had been written about the thousands of wealthy and middle class Chinese who had fled. Some said at the rate of one thousand a day. They had established themselves in Canada, Australia, Singapore, even Costa Rica, and the United States. The new taipans had taken over Monterey Park, a few miles from Los Angeles, where 55 banks served their money needs. With an inner smile, he remembered a bumper sticker he had seen recently, "Will the last American to leave Monterey Park please bring the flag."

He slept through the two movies. He achieved this minor triumph by glaring at the flight attendant the first time she awakened him. After two glares, she obviously decided there was nothing she could do with this curmudgeon.

The pilot took the plane over the South China Sea to the Hong Kong International airport on the partly man-made island of Chak Lap Kok, a 20-billion-dollar engineering and technological marvel.

The first time he noted the handsome, young Chinese was while standing in line at Immigration. Dave was having difficulty juggling three cases and an attache one when the Chinese, whom he thought might be a student, picked up one and said, "If I might, sir..." He was standing directly behind Dave who thanked him.

They started chatting with Dave taking the lead. The youth was nicely suited with a white shirt and string tie. His dark hair was cut short and well brushed. He spoke impeccable English. He said he was returning from San Francisco where he had a sister. He lived in Hong Kong with his parents in the New Territories, the mainland part, and hoped to find a job in the computer field.

They passed before the Immigration Inspector who checked an index to determine if they were on a wanted list. Next came the mechanical baggage mover carrying luggage past a Customs Inspector who politely asked if the two were carrying contraband. He motioned them on without opening their cases. Dave needed to change U.S. dollars and the youth assisted by computing quickly in his mind exactly how many HK dollars Dave should receive.

They walked out into a wide, long runway with crowds on either side waiting for friends or relatives. They left the building and veered to the left where roped off "runs" accommodated queuing up for taxis. The Chinese insisted on helping him with his cases into the cab. They shook hands and Dave thanked him. The young man added, "The taxis here are all metered and cheap. The drivers won't try to cheat you because you can report anything like that to a control office — the phone number is right there — see it? — and the driver will lose his license."

Dave checked into the prestigious Regent Hotel, the new show place of Asia. A short distance away stood the Peninsula, the grand old dame of another generation, another century, keeping its legends and character while moving into the modern world. It was to Hong Kong what the Raffles was to Singapore or the Waldorf Astoria to New York City.

An assistant manager showed him to an expansive room where the bath was all marble. Already waiting for him was a vase of gladiolas. A fruit bowl would be arriving shortly.

The side facing the harbor was all glass, a breathtaking view that encompassed sampans, junks, cargo vessels, lighters, naval ships, bedecked tourist boats, a "grocery store" serving foreign ships, and about everything man had conceived for water travel, except canoes. A storm was brewing. On the other side was Hong Kong island with its jungle of skyscrapers, ten or so Manhattans jammed together. Most were lighted. Here billions of dollars changed hands every day, where the Heng Seng stock market was the thermometer for one of the world's great financial centers. Huge advertising signs, some brightly lighted, dotted the harbor side across the way. He scanned them quickly. Fuji, Canon, Nissan, Citizen.

"No American or English?"

The manager shook his head. "The Japanese have moved in."

He asked the manager how he might go about finding Ming Toy. The manager said the hotel would locate her. He didn't seem to think there would be a problem. That was the advantage of staying at a hotel in Asia. The guest was someone special.

He showered and while dressing, ate a sandwich that Room Service had brought. He hurried, knowing he was running two hours late on his appointment with Mac's wife.

Chapter 5

Outside he showed the doorman the address. "That would be the Wong Tai Sin district, sir."

The taxi driver spoke mutilated English. "Take Waterloo Road. Nice homes. Rich people."

He fancied himself a tour guide. "American Baptist College, see? Seven thousand students. TV stations, see, TVB. You watch? No? Lion Road Tunnel soon. Shatin Central. You Shatin race track? Take you tomorrow? No?"

They were creeping bumper to bumper. Trucks and buses reduced the taxi to a toy. An ambulance tried to enter from a side street. The stench of exhaust fumes was overpowering.

And then all traffic stopped with a jerk. Truckers screamed, motorists sounded their horns. It was bedlam.

"What's happening?" he asked.

The driver shouted back. "Look. Man chase duck."

A peasant-type Chinese waving a broom was chasing a waddling duck up ahead. The noise leveled off.

The taxi driver said, "Duck, much money to man. Everybody know. Stop, let man get duck."

Another minute and the peasant cornered the duck. The truckers sounded horns in applause. For everyone, it had been an adventure, a break in the deadly monotony of negotiating the equivalent of a Los Angeles freeway. Dave thought, "In Los Angeles, no one would stop for a duck."

The driver said, "Here, duck have right-of-way."

The taxi driver turned the radio on high. A girl was singing in English with a background of traditional Chinese music, what Americans would term sing-song. The driver then got a friend on the two-way radio and shouted above the music. There was much laughter and Dave grew concerned. They had come a long way.

The driver sensed what Dave was thinking. "Soon. Soon."

A few minutes later, he pulled the taxi up over a curb to get out of the way of the traffic. "There. Two doors." The low white building was two-stories of flats (apartments). Dave paid him what the meter showed and added a HK dollar. He asked about getting a taxi back to the hotel. "No need phone. Step out on curb. 15,000 taxis in Hong Kong. One come, chop chop."

Her flat was on the ground floor, the second in from Waterloo Road. A potted geranium stood on a window air-conditioner. In the background, a gossamer lace curtain fluttered. He tapped with restraint, not wanting to disturb the neighbors at this hour, forgetting that the music of Hong Kong's counterpoint symphony filtered in from the street. Truck brakes whining, the growl of tires, gears grating. Day or night, it mattered not, the symphony would rise to thunderous heights, then drop occasionally to a low, monotonous drum roll.

The aging, dark door, which had suffered from repeated paintings and humidity, opened with a creaking, as far as the short inner chain would permit. In the faint light, he saw a beautiful face that seemed sculpted in marble.

"I'm Dave Anderson. Sorry I'm late but the plane —"

"Show me some identification."

He remembered the voice from the telephone conversation. A little husky. Definitely on edge, not hostile but not friendly, either. He fumbled for his wallet. He waited to open it until three rough-looking men had passed behind him on their way to another flat. He had been told at the hotel that this was a "good area." Still, back home there were stabbings and murders in even the best neighborhoods.

He offered a California driver's license which she studied, then released the chain.

"Sit here," she said imperiously.

The living room reflected money, copies of works by Gaugin and Monet on the walls, the chairs upholstered in embroidered velvet, the floor covered with a deep Oriental rug, several carved Chinese tables placed with a decorator's touch, and a child-size ebony elephant by the window.

Obviously, the most expensive fixture in the room was Heather Dunleavy. The eye went straight to two large diamond earrings. Somewhere in the 40-to-50 thousand range. She wore them well since she was tall, about five feet ten. She was in a black cheongsam with a slit-teasing skirt that when she sat, rode high on a bare, well-shaved leg. The collar was Mandarin, China's great gift to womankind, the most fashion conscious invention ever devised. It had a certain beauty, yet hid aging neck lines.

Her alabaster face was a fascinating study, a too-prominent jaw, lips that set too firmly, eyelids streaked black as if she had run a marker over them. Her shiny blonde hair cascaded well below shoulders that needed no padding.

Mac, he thought, you got what you wanted, didn't you? An elegant, $500-a-night hooker. "I want more than sex," Mac had said. "I want class, too." Class was a favorite word — and Heather Dunleavy had it.

"Sit here, please," she repeated. He took a chair opposite her, not more than a foot away. Her tone said she was accustomed to placing men where she wanted them. He was conscious there had been no "thank you for coming" or "did you have a good flight?"

He said, "I'm so sorry about Mac."

The same old bromide. He never knew what to say in time of death. A Christian believed in the after life, and by saying "I'm sorry" could infer he had no faith. After all, shouldn't it be a joyous occasion? The mind might rationalize but the heart never did. Death was a void, never to be filled. There would be no homecoming at an airport a few months hence. There would be no postcards, no phone calls.

He said now, "I 'feel' for you," and meant it. He added, "I'd like to help. Do something. You said you needed help."

"The problem has been taken care of."

That jarred him. He still had the romantic longing of male youth to help a girl in distress, the knight-on-a-white-horse kind of thing riding to rescue Guinevere. Only this was no Guinevere.

In spite of her manner, he sensed fear in her bright blue eyes.

She asked, "Did you bring the note Mac wrote you?"

He tensed. "No...no. I didn't think to. I didn't know you would want to see it."

"I'm to accept your word he wrote you?"

He felt anger surfacing. The words were accusatory — but the voice was still flat and husky, as if they were discussing vegetables to buy at a market.

He said evenly, "After Mac came here, we kept our friendship going by exchanging cards at Christmas with short notes. We never missed a year — and he never mentioned you until this time."

No matter how hard the serve, she returned the ball, "Mac was a very private person."

"How long had you been married?"

"For some time."

He thought to cool the situation. He said quietly, "I thought that as two Americans in a foreign land we might find common interests, common ground."

She sat up straight. "I am not an American, thank God!"

He was taken aback. "English?"

"Hong Kong."

"I don't understand."

"I was born here. My grandfather was an American. That was

back in the days of the great taipans...the Swires, the Jardines, Matesons."

For the first time, a trace of emotion slipped in, pride in being a native of Hong Kong.

The silence seemed endless. He caught a whiff of strong perfume. Mac should have told her that a whisper was romantic, to overdose was cheap.

He launched another attempt. "I came here tonight, Mrs. Dunleavy, because I felt a closeness to you. Because Mac was my friend, I wanted to help if I could. If I couldn't, perhaps we might comfort each other, recall stories about Mac, but somehow —"

She interrupted. "I detested the man. I don't know why death suddenly exalts someone to sainthood."

He sat forward, getting ready to leave. "I see. I had no idea."

He hesitated, then plunged ahead. He had nothing to lose. "Mac left me a small inheritance, a sampan. I need to talk with the sampan woman, one Ming Toy. Do you know where I could find her?"

Her eyes flashed. "I don't discuss my husband's affairs."

He was not about to be dismissed. "I've come a long way. I'm terribly tired. Fourteen hours in the air. I want to ask a few simple questions...because Mac was my buddy. Was he ill a long time? Did he suffer? Where did he die?...and where was he buried? I'd like to take some flowers to his grave."

She rose. The talk was over. "You come here, Mr. Anderson, and treat me as if I were on a witness stand. I will not tolerate such cross examination. You come here pretending grief and grill me like a common criminal."

Another time, with another woman, he might have felt shattered. He might have been convinced he had gone too far. But as she walked to the door, straight backed, he knew she was a master in the forensic arts. She had given him no information. Her answers were cleverly skilled to make him appear the scoundrel.

At the door, he said quietly, "I know you're in serious trouble and you're going to be needing me. You know where I'm staying."

He had no basis for the statement. He was guessing. If she were caught up in something, and events he knew nothing about took a certain course, she might call him. He had used that artifice many times in many countries. There was the situation in Tegucicalpa, Honduras, with a prime minister who wouldn't talk. In that instance, Dave had said, "I know you're in serious trouble with Washington." That same day he was called back. It was a deception as old as journalism.

As he returned to the street, he passed a shrub as tall as a person. He was too engrossed at the time but later remembered a movement, one of those little details that the mind files away, for recall if needed. And then he was on the sidewalk, caught up in a stream of people. An older man in the dress of a scholar came along tapping a cane, perhaps blind, and Dave side stepped him. He remembered a young woman in drab dress, holding a baby, jostling him, forcing him to step into the street. Later he would learn that this seldom happened, that no matter how great the crowd, Hong Kong people skillfully threaded their way without bumping another.

He raised a hand and within minutes a taxi careened up, brakes moaning as it came to a sudden stop. He opened the door, heard a distinctly loud gun shot, heard people screaming, and suddenly was alone as everyone scrambled for cover. There was a sharp break in the air as a bullet passed him and rammed into the cab door a few inches from his hand. He whirled about, and saw his assassin partially concealed by the tall shrub. He was so hidden that Dave could not recall later whether he was young or old or how he was dressed or what make of weapon he had.

He heard the taxi driver shouting at him to get in, get in. Then there was another gunshot from a different direction, and again he turned. Later he could not understand why he hadn't entered the taxi rather than standing there, but in the shock of the moment, not doing the logical thing, although his mind was screaming along with the driver.

He turned about to spot a young Chinese on the sidewalk with weapon raised, aimed at the assassin in the shrub. The young Chinese fired four shots in rapid succession. Then Dave tumbled into the taxi, and the driver pulled away from the curb with his hand on the horn, and the car door swinging wildly. Another minute and they were lost between two gargantuan trucks, and the driver slowed. Righting himself, Dave pulled the door closed. The taxi driver shouted back, asking what it was all about. Dave answered he didn't know.

Only one thing he knew for certain about the whole frightening episode was that the young Chinese firing at the assassin was the same Chinese who had helped him with his luggage when he had cleared Customs and Immigration and changed his money.

Chapter 6

Shaken, Dave walked unsteadily into the hotel. All the way back, he had tried to grapple with the situation, make some sense out of it.

A young police officer in uniform met him half way across the lobby. Unknown to Dave, the taxi driver en route had phoned 999, the emergency police number.

"May I talk with you, sir?" Dave nodded and led the way to a cluster of lounges. The time was almost midnight and few guests were about.

The officer, in his mid-twenties, identified himself as a constable attached to the Organized Crime Bureau. He reported that a police team was at the scene of the crime. He asked Dave to relate chronologically his movements in the Wong Tai Sin area, leading up to the shooting.

"I don't know what it's all about," Dave said. "I haven't been here long enough to have any enemies and I wasn't associating with anyone in Los Angeles who had any ties with Hong Kong."

"If you will. sir," the officer said, "start with the time you left the hotel, where you went, why you went there, whom you talked with, and recall anything that took place when you were on the street waiting for a taxi."

Dave got hold of himself and narrated step by step his activities. Without being asked, he gave Mrs. Mac Dunleavy's name and why he called on her, and the fact that the party opening fire on the assailant had helped him with his luggage at the airport.

Later, back in his room, he got out his diary. He had kept one since his college days. "Someone tried to kill me tonight. At first, I thought it was mistaken identity. But that couldn't be, since someone had assigned me a bodyguard. Who would do that — and why? Why would I need a bodyguard? Was Mac in drug running or something like that — and someone thought I was coming to take over his business? I have all kinds of questions?..."

The one undisputable fact in this maelstrom of nightmarish thinking was that someone had attempted to kill him — and might try again.

As the night wore on, he found the harbor scene pacifying. There was a contentment about the rhythmic lapping of the waves, the eerie sound of a far-off fog horn, the sampans, junks, lighters, ferries and tramps riding through the dark, thc ghostly forms of other boats in the distance, the dark, brooding cloud mass over the Peak, where the "old wealth" lived, and at dawn the silvery shine of sunlight on the walls of skyscrapers.

He was too exhausted to shower or shave. At 7:30 a.m. he tuned in the CBS Evening News which had run back home the day before, and afterwards CNN News which had become as universal as Coca Cola and McDonald's.

Somehow he found himself in the downstairs restaurant, which was glassed-in from ceiling to floor, affording a fabulous view of the harbor. On the wide promenade between the hotel and the water were Chinese of all ages twisting and stretching their bodies and moving arms in all directions. They were doing the tai chi chuan, 108 choreographed, slow moving exercises, centuries old, with such interesting names as "Finding Needle at Bottom of Sea" and "Grasping the Bird's Tail." Some had headsets, the same as joggers in other countries.

With alarm he noted that almost any guest could take a shot at him. Casing them, he scanned one table after another. Then he realized the waiter was asking for his order. "Coffee and rolls," he said, as if this were any ordinary day.

He was sipping the coffee when he saw the concierge approaching. With him was a Chinese in his mid-thirties, in a gray suit that had been slouched in too much. He wore a white shirt with unbuttoned collar and a droopy tie with a sleepy-eyed dragon on it. The most distinctive feature about him were squinting, roving eyes that stopped here and there long enough to snap a mental picture.

"I beg your pardon, sir," the concierge said. "May I present Inspector Peter Yeung of the Organized Crime Bureau. He would like to have a word with you."

Puzzled, Dave rose. Detective Yeung openly sized him up.

"I am sorry to inconvenience you, Mr. Anderson," the Inspector said, "and if this is not an appropriate time I could return."

Dave shook his head. "Have you had breakfast?"

Inspector Yeung smiled, "My son — he's four — wakes me up for breakfast every morning. He's a happy little bugger. But I will have coffee, thank you. It's very good here."

He nodded outside where the shadow boxers were. "I read that your American athletes don't think much of the value of our doing tai chi."

Dave recognized the technique. Lull the mind before delivering the punch.

He played along. "We're a huff-and-puff nation. If we don't fall exhausted...half dead...then we haven't exercised."

Yeung pushed his chair back and settled himself comfortably. He took out a pack of cigarettes and offered it to Dave who refused with thanks. The Inspector proceeded to put a match to one. He was a chain smoker, as were many Chinese. Dave thought: We Americans spend millions trying to stop drugs from entering our country from Columbia and Asia's Golden Triangle, yet we export drugs (cigarettes) by the millions to Asia.

The Inspector was saying, "The constable last night took down the basic facts which you most graciously gave him, and I have one or two questions. Perhaps I should call them observations."

He cleared his throat. He had an asthmatic condition. "Before we get into that, I have nothing to report yet about the investigation. We are pursuing this case intensely."

Dave nodded, waited.

Yeung continued, "I know you must be concerned about your personal safety. I have managed for the hotel security to escort you to and from your room, and for either the desk or concierge to notify you if any party has asked to see you. You will not, of course, open your door unless you know who is there. You can come and go anywhere in Hong Kong in the daytime since we have a small area and a big population — five and a half million — and our streets are crowded, and anyone even showing a weapon would be pounced upon. I would suggest that you go out at night only when you're with people — and people you trust. The point to remember is this: Never find yourself alone at any time anywhere. Is this acceptable, Mr. Anderson?"

Dave nodded. "I can take care of myself. I was a foreign correspondent for years, and in some tight spots. But I will take every precaution."

"Please do."

Yeung glanced at notes he had taken from an inside coat pocket. "The constable reports that you arrived in Hong Kong a little after seven, took a motor car to the hotel, and then went to call on Mrs. Mac Dunleavy whose first name is Heather. Is that correct, sir?"

Dave nodded and Yeung continued. "The fact you were talking with Mrs. Dunleavy within three hours after you arrived, would suggest to me that there was considerable urgency. Would you please tell me what the urgency was?"

Dave tensed. "I don't know. A few days ago she told me on the phone — I was in Los Angeles — that she needed help but when I talked with her last night she said the problem had been taken care of."

"And the problem, what was the problem?"

"She didn't say."

"You didn't ask her?"

"I may have. I don't remember. Anyway, she didn't tell me. She wasn't about to tell me anything. It was not a satisfactory conversation."

Yeung studied him while lighting another cigarette. Flushed, Dave thought, I probably look guilty. I always look guilty when I'm denying something.

Yeung continued. "The officer's notes advise that you were a close friend of Mr. Dunleavy. I should think that his widow would appreciate your interest in assisting her at a time like this."

"She didn't."

"You had never met her before?"

"I didn't know she existed before I received the note."

"Yes, the letter. I meant to ask about that. We wouldn't want to inconvenience you but would it be possible, Mr. Anderson, for us to see it?"

"I'm not sure what I did with it. It may be on my desk and if so, my secretary will fax it to you. If it's in my apartment, I wouldn't know where to have someone look."

Yeung set the cup down. "I've found that most business men have a system for handling their correspondence. I would assume that yours would be fairly heavy."

Dave found himself sweating. "I do for business. This one was personal."

"Of course."

Yeung paused to snap a mental picture of a quite gorgeous-looking young woman seated two tables from them who was focusing on Dave.

Yeung turned back. "I must write up a report, of course, and I don't have the date Mr. Dunleavy died or the cause of death."

Dave took a deep breath of resignation. "I asked his wife and she couldn't remember."

Yeung showed surprise. "I must say that is a very unusual lapse of memory. But never mind. I'll check Vital Statistics."

He turned over a page of the notes. "The officer advises that you informed him that you came to Hong Kong primarily to take possession of a sampan that your friend, Mr. Mac Dunleavy, willed to you."

He looked up and Dave nodded. Yeung continued, "I am curious and I don't mean to be overly so, but your airfare, Mr. Anderson, cost more than the sampan is worth. Furthermore, you could have sold it with a telephone call."

Damn this infuriating detective who was soft-spoken, yet took obvious satisfaction in weaving his nasty webs. Here, Dave was a victim, who could have been slain last night, and he was being treated as if he were involved in a criminal undertaking. He was about to explain about Ming Toy, and his deep friendship for Mac, but decided to end the conversation. Anything he said could be misconstrued.

Yeung sensed his anger. "I must apologize. I am most sorry to have inconvenienced you. You have been gracious about commenting on my observations. One more, please, and then I will leave you."

He took his time lighting another cigarette. "About this sampan woman you call Ming Toy?"

"Yes?"

"Would you please ring me up after you have talked with her — and let me know what you discussed?"

Dave said angrily, "I haven't located her."

Yeung took a slip of paper from his pocket. "Her name is Chan May Li, and if you will give this note to the anchor man on the dock of the Floating Jumbo restaurant at Aberdeen..."

He handed the slip to Dave. "Any taxi can take you there. It's quite a sizable barge. Miss Chan will come by in the sampan at 7o'clock this evening. You can thank the hotel for asking us to find her. And now, I will take my leave. Thank you, Mr. Anderson."

Chapter 7

At 5:30 Dave asked the doorman to summon a taxi. At the time he should have known something was amiss. The cab did not come the usual way. It moved out on signal from a herd of parked Rolls Royces and Mercedeses. Too, the doorman failed to instruct the driver about the destination.

"Aberdeen," Dave said to the driver, raising his voice. Mentally he kicked himself for that. Why did a person traveling in another land speak louder than normal, as if increased volume might help a native understand English better?

"Yes, sir," the driver said in good Chinese English, which was a slight Chinese accent and a slight London one, an intriguing combination.

Dave stiffened in the back seat to study him. He was young — just about everyone in Hong Kong was young, with better than 50 percent under 30. He wore an open nondescript shirt, pressed gray trousers, and gold-rimmed glasses. He drove with confidence.

He said, "The Shum Wan pier? Opposite the Floating Jumbo restaurant?"

Dave was edgy. "How did you know that?" he snapped.

The driver glanced in the rear view mirror. "Pardon me, sir, I should have introduced myself. I am Sergeant Tang Shunyan of the Hong Kong Police. Inspector Yeung thought you might be safer if I chauffeured you to Aberdeen and back."

Dave muttered to himself, Safer! The cagey Inspector has taken me prisoner. He's going to find out how Ming Toy and I react to each other, if we are strangers or co-conspirators. Well, for the present, I can't do anything. But what U.S. president was it who sneaked out on the Secret Service mornings at the White House to jog around Washington? Harry Truman. That was the one. Well, from here on I'm going to pull a Harry Truman on the Hong Kong Police.

The driver continued. "I will not be present when you talk with Ming Toy. You will not see me — but I'll be close by and on the watch if anyone tries to kill you."

Dave offered no comment. It was the faintly indifferent way the Sergeant said it that irked him, as if a murder was too commonplace to break up the monotony of the day's work.

Dave thought to himself, my basic trouble with the police is that I have guilt feelings. I have never mentioned the $60,000 in $5,000 increments that Mac mailed to me. I have withheld evidence that might mean something.

Several times he had been about to refer to the money but if the police knew, wouldn't they jump to the conclusion that he was actively involved with Mac in something illegal? People don't go around mailing money in such sums unless they are laundering or hiding it.

Even he himself could not explain away the $60,000. Except for the $5,000 Mac had sent for Laurie's Foundation, Mac had not mentioned the balance. At the time, Dave had thought that someone would claim it, probably his widow or Ming Toy. Or had Mac sent it as a gift to him and not wanted him to know that it had come from a questionable source?

He had been further perplexed when earlier he had taken a telephone call from a woman, obviously Chinese and mature, who invited him to a luncheon meeting the next noon of the Taipan Association, an exclusive, prestigious organization of Hong Kong's wealthiest business leaders. It dated back a century or more and was commonly known as The Club.

She had called him "a distinguished American." He answered that he was flattered, and she concluded to his astonishment that he had accepted. A limousine would be calling for him at 12:30 p.m.

He had not the faintest idea why the Taipan Association would invite him. He had no status, no money. The Club was so oriented toward England that it invited only celebrated English and Chinese. It considered the United States another colony.

Now Dave sat back in the cab, unexpectedly relaxed. He might be in a time bomb but it was moving slowly, smoothly through the heavy traffic, driver cautious, the day a warm one but not overly so. At the thought of meeting Ming Toy, he experienced a pleasant surge of anticipation. He could not picture what she would be like. He hoped it would prove a happy occasion, one Mac would have liked.

Outside the air-conditioned car, Ming Toy's world floated by. Teenagers, laughing, talking excitedly, but polite, courteous, restrained, like America's teenagers of decades ago. A young woman with a pole across her shoulders, with enormous baskets on each end, delivering food and drinks to offices. Well-dressed business men, ties and coats, shoes polished. Construction workers supported only by a bamboo scaffold ten stories high, bamboo poles knotted at the ends with rope. Workers would trust no other kind. A woman hawking toys on a street corner. Youngsters sitting on the sidewalk reading "Superman." Workers in their black "fragrant" cloud linen, stooped, moving fast in sandaled feet. Little old women with feet the size of five-year-olds — the result of having them bound tightly since childhood in the old China custom — taking mincing steps. A man with a slaughtered hog thrown over his shoulder. Jeweled women and amahs shrunken by hard work. Neatly-dressed children with their school books. Men in felt slippers and women in cotton pajamas. A tailor carrying a new suit. A cat asleep in a cardboard box in the midst of shoppers. A letter writer at a tiny table on an alley corner, busy with his brush. Bamboo poles jutting out of high up apartments with clothes drying in the wind, and other poles strung with fish drying for dinner, being "smoked" by the sun's rays.

Under questioning, the Sergeant told Dave about the sampan people. They were disappearing, he said. Not more than 19,000, he thought. The young people were taking to land. More money, more excitement, more opportunities. Yes, he said, the sampan people had to register with the Marine Department, and were given numbers, the same as with cars. They were licensed as kaido (small boat) ferries and could tie up anywhere without paying a fee. The people shopped for groceries and supplies at harbor villages. They had no mail service.

The Sergeant stopped the car and nodded toward the Floating Jumbo, the size of a football field, four decks topped with a pagoda, sitting on a barge a quarter mile out in the water, capable of serving 2,000 dinners at a time. Thousands of lights added a Christmas effect.

"You take the boat there, sir," he said, indicating a brightly painted shuttle craft bobbing a half block away. "I will park but when you finish, come back and I will be here."

The shuttle was half filled, some twenty customers from a dozen nations on their way to dinner. The boat passed a marine center on the left where junks had once anchored but now million-dollar yachts graced the harbor. Gradually, the junks were disappearing, those flat-bottomed boats with tremendous bat-wing sails and a high poop, the logo of Hong Kong for a century.

At the Jumbo's dock, Dave handed the anchor man the note in Chinese given him by the Inspector. "She will stop over there." He indicated another landing.

Dave paced about impatiently. He watched a very happy little boy climb off another shuttle and suddenly start screaming and sobbing. He had looked up at a gold-and-red Chinese dragon curled around a pole, an immense monster with a ferocious face and white fangs a foot long. The little boy thought the dragon was going to get him.

Then a sampan pulled up to the landing, motor throbbing, water splashing, and a voice called out loudly, "Mister America. Got customer. Back soon. You wait? Please?"

He shouted back, "Yes!" Two older Americans on the boat waved and said something, and the sampan was gone.

So that was Ming Toy at the steering arm in the back, much younger than he had expected, in Levis (501's, she proudly told him later), a coarse dark shirt and a wide-brimmed, straw hat with a three-inch black fringe hanging around the circumference which marked her as one of the Hakka people. Centuries ago they had lived north of the Great Wall but had been driven gradually south. Most lived in Hong Kong in six walled villages, built in the time of pirates and bandits.

He noted the sampan was painted a dark color with a blue curved awning top overhead. As customary, the boat had a necklace of old tires fastened around the outside perimeter to protect it when pulling in to the pier for tying down.

Not more than 15 minutes later, she returned. As he climbed awkwardly down into the boat, she reached out from her seat by the steering arm to shake hands. "American style."

"Wish happiness," she said. Her dark eyes danced in the evening glow, the way Laurie's had, and she had the same outgoing spontaneity.

She piloted the sampan to the other side of the Jumbo and soon they were in a vast field of boats tied up to boardwalks.

"Go to office," she said, laughing. She tied up between two other sampans. "Happy meet you, Mister David. Me call you David. Right? Call me Ming Toy? Right?"

"Right." He felt the tenseness of the last few hours fall away. She was smaller than he had expected, not much more than five feet, and had a slender, hungry-looking body, like many Hong Kong Chinese, not from lack of nourishment but from long hours, hard work. She had glossy black hair knotted at the neck-line which framed an oval face highlighted by a hands-in-the-cookie-jar look.

She turned off the motor, rose and stretched catlike. "Please to sit here." She turned on a weak light bulb. By now night had crept in, interrupted by pinpoint lights across this vast "parking lot." In the adjoining boat, a mother was cooking dinner for two small children over a little burner, and on the other side, a father and his teenage son were repairing a motor.

Idly, he wondered which one would report back to the Inspector. He thought more of the deep darkness, no moon, no stars. He was a sitting duck. He scrunched down on the bench that circled the inside of the boat.

"Mister Mac say you come." She spoke very low and there was grief in her voice. "Mister Mac came, say dying. I cried. Said no, no.

Asked how dying. Said bad disease. I think, cancer. What do you think?"

"He didn't tell me."

She talked fast, all of the packed up feelings of recent days spilling out. "He good man, Mister Mac. Ming Toy love Mister Mac. I sick, need operation. He take me to hospital, pay, bring flowers. Neighbor..." She indicated the woman in the next sampan. "She sick. He take clinic, bring back. She get well. Mister Mac good man."

"I know. We were close friends." His heart went out to her and the feeling surprised him. He lived in a hard world that was not cruel by premeditation or indifference but one in which people had no time for compassion, even though they wanted to help those about them. They themselves were struggling to survive, fearful of what tomorrow would bring, always fearful, especially in the dark, sleepless hours when the problems seemed insurmountable.

"Mister Mac say you come. He say you good man. He say you take care Ming Toy."

"You needn't worry. I will." It was good to have someone need you. Laurie had.

He jumped at a splash nearby. Someone swimming? At this time of night? Fearfully, he listened but could peg no further sound.

He continued, "When did Mister Mac tell you he was dying?"

"Monday before Monday. He come always Monday. We divide money. Here..." She reached under the seat and brought forth a plastic bag stuffed with Hong Kong bills and small change. "Your money. Twelve hundred dollars."

He calculated that would be almost $150 US. He handed the bag back. "It's yours."

She sounded angry. "You take. I honorable woman. I keep record. Your share." She handed him several sheets of school notepaper. She had listed every trip for each day and the sum paid by each person.

"I can't..." He saw the fire in her eyes and relented. She wasn't all sweetness and light.

"When did Mister Mac die?" he asked.

"No know. Monday come, he not come. Called home, wife said he dead. I said, I want come..." She couldn't find the word.

"To the funeral," he put in.

"Yes, what you call funeral. She said too late. I said, want bring flowers. She said too late. She not good woman, I think."

"What business was Mister Mac in?"

"Many businesses. He buy here cheap, sell outside."

"Did he have an office?"

The shadowy form of a burly man took shape on the boardwalk, staring down at them. Dave tensed, preparing to fall flat, his heart pounding. She yelled in Cantonese and he moved on.

Dave took a deep breath. "I live in Los Angeles, far from here."

"Mister Mac tell me."

"I will have to sell the sampan but —"

"No, no!" she shouted. "Why sell? Sampan make much money. Ming Toy honorable woman. You make half, I keep half."

"But I can't stay here. I have a business —"

"No need stay here. I mail money. I honorable woman. You ask. People say Ming Toy okay."

All of his life he had not known how to cope with women who were angry or furious or otherwise emotionally upset. He could handle men. He could tell them to go to hell if it came to that. He could walk out on them. He could threaten them.

"We'll work it out." That was a feeble retreat.

She enthusiastically agreed. "Yes, work out. Keep sampan. You happy, me happy. Mister Mac said you good man."

By now he wanted to send "Mister Mac" to the nether regions if he had not already arrived there.

They talked for an hour. He learned that she lived with her mother in a sampan a short distance away. It had a built-in wooden shelter at one end that protected their beds and possessions. Her father had died in a village, Yongfu, south of Guilin in Guangxi province. Afterwards she and her mother had walked to Hong Kong, some 100 miles, carrying what necessities and keepsakes they could manage.

"How did Mac come to own the sampan?" he asked.

She laughed. "Won it in mah-jongg." Mah-jongg was a favorite with the Chinese, a noisy game played usually with ceramic tile. As the players slapped the tile down, the racket could be heard all over the neighborhood.

"He got me. Old boss make me work for food. Mister Mac gave me half. Expenses first."

"You work for police?" she asked. It was so unexpected, it left him speechless. She continued, "Police say you here. Want see me."

"I do not work for the police."

"You like picture Mister Mac?" On either side of the steering arm hung a picture, one of Mac and the other of a Chinese figure, each draped in red ribbon.

She pointed. "Tin Hau. She goddess. Help boat people. We go temple Poi Toi, thank her. Help boat people much. Stop storms, shipwrecks. Mister Mac, he god, too, no?"

So now Mac was a god.

She continued. "Mister Mac Christian. One God. I Buddhist, one god. But big world, God, Buddha. Need much help. Have many assistants. Tin Hau busy with sea people."

She added, shyly, "Ming Toy like you, Mister David."

Back on land, he walked slowly toward the taxi. He had $1200 HK in his pocket. He felt like a pimp.

Chapter 8

He slept fitfully. It was as if two controls were vying for his brain. One instructed him to sleep, sleep, sleep. The other, to wake up, wake up.

He showered and that helped. He telephoned Marge in Los Angeles. He had to talk with someone. She was ending her day, which was yesterday.

Somehow sanity returned when she gave him a rundown on the day's activities. This was his world. He could make decisions. He was in control. She reported that a British bank had requested a scan on Abu Dhabi, one of the United Emirates. Did the ruler, Zayed Bin Sultan Al-Nahayn (whose oil income was reputedly one billion a year) have the support of his people? Had the failure of the Bank of Credit and Commerce in London, in which he had a 70% interest, endangered him financially? Was he still favorable to the western powers? Dave informed Marge that they had an informant in the neighboring sheikdom of Dubai and to dispatch Rashid, after he finished in the Sudan, to talk with him.

He asked her to fax a copy of the note Mac had sent. "I remember vaguely putting it in the middle drawer of the desk."

"You put everything in the middle drawer."

"You're fired."

"So what else is new?"

He asked her to pay his personal bills. And how was Old Boy doing? Old Boy was his ten-year-old collie. Marge had promised to run by and feed him although Old Boy had never "cottoned" to her.

"He's quit barking at me. Figures I'm from the Community Food Bank."

He felt better. Talking with Marge helped.

He spent the morning in his room. As usual, he had brought papers with him from Los Angeles, letters, reports to read, and newsmagazines. But he found his thoughts wandering. He couldn't concentrate.

He got out his diary. It was like a pacifier. He wrote, "Ming Toy proved a surprise. I had expected a sex kitten and here she was radiating goodness — although one can never tell. I remember meeting a Dallas News columnist in Papeete who had gone there on vacation with his wife — and ended up packing her home and quitting his job for a Tahitian girl who met his every wish, whether it was running to get him a beer or making love any time day or night. I don't understand why Mac would have taken half of what Ming Toy makes. It's not like Mac. Maybe he's changed. The years do that. You meet someone you haven't seen in a long time and they're not the same."

Shortly before the limousine was to take him to The Club, the concierge delivered a note in Chinese that had been left at the desk. The concierge translated: "The Cricket Man has a message for you. Do not send anyone. Pick up yourself."

There was neither a salutation nor a signature. The characters were hand sketched on expensive stationery.

The concierge said the Cricket Man wove crickets out of bamboo shoots. He sat on an old, beaten up chair on Salisbury Road, just beyond the Peninsula Hotel and the Y.M.C.A. He did a brisk business selling his product and when he was idle he wove more.

"He charges $25 HK which is a little more than $3 US," the concierge said. "I know because last week I bought one for my son. He's 10 and been wanting a live cricket but his mother wouldn't permit a live cricket in our house. You may not know, sir, but crickets — live ones, that is — are kept as pets in many homes."

He added, "Nice chap, the Cricket Man."

The limousine was waiting and Dave went off, wondering what could possibly be in the message.

Exchange Square rose tall off Connaught Road Central. Here was housed the Heng Seng stock exchange, one of the world's largest. Farther along, near the old Bank of China tower, they pulled to a stop before an imposing building that looked like a transplant from London.

At the curb a guide was posted to escort Dave inside. They waited a few seconds for the lift, and as the elevator door opened, Dave took a step back in shocked surprise. Leaving the lift was the young Chinese who had helped him with his luggage at the airport and opened fire on the gunman.

Recovering quickly, Dave stopped him. He blurted, "I'm glad to find you. I want to thank you — for saving my life."

The Chinese stared unbelievingly. "I don't understand."

"Can we go somewhere to talk?"

The Chinese started away. "You have the wrong person."

Dave took a step with him, "I'd know you anywhere."

The Chinese stopped, smiled. "You know what you Americans say, all Chinese look the same."

He quickly melted into the crowd leaving the building. The guide said, "Please, sir, we have only a few minutes."

If he had been hit over the head, Dave could not have been more bewildered. He could not have erred. That face would be stamped in his memory forever.

He walked by rote into the lift and left it the same way. The guide entered a door with a modest sign, The Fragrant Harbour Room. Apprehensively, he walked into a place of grandeur, with high ceilings that made it look larger than it was, walls of rosewood over which hung paintings of the great taipans of the past. A thick Oriental rug covered the floor. Twenty tables for four each had been set, covered with hand embroidered table cloths from China, and set with English silver, gold-etched Spode plates and Waterford crystal. Each table had four high-rise handcarved chairs in the Chinese style, black lacquered with velvet seats. In a corner, a chamber group of three played the classics.

Distinguished-looking men in their tailored best, mostly with white shirts and conservative ties, stood about chatting. One quickly came over, "Mr. David Anderson," he said, beaming. "How very good of you to come. I am most honored to be your host, Alfred Kwan. I thought the interview you wrote on Margaret Thatcher some time ago was truly a masterpiece."

Dave corralled his careening thoughts. "Thank you, Mr. Kwan, for inviting me. I am the one honored."

Alfred Kwan was pleased with his guest. He had said the right things. He would fit in. Kwan was in his fifties, fairly tall, well-built though slender, with graying hair turning white, sharp, inquisitive eyes, the smooth skin of a 20-year-old and manicured fingernails. He was the kind of affable and diplomatic financier who would have graced any stock market in the world. He was the cosmopolitan entrepreneur.

"Come," he said. "I want you to meet some of my friends."

Dave thought, I could be back home at the Jonathan Club in Los Angeles. Around him the conversation turned to the same kind of remarks. "I don't think the Japanese stock scandal will affect the market." ... "What about London? Isn't it in for a stiff slide, what with the economy." ... "Something has to be done about the Vietnamese refugees. We can't take in all of Vietnam." ... "Prince Charles had better shape up." ... "Did you know we have the largest facility in the world at Kwai Chung for loading containers. Two thousand lighters working that harbor."

And over and over conversation about the take-over by the People's Republic of China. Would China respect its promise to keep Hong Kong as it was for 50 years?

By now, Dave learned that Mr. Kwan was Managing Director —

the equivalent to CEO in the United States — of South China Shipping, Lt., and consultant for Lloyd's of London, the famous insurance group. He had been graduated from the University of California at Berkeley and taken his masters at "The Farm," as he called Stanford.

"I didn't speak a word of English when I arrived in the States from China," he said, "but when you're young you pick up a language quickly."

Dave talked puppet-like but only half knew what he added to the conversation. His eyes scanned the room. He sat with his back to the wall, a good protective position, but at the same time open to attack.

Back in the hotel, he had thought, what a good opportunity to do a piece about Hong Kong. How much money was being taken out and where was it going? Would the real estate market collapse? Is there a serious "brain drain"? Had the tourist trade, one of Hong Kong's major "industries," dropped considerably?

But while Alfred Kwan answered his questions graciously, nevertheless he cut the conversation short. He had other matters to discuss and he riveted in on them with the same persistence with which he had built his empire.

The first surprise came shortly after salad. "My friend, Inspector Yeung, tells me you knew our friend, Mr. Mac Dunleavy."

Dave nodded, waited.

"Are you taking over his business?" The affability had disappeared.

The entrée, Chateaubriand, arrived. "I don't even know what his business was, Mr. Kwan. We hadn't kept in touch in recent years except at Christmas."

Kwan hesitated a brief, telltale moment. "He was a small operator, in the export business. I knew him only slightly and through a rather unfortunate set of circumstances that I never discuss. He was a gambler, and lost what you Americans would call his shirt. He had a ship go down in the South China Sea. Lost everything...cargo, everything."

He continued, "The Inspector tells me he left you a sampan," Kwan laughed. "Not a very sizable inheritance."

"He wanted me to look after the sampan woman."

"Miss Chan." He repeated the name. "Yes, Miss Chan. I believe she calls herself Ming Toy. She had a little difference with the authorities, nothing major, just a small matter, and Mr. Dunleavy asked that I intercede, which I did. I promised to keep the matter in confidence. I did not understand his interest in the Chan woman. I cannot conceive that he had a liaison with someone so far beneath him."

"She's quite attractive," Dave said.

"I suppose so...but...well, we respect all people here but we do stay loyal to our class when it comes to relationships."

Dave folded the napkin. It was too expensive to be squashed up. "I assume class means money."

Kwan stiffened. "Not so. Class means family, your heritage, who your ancestors were. Right now, I am arranging for my earth burial, an omega type grave up in the Tai Mo Shan country, which will be important to my children. It will be expensive since ground here is scarce and most are cremated.

"First, I must have a conference with my feng shui scholar. In your language, a geomancer, one who is knowledgeable about winds, storms, all the forces of nature. He will instruct me in regard to the direction I will lie, probably in the lee of a hill, facing the sea."

Kwan's piercing eyes studied Dave. He continued, "A century or so ago one of my ancestors was buried in the wrong direction and for years the family suffered misfortunes before they consulted a feng shui master. He found the mistake and my most worthy ancestor was re-buried, and ever since our family has had good fortune."

He saw Dave's skeptical look. "An American or Brit would not understand. Yes, I am a graduate of Berkeley and The Farm, and have made millions, but my heritage — the ancestors who made me what I am — and my family are more important to me than all my earthly possessions."

Dave leaned back, comfortable for the first time. "I must admit I don't understand but I do respect and admire a culture that places value on the important things in our lives."

Dave added, "I do think it's a tragedy that in our western world we don't think more about those close to us who have gone on. I don't mean to honor them just to honor them but to remember the guidance they gave us and the good they did. Our grandparents die and within a few months, we have forgotten them — when they may have shaped our lives, sometimes inspired us, always taught us about caring."

He recalled a quote he had read from Irmagene Nevins Holloway: "The memory of those who were before us is within you; the memory of those who were before us is among us, and those memories are at our door and give us strength, peace of mind and we are thankful."

Kwan shoved back his chair, ready to leave. He was all business again. "By the way, my wife and I will be celebrating our 25th anniversary the end of the month. She's the girl at Berkeley who taught me English and I taught her Cantonese. We'd like you as our guest."

The end of the month. He wants to know if I am going to be here that long.

Dave started to thank him but never finished. The sound was that of a shot exploding, a tremendous crash, and then the walls themselves seemed to reverberate. He dropped to the floor so instantly that there was scarcely movement of body, and in doing so, knocked over the chair which struck like another gunshot. He heard men talking loudly and then their voices were cut off knife-like and there was once more only the familiar murmur.

"I apologize," Alfred Kwan said. "The waiter dropped a tray. The Inspector told me you were in some kind of danger but I had no idea..." He trailed off.

Chapter 9

Never had he been so baffled. Alfred Kwan had not invited him to the luncheon to chat about Mac and Ming Toy and the feng shui scholar. Kwan was definitely not the social type. He didn't bother with anyone unless there was profit or advantage to be gained. He had not built a great shipping empire by entertaining total strangers.

Dave analyzed what had happened since he left Los Angeles. He had been buffeted about by events and people he did not know. For the first time in years he had lost control. He had come to claim a sampan and help a woman. Nothing more.

He had to gain control. He remembered in high school, his mother talking. "Most people just drift. They go willy nilly with the crowd. They do as others do or tell them."

Control. He knotted his fists under the table.

The limousine returned him without incident to the hotel. He debated about taking a taxi. The Cricket Man was only four or five blocks away, up crowded Salisbury Road. He decided to walk.

He was passing the desk when the assistant manager called, "There's a young lady waiting for you."

Dave turned. A smartly-dressed Chinese woman in her mid-twenties was approaching. She was in a belted, summer-print skirt that hugged a waist unbelievably small and a thin blouse that outlined small breasts. She had on dark glasses which might be the vogue in Hollywood but were the exception in Hong Kong. What really would mark her in anyone's memory, however, was a three-inch knife scar on her right cheek which was partly concealed by pancake make-up.

She was smiling.

"Mr. Anderson?" She had a soft, whisperish voice, word gossamers blowing in the wind.

"Yes?"

"I beg your pardon a thousand times for being so bold and brazen — in accosting you without an introduction. I am Felicia Yee and I study at the Chinese University out in the New Territories. We have two universities, Hong Kong University and Chinese University."

He broke in. "Why are you telling me this?"

She looked up at him with bright, beseeching eyes.

"Do forgive me. My professors tell me I must get to the point. I wanted you to know that I am a responsible and trustworthy person. You may ring up Chinese University —"

He started to move on. In the most innocent way, she blocked him. "I apologize for taking your time. I am earning my way through the university by selling information. My fee is quite reasonable. One hundred HK a day with a minimum of one week. That would be $12.82 US."

"Information?" This was a new approach. In Paris, they sold you postcards. In Bangkok, $10,000 Rolex watches for $50. In Mexico City, "ancient" Aztec pendants for $5. In western U.S., homemade Indian arrowheads. "Sorry, no." He was brusque. He pushed past her.

"I will give you a sample. The gentleman in the gray suit over there by the lamp, he is following you."

Dave stopped abruptly. The "gentleman" was a little man reading a newspaper. He had the anonymous look that surveillance agents cultivate. His clothes were muted, his hair long, and his face just one more tossed out of a box of rejections.

"You're crazy," Dave said, resuming his walk.

She followed. "You do need information. This is the information age. Everybody has to have it. You need to know why he is following you and what he's after. If you should want my services, call this number."

She pushed a slip of paper into his hand and disappeared down the corridor leading to the New World malls.

He walked briskly, angry. Just one more of Inspector Yeung's tricks. She would find out where he was heading and what he planned to do. And he would be paying for it. Every day.

To throw the "dogs" off his trail, he did a switchback and entered the legendary Peninsula Hotel where the moguls of Asia and the millionaire tycoons of the western world once gathered, and where spies of many nations still congregated. This day, seated at little tea tables inside a vast ornate lobby were couples from America's Midwest, English ladies who lived on the Peak, and Chinese businessmen and women. They were enjoying tea (no tea packets, please, the very idea was abhorrent), cakes, biscuits, scones and finger sandwiches. After each chamber music number, they patted fingers of one hand on the palm of the other.

He walked swiftly through the milling throng, then back on Salisbury past the Y.M.C.A. He had gone no more than the next stop sign, when he discovered the little man a few steps behind him.

For a moment he stared into a window at a collection of crafts from old China, debating whether to continue, then decided it didn't matter if the little man learned he was visiting the Cricket Man. He wouldn't know what was in the note unless he had already bribed the Cricket Man.

Dave had to wait. The Cricket Man was busy with a very young customer. A little girl wearing a T shirt that reported she was from Chicago had bought a bamboo cricket and was taking a picture of the Cricket Man who was short, roly-poly, and good natured.

When she was gone, Dave looked a cricket over and asked the price. Marge's daughter might like one. While the Cricket Man was wrapping his work of art, Dave whispered, "You have a letter for Dave Anderson?"

The Cricket Man's hands stopped still, then he resumed the wrapping. While he made change, he blocked with his body the view from the street and extracted a letter from under a pad on a little table where he worked. Dave slipped it in his side coat pocket.

"How much?" he asked.

"No charge for postal service. But don't let Mail know I am stealing business from them." He laughed uproariously. "Come back soon. Christmas come, you need many crickets for small fry." He laughed again. "Speak American, no?"

Two doors away Dave struggled through a mob of teenagers buying ice cream cones.

In this melee, he managed to open the letter, and as he feared, the message was in Chinese characters.

He remembered a one-hour photo shop, and inside found an older teenager busily taking in exposed film and writing up receipts. He asked the boy in a low voice if he could take time to read the letter. He slipped a $10 HK bill into the boy's hands.

"Please, sir, this way." He led the way a few steps into a cubicle. He scanned the note before translating. "Will you please keep this in confidence?" Dave asked. "If anyone comes around..."

Until now the boy had been efficient and courteous but reserved. Suddenly he became enthusiastic. He was a co-conspirator in some kind of drama.

"Don't worry," he said in rapid fire English. "I never talk."

Dave handed him $30 HK more.

The boy read. "Very Honorable Sir: I am privileged to invite you to meet me at the Bird market at 9 o'clock tonight. I will take the liberty to approach you since you do not know me. My venerable ancestors wish us to meet and settle a matter of importance in peace and harmony and in accord with the teachings of Confucius. Do not worry about your safety. I will have armed guards with me. If you do not come, I wish Miss Chan happy fireworks."

It was signed: "The Chrysanthemum Man."

Poker faced, Dave thanked the boy and took back the letter. He had decided in advance he would report no development, no matter how much inherent danger there might be to himself, to Inspector Yeung. He would be in sole control.

He asked the boy about the Bird market. It was on a street somewhere off Argyle in Kowloon. The boy had never been there. Birds, he explained, were Hong Kong's favorite pets. There was no living space for dogs or cats, and anyway, they cost too much to feed. Mostly the Bird market's customers were old men, seldom women. Clad in slippers and traditional dark Chinese suits, they came to buy wah mei thrushes, seung see warblers or other singers from mainland China. They cost $150 HK (about $20 US) to $900 HK ($112). Hand carved cages were for sale, too.

Then mornings the senior citizens would take their pets out for a stroll. They would end up for dim sum (snacks) at a teahouse and hang the cage up on a pole over the table. Sometimes they would get into heated arguments over which bird was the most melodious. The Chinese teenagers had their headsets, the same as in England and the United States, and the older Hong Kong citizens their birds. A poll taken by a Hong Kong newspaper revealed that the readers overwhelmingly preferred the birds.

On his way out, Dave saw the little man approaching. Dave blocked him. "I hope you enjoyed our walk," he said. "Too bad I didn't have time to invite you to tea at the Peninsula."

The little man smiled, shrugged and walked by as if he didn't understand English.

Armed guards to protect whom? And what was the meaning of "I wish Miss Chan happy fireworks."

He would place the letter in the hotel safe. He might need it for future reference. He had no intention of keeping a rendezvous with someone he didn't know to talk about a matter he knew nothing about.

Chapter 10

He walked deep in thought, not seeing anyone, as one does in a big city. Then he heard a voice calling out.

"Good day, Mr. Anderson."

Felicia Yee was passing him at an intersection.

On impulse, he whirled about. "Data girl?"

She stopped, turned. That eternal smile. It irritated and captivated him at the same time.

"Happy we meet again," she said. As if it were happenstance, he thought.

"I've got a question," he said. During the walk, he had remembered that once years ago he had been sold "information." It was in Colombo, Sri Lanka, during the Tamil uprising. A hotel bellman had kept him informed on a day-by-day basis about the fighting and had given Dave some of the best series he had ever written. The bellman had intrigued him at the start by saying he was in the "news" business. Now, the computer age had promoted "news" to "information" and "data".

"Too crowded here." She led the way toward a steep hill marked, "Marine Police Station." She found a recess away from everyone under a giant tree. "A question?"

He backed a couple of feet away as if her physical presence might soften him. "How come you knew that little pip squeak was shadowing me?"

"Pip squeak?" She laughed softly. "Good American word. I must remember. I have sources."

"I just picked up a letter." He stared to see her reaction.

Her low laugh was teasing. "I know."

"All right," he said flatly, "I'll make a deal. If you can tell me what is in the letter, I'll hire you."

Of course, she didn't know.

"You mean," she said, "subscribe to my services? Hire is crude."

He had had about enough of her. "Quit stalling."

She sobered. "You are to meet a man in the Bird market at 9

o'clock tonight."

He took a deep stunned breath. How could she possibly know? Unless she had written the note, or knew the party who had, or was privy to whatever was going on. He took a closer look at her and realized he should have sooner. The face was a little too mature for the usual student, with faint ant trail lines across her neck. True, students came in all ages now. But her voice, her attitude and her language were of a woman of experience. She could be thirty. The scar, too, suggested experience, possibly of a sordid nature.

"You win," he said laconically, handing her $500 HK. "Where is this Bird market?" While he had no intention of presenting himself as a sitting duck, he would play along in the hope she might disclose her part in this maddening enigma.

"Beyond the Grand Tower Hotel. Fu Lock street. It's difficult to find. A narrow alley. I'll take you if you want me to. I won't go in and if you don't come out in a reasonable time I'll go home. I won't report it to the police since that is not a part of my services."

"Are you telling me," he asked slowly, "someone's going to take a shot at me?"

Unexpectedly, she was all business. "I supply information. I don't advise. I will give you this much data. You will be in a busy alley. It would be difficult but not impossible for anyone to use a weapon. Maybe a knife, although that, too, would be high risk for a hit man."

He couldn't believe that someone so outgoing, laughing and smiling, could become hard and pragmatic. "You make it sound clinical...technical...cold."

"Facts are cold, Mr. Anderson. The computer is cold, the printout mechanical. We are not living in an age of emotion."

She added, "Except I wouldn't want to lose a new client. Shall I go with you?"

"I'll find it," he said stubbornly, with finality. "What about the pip squeak?"

"Inspector Yeung thinks you might lead him to something important in a case he's working."

"Does Mac Dunleavy figure in it?"

"Yes."

"Look," he said sharply, "I don't like yes-es and no-es."

"I'll make inquiries. Tell you tomorrow."

"Another question."

"Yes, sir." She was so blasted polite. You can't trust a Chinese, a friend had told him. They're courteous while they're picking your pocket. Of course, he had known a few Americans with the same modus operandi.

"A certain party says he wishes another person happy fireworks if I don't show up. Oh, what the hell, you know what's in the letter."

She hesitated. A dark cloud crossed her face.

"Old Chinese custom," she said slowly. "They set off fireworks when a loved one dies to let the spirits know — or something like that. I do not understand the old ways."

A puzzled moment passed and then the situation struck him suddenly and his heart increased its pounding until he imagined his body shaking.

If he did not keep the rendezvous tonight, Ming Toy would die.

"I don't understand." He could scarcely be heard. "I don't know what's happening."

She put a hand gently on his. "You love Ming Toy."

"No, no...but I had a friend who loved her...a little...maybe...I don't know. I promised him I'd look after her."

The silence that followed was loud and unbearable Finally she broke in. "Please...don't die for a friend. A dead friend."

Chapter 11

It was a nether land out of a horror story. A slashing, slanting rain blinded him, turning the world about him into a murky one without shape or distance. The night closed in black and frightening, and only vague points of light bobbed and disappeared and bobbed again, as if carried by lanterns.

He stood drenched to his shivering skin at the Jumbo landing. He heard voices close by and saw no one until the voices were upon him and then they were emanating from ghostly figures. He was listening for one voice in particular. He had returned to the hotel to find a message telephoned in by Ming Toy's cousin. Or so he said. She was in a desperate situation. Could he come at 6 o'clock to the Jumbo landing where they had met the night before?

It was now twenty minutes past 6 and he was growing ever more apprehensive. For one thing, if the rain persisted, the Bird market might not be crowded, and he had depended on that for his safety. That and the little anonymous man. Dave had swung a hundred and eighty degrees, from wanting to lose him to desiring to keep the surveillance going. In case Dave was trapped, the little man might rescue him. Now, though, there was no way of telling if the detective was about.

The sampan hove into sight, swaying like a drunk. Any minute the waves threatened to engulf it. Ming Toy clung with one hand to the steering arm and with the other grasped the anchor pole. He half fell, half slid into the boat. She lost no time navigating out into the harbor. She was shouting something but the words lost themselves in the crashing of the waves. Within a few minutes, she took shelter half way around the Jumbo in an overhang of the restaurant barge. He floundered about as he reached out to tie up the sampan. Here the boat rocked but it was a baby rock, and there was a silence broken only by the distant thunder of the storm.

There were no pleasantries. She was too distraught. She blurted out, "Two men come. Say kill me. Kill boat. Very mad."

When she couldn't go on, he asked, "Did you know them? Had you seen them before?"

"No see. Not Han people. Maybe Mongol. No know."

"What did they want?" He had forgotten he was soaked, that water was running off him as if he were a sponge being squeezed.

"Say Mister Mac owe much money. I say lie. Mister Mac honorable man."

"Go on."

"Say where money? I say what money? They get mad. Hit me, twist arm. Say I know where money is."

Suddenly a yacht seemed upon them, about to crash into the barge. He saw only a white form, then it slid past, within a few feet. He realized how vulnerable they were in the storm.

"Did Mr. Mac leave you any money?" he asked.

"Why leave money? Make much money with sampan. No need money."

He wanted to reach out and put his arm about her. She looked so frightened and forlorn.

"Did they say why they thought you knew where the money was?"

She hesitated. She hated to put it into words. "Say Ming Toy girlfriend of Mister Mac. I shout they lie. They no like. One has gun. Say kill me tomorrow. Blow up boat with me in boat. People think accident."

He did take her into his arms. He felt her quivering body calm. He understood why Mac had loved her, whether it was a platonic love of a friend or the love of the womanizer he was.

"Listen, Ming Toy," he said. He wasn't sure he had her attention and raised his voice. "Do you hear me?"

"Yes," she whispered, clinging to him.

"Look, they're not going to kill you as long as they think you know where this mysterious money is. Tell them you gave me the money and then you set up a time for me to talk with them. Act as if you're betraying me, to save yourself. You've got to be an actress."

"Like Do Do," she said softly.

"Yes." Do Do Cheng had been the darling for years of Chinese movie audiences.

He asked quietly, "Were you in trouble with the police once?"

She broke his hold and sat rigid. "Who say?"

"Were you?"

"Police make trouble. Ming Toy make no trouble." She was angry. The wildcat in her could spring to life so fast.

"What was it about?"

"Poor man. He drowning. Ming Toy save. Police come. Asked why? I said he drown. Police no care. Police make much trouble. No like Hakka. Me Hakka."

"When was this?"

"Tuesday before Tuesday. Long day. Hard day. Much tired. Take sampan out night. Need rest, quiet. Hear man calling. No understand what say. He Vietnamese. No speak Chinese. Get him in boat. Take to land. Ming Toy feel good. Saved man."

"What time of night was this?"

"Two, three hours before come up sun."

"Was he from a Vietnamese refugee camp?"

"Man drown. You no ask. No time."

"Did he give you money?"

"Gave reward. Police say pay. Help man escape. No pay. Like tip."

"How much did he tip you?"

"No remember. Maybe two five bills."

"Two $500 HK?"

"Maybe. Not sure. Give half Mister Mac. He talk with friend. Police make no more trouble."

He wanted to emphasize the seriousness of the crime but at the same time not hurt her. She had been through so much.

He said softly, "Some people would say you arranged in advance for a certain payment to pick up this man...perhaps he waded out to the sampan...and take him to a crowded area where he could hide out."

"Who say?"

"Some people."

"Tell some people go hell. Ming Toy did good thing. Mister Mac like do good. Make much money. You no like?"

Damn Mac! Even in death, he came out top dog.

"Look, why don't you just take the tourists around the harbor...and nothing else."

"You no want do good?'

"Not too much. No, not too much."

He had to get off this subject. "When did you say the two men will be coming back?"

"Tomorrow."

"You set up a date for me to meet them. It can be any place, any time. And don't worry. If they think you are playing ball, they won't hurt you."

"Playing ball?"

"A slang expression. Means working with them."

"Okay, play ball." She smiled, and added, "Not do much good."

He didn't believe her. She was like a cat. Did what she wanted to do when she wanted to do it. But a very lovable cat.

He wrote in the diary that night: "At home people ask me why I am fond of Hong Kong and I have trouble telling them. Maybe it's the excitement...everything moves so fast...the poor guy who had shots fired at him when he escaped from Vietnam runs a vegetable stand a few months later. The capitalist puts up a skyscraper and has to get his money back within three years. Fortunes are made every day on the stock exchange. High school kids get jobs at low pay and within a year some are running the companies. Maybe it's the color: the sampans and junks, the mobs, the celebration with dragons and fireworks, the temples (anything possible that can be prayed to is prayed to, goes an old saying). Maybe it's the people. Nowhere is there so much hope, so many visionaries. They will work 15 and 16 hours a day to make their dreams come true. Nowhere is there more belief in families, from ancestors long dead to toddlers. Maybe it's history. They were mostly refugees and took an island of stone and made it into one of the world's great cities."

Chapter 12

The storm had passed and the night was a warm, balmy one. Only a dark mass over the Peak was a reminder of how swiftly old man weather could change his mind.

Dave was reassured when the doorman raised a hand in signal and a taxi on the street below came in answer. It had the lighted "For Hire" sign which the driver turned off as he pulled up. Inside were the usual meter and license prominently displayed. The driver looked like a cabby, too, which the police officer of the night before had not.

"Where to, sir," the doorman asked.

"Holiday Inn on Mody Road."

As they pulled away, heading for Nathan Road, "the biggest bargain basement" in the world, Dave engaged the driver in pleasantries. Had he had a busy day? Many tourists this time of year?

The cabby said he was thinking of moving to San Francisco. Could he buy a taxi and get a license? How much could he make? "We just got married and want several children. A big family."

At the Holiday Inn, Felicia Yee emerged quickly from a tour crowd waiting for a bus. Once she was in, Dave said to the cabby, "The Grand Tower Hotel. Fast."

The taxi shot down the jam-packed street as if they owned it, back to Nathan and north.

"You okay?" he asked her. She was in acid-washed jeans, a dark blouse, expensive carved boots, and the dark glasses she never removed, even at night. And she was smiling. He had discovered that her smiles were different. One would be pleasant and ordinary, another teasing and others, taunting, sarcastic, mocking, even sad.

"Where have you been?" she asked. The scar seemed even more pronounced. "I tried phoning you."

"You know where I was. Let's quit this cat-and-mouse game." He had debated about taking her along. His mind told him definitely that she might be a key part of a set up. His intuition...that she was what she seemed, honest, forthright, truthful. His mind came up with a rebuttal. He was like many young males. Suckers for pretty, young women.

She said plaintively, "That hurt. I wish we could be friends."

"I do, too. We could be if —"

"If you were sure of me." There was a long awkward pause. She was sitting close to him. He caught the faint whiff of her perfume (Shalimar, he guessed).

"You arranged the meeting," she continued. "You asked me to go with you. I had nothing to do with it. I'm coming along because I wanted to get better acquainted with a client — and I like you. I don't want to see you hurt."

He was touched. He believed her.

"Is someone setting me up?"

"I'll let you know soon." She took a small cellular phone from her purse. Hong Kong had more cellular phones per person than any city in the world. At some bars, you couldn't see the drinks for the handsets.

They passed the Mosque, glistening white, in Arabic design. Here a small Moslem minority worshipped.

"Why the Bird market? Why not an office, a hotel room?"

"Simple. They have friends there, around them. They may even own some of the stalls. And in case the going gets rough, they can vanish within seconds. The streets around are rabbit hutches and the shops the same."

"You talk like an American."

The smile was a happy one. "I'd like to be. I spent two years at the University of California in Los Angeles. I've an uncle living there. I'm as American as a Chinese girl can be."

She was born in Shanghai, she said, but at three, her parents moved to Hong Kong where her father ("I hate him") was a small time entrepreneur. "I love Hong Kong and I'll stay here...for a time."

They passed Jordan Road, a thoroughfare. Everywhere the sidewalks were crowded with young people, out for a movie or a disco or just strolling, holding hands, finding more privacy in the crowds than at home where the living quarters, possibly 10 by 20 feet, were shared by the entire family.

She said, "I visited a friend the other day in a home that small, and she had a piano in it. And three lived there. Some of us are happy with very little. You Americans expect too much. You want more and more and more."

He agreed, although his thoughts were elsewhere. They were nearing Shantung Street, and he was growing uneasy. Maybe he had made the wrong decision. Perhaps he should have notified Inspector Yeung. However, he had to come, and alone. Otherwise, if the police moved in, they might have jeopardized Ming Toy. "They," whoever "they" were, would have closed in on her — and him — if "they" had learned he had called the police.

"Where can I get a gun?"

She was startled. "Tonight?"

"No, no." He was thinking of the two hoodlums who had threatened Ming Toy, whom he would have to meet soon. "I can't go around without some protection."

She said, "A permit will cost you almost $500 US, but I don't think they'd give it to a foreigner."

"I'm not asking about a permit. I'm asking where I can get a gun?"

"What kind?"

"A .357 Magnum."

He felt her soft body tense and realized she was leaning against him.

She thought to dismiss the request. "I don't think little boys should be playing with guns."

He resented her injecting humor into a deadly serious matter. "There's got to be a black market."

"I'll get you a Magnum tomorrow morning."

"You can get one? Where?"

She pulled away, stiffened. "Look, we will have an understanding now. I don't reveal my sources any more than a newspaperman does his. Okay?"

He nodded. "What about you? Are you carrying something in your purse?"

"It's none of your business."

"I think it is. I might need —"

"I've told you before..." She said it quietly but firmly, not in anger but matter-of-factly. "I'm selling information. I'm not an advisor or a bodyguard. You're on your own."

"You're right. I apologize."

The Grand Hotel came into sight. In English, she instructed the driver to turn left at Shantung, right the next corner, left at the next.

The cellular phone sounded. She was still talking, very low, in Chinese, when the taxi pulled to a stop at Fu Lock street.

Putting the phone down, she whispered to Dave, "At the time of his death, Mr. Dunleavy had just wound up a business deal involving many millions of dollars. The man you're seeing wants his share of the profit. I don't have any details."

"Oh, God!" Dave exclaimed.

"I'll say a Buddhist prayer for you, Dave." It was the first time she had used his first name. "I'll leave God up to you."

Chapter 13

The moment he stepped out, he heard a babble of songs intermingling noisily but affectionately with each other. It was as if he were in a forest of a thousand birds.

He glanced back. She was leaning against the taxi. She gave him a sign, lifting her hand. He didn't understand but was oddly assured.

The passageway couldn't have been more than eight feet wide. He entered a corridor with birdcages stacked like so many crates, six and eight on top of each other. Near the entrance, a cage maker sat on the ground sawing and nailing. Nearby was another carving with a razor edge knife. To his surprise, he found crickets as well as birds for sale.

He paced slowly, stopping occasionally to scrutinize a bird.

He passed mynah birds, always talking, never permitting you to get a word in. They bothered him, especially tonight when he wanted no distractions.

He kept on the qui vive. He checked out every person he saw. Every few feet he would stop to case the alleyway ahead as far as he could see, and then turn about to check out the way he had come.

After the mynahs came the parrots strutting around in their colorful plumage. They were also talkers. A friend called his parrot "motor mouth."

Because of their attire, often in bright blues and reds, the parakeets drew the younger set. One bird called out to him, "Hey, chick, whatcha doing?"

The canaries were the Met singers. They had songs well rehearsed.

He passed men — and not all old — in all kinds of strange positions. Here was one on hands and knees with ear pressed up to a cage, another standing tip toe to listen to a bird in the top tier. Others were bent over to get a better fix. This was a quiet people market, little talking, and the customers were as intent as those aficionados back home listening to a compact disc.

The arrangement was perfect for the party meeting him. The party could choose the location and there was no way the police could set up a trap in advance. If he suspected he was being cornered, he could change his plan on the spur of the moment. Another location, another time. It was the mark of a professional who lowered his risk.

For some inexplicable reason, Dave had lost his fear of foul play. This was a lulling scene, and perhaps it had been chosen for that purpose. Silently, men came and went with their buys, and a lone woman with a little girl who was as excited over a bird as any child getting her first dog or cat.

He was taller than most and stood out because he was Caucasian and his clothes were American. Yet no one glanced his way. He was only another of Hong Kong's customers. There were so many, and so welcomed, that somehow they faded into the scene.

He had gone 100 feet or so when a low voice from behind him asked, "Mr. Anderson?"

Although he had anticipated the voice, he turned startled. The voice belonged to a short, thin, well-tailored Chinese with an imposing, commanding personality.

"If you would, kind sir." He led the way between several stacks of cages to a small open space. "Better for talking."

He displayed the attributes of wealth. His expensive Rolex watch, tailored dark blue suit, handmade black leather shoes, and a diamond ring the size of a dime indicated he was not adverse to advertising the fact. He was in his early fifties, but his unlined face and full shock of black hair suggested he could have passed for forty. He had a chrysanthemum blossom in the right lapel of his jacket.

"I knew you would come," he continued, "although my associates said that this was all part of a deception. I told them they were wrong. I told them that Mac Dunleavy was a person of honor and that you would be, too. One or two suggested that we use more forcible tactics but my family has always been faithful to the teachings of Confucius and we would do that only as a last resort."

He quit, waited. The silence that ensued was appalling to Dave. "You'll have to brief me," he said hesitantly. "I don't know what this is all about."

The man shot him a stony, killing glance. "You disappoint me. My friends will tell you that I don't like to be disappointed."

The softness had turned to stabbing firmness.

Dave said slowly, with authority, "You think I am covering up, lying. Yet if we are to get anywhere, you will have to assume for the moment that I am honest about this. It will be to your benefit to assume that. You cannot lose by explaining in detail what it is that you think I know and don't. And what you think I should do, and don't."

Unexpectedly, the man shifted gears. "Who is the woman waiting in the taxi for you?"

Dave was jarred but quickly recovered. "I am in the news business, as you know, and she is secretary to my correspondent in Taipei. I use her when I come to Hong Kong as an advisor on Chinese matters."

"What's her name?"

"Samantha Chen. May I have yours?"

"Not necessary."

Out of the corner of his roving eye, Dave caught a glimpse of the little, anonymous detective in the gray suit walking past them. The Chrysanthemum Man saw him, too, and raised a hand in signal. There was a ping from a silencer, the detective fell over, and almost in the same moment, two men appeared so suddenly that afterwards Dave could not describe them, and vanished carrying the body.

The Chinese turned back to Dave. "He was a danger to society. My associates and I have sworn to eradicate all criminal elements from Hong Kong."

Dave offered no answer. He took time to steady his shattered nerves. He had no weapon. He was outnumbered. He had to play along.

The man said quietly, "My associates and I entered into an investment with Mr. Dunleavy that resulted at the time of his death in a profit of approximately 12 million Hong Kong. We have about six million coming to us — and there are only two people who know where the six million is. You and his widow."

Dave broke in. "What kind of investment?"

The man ignored the question. "We have interrogated her thoroughly and are convinced that she barely has enough to live on. That leaves you. Since you arrived here just two days ago, you may need a little time to get into Mr. Dunleavy's affairs. Make arrangements with his widow. We will expect the six million from you 48 hours from now. I will call and let you know where to deliver it. That is all. I have nothing more to say. I hope you are an honorable person."

Dave started to comment but found he was alone. The man had disappeared as quickly as he had come.

Dave retraced his steps. Everything inside him cried out to run, to escape this nightmare he had been catapulted into through no doing of his own. He controlled himself, making his way slowly through the crowded alley. He kept on the alert, his head turning constantly. No one blocked him, though, no one even touched him, and no one called his name. The same mynah bird called out, "Hi, chick," and the same chorus agreed. The same thrushes and meadowlarks assured him all was right with the world.

As he neared the taxi, he saw Felicia putting a lighter to a cigarette. For a second, her right cheek was spotlighted. The scar was more prominent than ever. In the front, the driver slouched as if asleep.

When she saw him, she opened the door. "You all right?" she asked with seeming concern.

He nodded. "Nerves shot, that's all."

She pulled over to make room for him and their bodies touched. He was mildly stirred. In a normal situation he would have been aroused.

She gave the driver the Holiday Inn as the first stop. She would leave Dave there and he would continue to the Regent. She had already informed him that she could not meet him again at the Regent. She gave no excuse.

As they passed through miles of brilliantly lighted streets, more garish even than Las Vegas', that advertised everything from Nina Ricci to Wing Fat Dispensary, he related briefly what had transpired. He held his voice low and steady, so the taxi driver wouldn't hear. He described the Chrysanthemum Man in detail, hoping for recognition but she failed to react. He went over their conversation, and again, she offered no comment.

Then he told her about the gunning down of the anonymous little man. "Oh, no!" she gasped. He felt the tremor running through her body. "Why? Why would they do that? He wasn't hurting anyone. He was just an innocuous little guy. He was a dear little man."

"You knew him?" Dave asked in surprise.

She hesitated, and the hesitation was an admission. "Not personally. I have a friend who knows him."

The cover-up was too smooth, Dave thought. The product, though, of a very quick mind. However, why had she lied? What did it matter whether she knew him?

He followed up quickly. "Did your friend identify the Chrysanthemum man?"

She measured her words. "I'm not sure."

"Then you do know?"

"If I do, I'll tell you when I can."

They passed the police station at the intersection with Austin Road and then Kowloon Park.

He tended to raise his voice when he didn't like the way a conversation was going. "Tell me, Miss Yee, were the two men who threatened Ming Toy sent by the Chrysanthemum man?"

She took a long drag on the cigarette. "I'll find out."

He was angry. "What kind of a business deal could Mac Dunleavy have been in that showed a profit of millions in a very short time?"

She said flatly, bitingly, "I don't know."

"Maybe you do," he retorted in the same tone, "It's drugs, isn't it?"

She rubbed out the cigarette and stared out the window on her side.

As they neared the Holiday Inn, she reached over, put a hand on his arm. "I wish I had met you at a different time, under different circumstances. I think we could have been friends. Maybe more than friends."

She was out and running for the hotel entrance.

He had strong guilt feelings. He had been rough.

He wondered if he would ever see her again.

Chapter 14

Dave had scarcely stepped out of the taxi than he was approached by the police sergeant who had driven him to Aberdeen the night he first met Ming Toy. "Inspector Yeung would like to talk with you, sir. If it's convenient for you, sir. He has asked me to drive you."

"Am I under arrest?" Dave asked.

The Sergeant shrugged. "No, sir. The Inspector would like to meet you at the Restaurant of a Thousand Flowers. He would come here but he thought this was too public a place."

"I've had a rough night," Dave said, stalling. He had been through too much to confront the Inspector. He needed, too, to get his thoughts lined up. He never entered into a verbal duel without marshalling his plan of attack. You didn't quarterback without knowing what play you were going to set after reading the defense.

The Sergeant was smooth. "The Inspector will come here if that is more convenient for you."

Dave capitulated. One way or another, the Inspector would corral him.

He sat with the Sergeant in an unmarked car. He was apprehensive that the Restaurant of a Thousand Flowers might turn out to be a police station.

The Sergeant was talkative. "You ever been in South America, in Rio or Sao Paulo?"

Dave had. "Then," the Sergeant continued, "you've seen those miles of horrible slums that march up the mountain sides. We used to have the same here. Most of us were refugees and we had nothing. But working together with the Brits we built thousands of those big buildings of flats that we have all over the place. It isn't much, a cubbyhole, but it's a place where we can sleep and have a community toilet, and little burners in the hallways and balconies where we can cook and hang our clothes out on poles to dry.

"So we worked hard, some of us 16 hours a day, and we got a little money together and could live better. And with all of the refugees came those smart asses from Shanghai. And they started up little plants. Maybe only 20 or 30 workers"

He took a deep, exuberant breath. "We did it! We showed the world that a little island that didn't have any oil or minerals or anything, not even enough land to farm on, could outdo even the States."

Well, Dave thought, I've had my civic lesson for the day.

The Restaurant of a Thousand Flowers covered half a city block. A mob of well behaved young couples milled about the entrance, waiting to get in. The Sergeant held up his credentials as he waved his way through. Inside was a vast expanse of tables, perhaps 400 to 500, with a band under hot spotlights playing at one end, and a dance floor the size of a basketball court, jammed to capacity.

A fawning maitre d' ushered them along the right, past little stalls with tables for four, red Chinese lanterns overhead, and silk curtains that could be dropped at the entrance to each. Dragons and other creatures of past centuries adorned the curtains.

The maitre d' led them into one and asked what they would have. Dave ordered a Carlsberg beer and the Sergeant, Dewars on the rocks. The maitre d' advised that the Inspector had telephoned he would be late.

"Did you know that the police commander here in Kowloon City is a Chinese woman? Came up from the ranks. Commands 1,000 officers. She's all woman — but she's a tough commander, sir, and fair."

Shortly afterwards, the maitre d' hustled in bringing a phone which he plugged in to a wall socket. "Los Angeles. A woman." He was impressed that he had a customer so important that an overseas call would be routed to the restaurant.

Marge's voice came over as clearly as if she were in the adjoining room. "Can you talk?"

"No." The Sergeant was presumably studying a menu. If his ears had had traction they would have stuck out a foot.

"I'll be brief. There seems to be some urgency. It's two ten here and I promised an answer by five. I had a call from Mae Hong Son."

His memory zeroed in fast. Mae Hong Son was a remote town in Northern Thailand, not far from the Myanmar border (Burma). The journalists called it the Golden Triangle, a land of jungles, mountains, and thousands of acres of poppies, which in some years were transformed into 600,000 pounds of pure white heroin, known as Heroin No. 4, worth a trillion or more U.S. dollars.

"Go on," he said, The Sergeant leaned forward.

"The party said they wanted to reach you, that it was an emergency."

The "party" would be Khun Sa or one of his aides. Khun Sa was the warlord who ruled the Shan States of the Golden Triangle where the borders of Thailand, Myanmar and Laos met. In his late fifties, he commanded a highly disciplined and well-equipped army of

15,000 dedicated to fighting for the independence of eight million Shans from Myanmar. Rumor had it, though, that the government in Yangon (Rangoon) had a secret agreement with Khun Sa. To simplify, neither would bother the other. Khun Sa could rule the Shan States and Yangon would look the other way, provided that Khun Sa only feinted in any attacks on the government.

Dave said, "What do they want?"

"The party said they couldn't discuss it over the phone. They would send a courier with a message."

His memory spun back several years. He was stationed in Bangkok, writing sweetness-and-light pieces about the King of Thailand, and his remarkable rapport with his people, and other similar articles. Then one day he met an agent with the U.S. Drug Enforcement Administration that was spending millions in an attempt to destroy the opium trade of the Golden Triangle. Working in collaboration with Myanmar, they were using serial defoliation to wipe out 200,000 acres of poppy fields.

At that time Khun Sa was the little known name of a half Chinese, half Shan (correct name: Chang Chi Fu) military genius. Why not interview him and find out what kind of man he was, what his plans were for his people, and more importantly, how long did he believe he could hold out against the American campaign to destroy the poppy fields?

Dave had no contacts. He knew mostly through gossip that Khun Sa lived in a village called Homong, an 11-hour mule ride through the mountains from the nearest road. He had a wife, five grown children, a collection of beautiful horses, and he drove the few miles of roads around Homong in a white Toyota pick-up truck with 10 bodyguards and a machine gun on the roof.

Dave flew to Chiang Mai, a large city for Thailand, near the Golden Triangle. He checked into the Rincome Hotel. Before he had unpacked, he had a drink at the Lobby Bar, which had large ceramic elephants on the stairway approach, and afterwards lunch at the Lanna Coffee Shop where hand painted umbrellas covered the ceiling. That night he had dinner at the Thong Kwow restaurant, set inside lovely teakwood walls. In each place, he let it be known to the waiters and anyone within hearing distance that he hoped to interview Khun Sa for the world's newspapers.

He was awakened early morning. He was never the one to leap out of bed "bushy tailed," as his mother would have put it. He mumbled something into the phone and was startled when the voice at the other end said, "I'm the PR guy with the Mong Tai Liberation Army and I hear you'd like to talk with my boss."

Never had Dave expected to hear colloquial "American" spoken by anyone associated with Khun Sa, and the use of "PR" and "boss" stunned him. He could only say, "Yes?"

"I tell you what. There's an old temple near you called Wat Chedi Luang. Take a taxi. Everyone knows it. I'll meet you, say, two hours from now. Ten o'clock. And we'll set it up. Okay?"

"I'll be there." Dave hung up in disbelief, not knowing what to make of this rapid fire dialogue. He might as well be in Los Angeles.

The taxi coughed repeatedly as it struggled up into the hills, into a cool morning mist that shrouded in the distance the holy mountain of Doi Suthep. At the temple, Dave climbed rough, stone stairs covered with weeds, and at the top looked into the thoughtful, trance-like eyes of a golden Buddha recessed a few feet into an archway. He had barely had time to look about when a roly-poly Chinese, a foot shorter than Dave, and in his fifties, came up behind him. He was in army fatigues, not too different from those worn in the U.S. a decade ago, and packed a weapon in a side holster. He offered a strong handshake. "Call me Barney. Just Barney. You from L.A.? I'm from L.A. Nineteen years ago. Worked on the old *Herald-Express*. You know the *Herald-Express*?"

Despite Barney's hail-well-met American attitude, Dave was edgy, and the feeling was contagious. If Barney feared he had been followed, and might be gunned down, then Dave was in the same danger zone. This was always the hazard in interviewing any guerrilla leader, that the enemy might pull off a surprise raid and wipe everyone out. Later, the opposition would send "deep regrets" that a journalist had been "accidentally" killed.

Barney spelled out the program in a few terse sentences. If Dave would fly to a town called Mae Hong Son the next morning, he would be met by one of Khun Sa's officers and taken into the hills not too far away where he would interview Khun Sa who was holding a war council. Barney said a battle was imminent with the Wa guerrilla forces over an opium smuggling route the Wa soldiers had seized.

Mae Hong Son proved a boom town of 20,000 where hotels had taken over the rice paddies and banks had moved in that used only cash. In fact, the town was a cash one, no credit cards, no ATMs, no checks, no promissory notes, no CDs, nothing but hard money, not unlike the days of California's Gold Rush.

The officer who met Dave at the small, backwater airport spoke no English. He was dressed in a well-pressed, smart, darkish-brown (to fade into the jungles) jumpsuit, open at the neck. He had no medals and no insignia to identify him as one of Khun Sa's aides.

He had a driver, and the 1975 Chevrolet was black, with even the chrome painted black. They climbed high into the mountains. They passed elephants working, rolling logs about, the saddles constructed crudely of wood, and then a hill tribe, the Hmong people, who scratched out a living from poor soil but nevertheless maintained dignity, as shown in their homemade, embroidered clothes. The children with their pretty, innocent faces and gracious ways touched him. He bought one of everything they offered for sale.

Several hours out of town, they left the car hidden in a grove of trees and walked into a clearing. About the same time, Khun Sa emerged from the jungle behind them, over a foot trail. He was accompanied by his bodyguards, eight in all, and Barney. Khun Sa was in the same dark brown uniform as the others, also open at the neck. He sported no medals. He had small patches sewn on each arm of the jacket. The patches had red backgrounds with an inset of a star on a yellow sun, the markings of the Shan peoples in their campaign for independence. He was a tall, wiry man who looked more like an Iowa farmer than a warlord.

He offered no handshake but a slight, welcoming smile. He indicated a grassy spot where they would sit for the interview. The bodyguards dispersed themselves about the area. They were heavily armed, not only with handguns, but also grenades and knives.

Barney translated. Dave led off the questions about the Liberation Army; a subject that opened up Khun Sa whose pride in his troops was evident. He spoke softly and despite his power and wealth had none of the grandiose words or trappings of egocentrics Dave had known in other revolutionary settings. This was no guerrilla army, in the stereotyped sense. They were well equipped with mortars, rockets, recoilless rifles, and some old tanks cadged from the Chinese. They operated their own farms for food, had modern barracks, a 70-bed hospital, and maintained schools and a Buddhist temple. For entertainment, they had American films on home video, a disco Saturday nights, and daily CNN News from a satellite. The operation cost $600,000 monthly. The funds came from a 40 percent tax levied on a dozen or so opium "factories," the laboratories that employed some 50 chemists and other highly paid scientists to refine the opium into heroin. The "sales force," once managed by the Mafia and the Marseilles "mob" (as set forth in the film, "The French Connection"), had been taken over by ethnic Chinese organizations, such as the Triads in Hong Kong.

Khun Sa stressed that the Liberation Army grew no poppies, processed no heroin, and did not engage in marketing. Dave challenged him on that. The financial base was opium, no matter how the poppies were sold or marketed. Khun Sa was quick to admit that.

Talking slowly, he outlined the problem, as he saw it. The farmers could not exist without growing the poppies. It was their livelihood. Otherwise they and their children would starve. However, if the United States would offer economic aid over six years to the growers, which would run somewhere between 150 and 300 million, to help them during a change over to other crops, he would use his army to see that the opium trade was banned from the Shan States. He said he strongly opposed the use of the drug and that if he caught any of his Mong Tai troops using it, they got a warning first, then if they persisted, six months of treatment, and then if they would not or could not give up the habit, execution.

"The Americans are to blame for the opium trade," he said. "You spend millions trying to eradicate the growing of poppies when you should be taking this money to eradicate your addicts."

He rose to signal the end of the interview. The bodyguards who had been moving about the perimeter closed in. Khun Sa thanked Dave for coming. He raised a hand in goodbye, and with his bodyguards disappeared down the trail into the jungle.

Barney remained behind. "Great guy, isn't he?"

Dave did a quick side step. "He has charisma." Dave was remembering what Khun Sa's critics had said, that he was ruthless, played all sides, and would stop at nothing to keep the opium trade going. His men swore by him, however, and so did the people of the Shan States. He, and the opium, would be around for a long time to come.

As for Barney, Dave was to learn later that Barney's predecessor had been a highly respected American newspaperman. Khun Sa had an inherent instinct for public relations. He paid the best money for the best PR people. Unlike Barney, though, his predecessor had been more the quiet, straightforward, objective type.

Chapter 15

The band at the Restaurant of a Thousand Flowers burst into a lively number. The dancers flowed back on the floor. Dave had to talk louder. "It's okay," he said over the phone to Marge. "Tell them where I am."

"Are you sure?" she asked, always the mother hen. "You may get involved in something."

"I can handle it. How's Old Boy?"

"He made advances."

"Advances?"

"Licked me full on the mouth."

A half-hour later, Inspector Yeung arrived. He was strictly business. He had just come from "the scene of the crime."

"He was shot down in cold blood. Never had a chance. Two 38's in his chest. Died immediately. Did you see it? Where were you?"

Dave went on the offensive. "I don't understand why you were running tail on me."

"Running tail?"

"A surveillance."

"Why not?" the Inspector shot back at him. "You arrive in Hong Kong and immediately someone tries to kill you, and you tell us nothing. We have every right to keep you under surveillance until we find out what this is all about — or until you tell us. We might not have lost a good man if you had cooperated."

Dave countered, "I didn't ask for the surveillance. I've told you everything I know which you haven't me. I've worked with the police all over the world and never had any problem until I arrived in Hong Kong."

The Inspector took a deep breath, sank back into the chair. "He was always ready for any assignment, and when anyone was sick or needed help he was there."

The Inspector covered his face. It was a moment before he could speak. "Why don't we talk this out calmly, professionally?"

Dave recognized a trap. "I certainly will, as far as possible. I have to protect the interests of Mac Dunleavy and myself. But I will cooperate as much as I can within that perimeter."

The Inspector took his time lighting a cigarette. "It will be to your advantage, Mr. Anderson. Otherwise, in a day or two we could be cremating you and brown bagging your ashes back to the States."

He toyed with the cigarette. "In all fairness I must tell you this. You were not responsible for the detective's death. He had been investigating the subject you call the Chrysanthemum Man."

He took a deep breath. "We have four men working on the attempt to assassinate you the evening you arrived."

"You know the identity of the man who attempted to kill the assassin?"

"I won't discuss that."

"I ran into him by chance — but he pretended he didn't know me."

"Perhaps you were mistaken."

"I'd stake my life on it."

The Inspector shrugged. "Let me continue with my report. I talked again with Mr. Dunleavy's widow and found her antagonistic and evasive. We checked Vital Statistics and there is no record of the death of anyone by the name of Mac Dunleavy, and no record of a cremation. I should add that sometimes the family is too poor to have a proper farewell, and they take the body out to sea. This is often a spiritual thing. We love the sea and with many there is a strong emotional attachment."

Dave started to interrupt but the Inspector plunged ahead.

"I have one more matter I want to discuss with you."

The Inspector stubbed out the cigarette, lit another. "We have a law that permits a sampan man to bring a bride to Hong Kong but she cannot work and must live on his sampan."

Dave sat upright, tense.

The Inspector continued, "We have a report that one such bride did take work and was arrested and ordered deported. The report states that another sampan woman helped her escape. Your Ming Toy — Miss Chan.

"I would suggest, Mr. Anderson, that you discharge her and find another 'tanka.' Miss Chan will have no problem obtaining employment on land and it will be the best for her. Otherwise one day she will go to prison."

Dave shuddered. "I'll talk with her."

"That won't do much good."

The Inspector continued, "For your information, we have checked with Chinese University on Miss Felicia Yee. She is taking one class, in Chinese Culture. They think highly of her. I might add that you are her first client in this 'selling information' business, and that leads me to believe she may be a plant."

"For whom?"

"I don't know."

"Am I in danger from her?"

"It's not within my province to say. I can tell you she lives with her mother, one Martha Yee, near the university in a block of 70 flats. Her mother works at a firm manufacturing IBM clones, and her daughter, Felicia Yee, as a part time receptionist — three hours a day — for Chester, Ltd., a small construction company. We know little about the father, Phillip Yee, who reportedly deserted them many years ago and whose whereabouts are unknown. Three years ago Miss Yee and her mother moved to Los Angeles where they lived until a year ago. Neither has a criminal record."

He rose and stretched. He was weary and barely audible. "In every police station in Hong Kong we have a shrine to Kwan Kung who protects us who are in police work. I will ask Kwan Kung tonight when I return to the station to help us on this case — and may these evildoers die a thousand deaths."

Back at the hotel, a call was waiting from Marge. He had asked her to check out Felicia Yee during the two years she and her mother had lived in Los Angeles.

Marge reported, "She gets good grades from everyone. I talked with two of her UCLA professors, several neighbors, and her supervisor at the Bank of America's telephone pool where she worked part time answering questions about accounts. She dated both Chinese and Caucasian students. Excellent character, good student. Are you planning to marry her?"

Dave laughed. "Come off it, Marge."

Before he retired, he wrote in his diary: "I am getting involved more and more in something I know little about. Ming Toy is what she is. Nothing devious. Mac's wife, Heather, is what she is, conniving, unpleasant. About Felicia Yee, I'm torn. She is beautiful, sexy. I could fall for her if she is playing it honest which I have doubts about. I've got the warning signal up about her — and Inspector Yeung, a very clever detective who sets his traps well. I could probably learn what this is all about if I delved into Mac's business but I am not here for that and don't have the time or reason. I'll take care of Ming Toy and get out."

Chapter 16

Shortly after 8 o'clock the next morning, Dave stood on the dock used by the shuttle boats to the Jumbo restaurant and waited patiently until a sampan showed up, ferrying people from the other side of the harbor. He told the old 'tanka' he wanted to see Ming Toy.

She stared up at him out of a wrinkled, weathered face that had seen many hard years go by. "You know Ming Toy?" she shouted.

"Mr. Mac died," he said. "I own the sampan now."

She gave no indication she had heard. Land people were barely tolerated in her world. They were a strange breed that dressed oddly and looked as if a good puff of wind would blow them away.

Somewhat to his surprise, about 20 minutes later Ming Toy swung her boat up to the dock. "Happy morning, Mister David," she called. Her eyes were dancing and there was that exuberance of youth that wiped away all thoughts of the night before.

She held the anchoring pole while he stumbled in. He doubted if he would ever manage a graceful entrance.

"Take trip," she said, laughing. "You come only night. No see harbor."

A trip wasn't what he had wanted, not for a serious talk. But it was a morning to savor, the waves gentle, the sun casting a silver glow across the water, and the temperature at that level which puts tingles dancing through the blood stream.

"How you, Mister David?" she called above the purring of the motor. They were breaking water like a porpoise at play.

Before he could answer, she continued, "Got new Levis. 541s." She spread her legs to show him. "Mister Mac bring last time. Look good, no?"

"Did he give you the ring?" Dave asked. She was wearing a gold one with a modest diamond but still one more expensive than a sampan woman would have.

"Year past. Mister Mac. Anniversary."

Anniversary of what?

She continued. "Mister Mac buy me coins. You buy coins? I give money you. Buy China gold coins. Panda one side. No put money in bank. No buy stocks. Only gold."

He said he would and she handed him an old, much used envelope. Later he counted out $7,000 HK, about $900 US.

"Men no come," she said

He described the Chrysanthemum Man. "No, no," she said. "Never see. Men rough come. Clothes rough. Talk rough. Bad men."

Without further chatter, he launched the attack. "A police inspector came to see me last night."

Her lips and eyes tightened. "He said you helped a bride escape who was being deported."

She nodded emphatically. "Yes, help bride. Poor girl. She starve, die. Love husband. Good man. I help. Do good."

"Look, Ming Toy," he said slowly, wanting her to understand every word. "I don't agree with the law any more than you do. I don't know why a bride can't come, and live on her husband's boat, and work. But we have got to do what the law says or you will go to prison. Do you understand, Ming Toy? I am trying to keep you out of prison."

She looked away. She was idling the sampan. When she offered no answer, he said gently, "Did you hear me, Ming Toy? I want you here every day running this boat, not in prison."

"Girl starve, die. Do much good."

"With some money thrown in?" He couldn't resist saying that.

She was near tears and he felt like a cad. "Why scold Ming Toy? Do much good. Make thousand dollars. You get half."

She handed him a $500 HK bill. "I don't want the money!" He raised his voice without intending to.

"Why you mad?"

"I'm not mad!"

"I hurt." She was sobbing. He looked away. He couldn't bear to see her cry.

"Okay, okay," he said. "Let's forget it. But no more rescuing brides."

"You got it."

He laughed. "Where do you get these expressions?"

The tears disappeared as fast as they had come. "Tourist talk. Good American, no?"

"Good American, yes. You promise? No more helping brides."

She nodded. "No more do good."

She would, he knew. She was about as repentant as a drunk taking one more swig. He had to end it right here and now.

"I'll sell the boat..."

He never finished. She was red cheeked. "You sell boat! You sell Ming Toy!"

He had gone down for the count before but not this time. "You're not a slave on the old plantation."

"Plantation?" she yelled, not understanding.

"Forget it," he said.

"No slave! I free! Do what want!"

He hurried on. "I'll get you a good job and buy you and your mother a nice flat. You can pick out the furniture and the wallpaper and everything."

"No!" she screamed. "No land job! Love boat. Love life. Why punish me. What I do?"

He realized he had just been knocked out. "We'll talk about it later."

"Yes, later. Keep boat. Make much money. Mother want meet you. Okay?"

He nodded. At this point he would have gone anywhere to meet anyone.

Her mother proved a surprise. She spoke English better than her daughter. It was stilted English and slow in coming as she silently translated from English into Cantonese and then the reverse. She had learned English, it turned out, in a Methodist mission school in Kowloon.

Her gentle round face had not a wrinkle in it although Dave estimated she must be about 60. Her eyes had the same sparkle as Ming's. Her hair was raven black, dyed no doubt, as many older Chinese women did, with a syrupy kind of charcoal. She was in the customary black cloud pants and a Mao jacket buttoned at the neck.

"I have pleasure to meet you, Mr. Anderson," she said. "I honored you come to our simple home. Please to sit."

He sat with Ming on a bench that ran along one side of the upper part of the sampan. That part was covered over with rough boards slapped together to protect them from the elements. A burner for cooking sat in one corner, a red box that served for keeping food was nearby, and there were the usual pots and pans and dishes on rickety shelves. A low bed, only a few inches from the floor, was in another corner. Here and there, hanging from the walls, were magazine pictures of Diana, Queen Elizabeth and Confucius. In a corner, lighted by a candle and with joss sticks nearby for burning at prayer time, was a shrine to Buddha.

Ming Toy was solicitous about her mother. "Bring tea?" she asked and her mother nodded. Ming Toy served the three from a battered tin pot. The tea was strong and unsweetened.

"You like Hong Kong?" her mother asked. It was the same question everyone put to a foreigner.

Dave said he did. "Hong Kong good to us," her mother continued, "but I want die in China where room for earth burial. Near ancestors. China my country."

She asked, "Are you married?" It was the kind of straight-forward question that the Chinese asked, that had shocked Dave in his first encounters. How old are you? Do you dye your hair? How many children do you have? No children. That is sad.

He thought that was an opening to ask Ming Toy, "Do you have a boyfriend?"

"No man. Man only make trouble. Make baby. No want baby."

Her mother smiled. "When she meet right man..."

Ming Toy laughed. Dave felt the closeness between the two, the love in Ming Toy's eyes as she watched her mother. Only half listening, he studied her. She had the beauty of body and face, the sharp mind, and the fiery determination to go far if she were transferred to Los Angeles or some other American city, and if someone financed her for a couple of years while she studied. In his travels he had encountered many Pygmalions who only needed a different setting and a chance at education to achieve a potential they didn't know they had.

In recent times, the fact had been proven repeatedly as Asians with little background had come to the United States and by sheer determination and hard work proved that they could become somebody, good citizens, in a different culture.

He remembered once saying to Mac, after returning from Calcutta, "It's all a matter of geography, the luck of birth, where we are conceived and where we grow up. We think we've done a lot on our own but we couldn't have if we hadn't been born in the right place to the right parents."

He wondered about Mac and Ming Toy. Had they been lovers? It was possible. Even in her temper flare-ups there was a naivete and a sweetness about her and an earthly sensuality.

"My daughter like you," the mother was saying. "She say you are like Mr. Dunleavy. He bought this sampan for me. We have papers. He was good to us."

She continued, "She work hard. Sometime work all night for Mr. Dunleavy. She work hard for you. Worked all last night. She like work hard."

Ming Toy rose quickly, glancing at her watch. "Got go. Tourists come. Make money."

They said their good-byes. Her mother whispered, "Thank you for being kind to my daughter."

Back in Ming Toy's sampan and headed for the dock, Dave said accusingly, "Should I expect a call from the police when I get back to the hotel?"

She laughed. "Police no know. Ming do no more good. Ming Toy promise. Okay? You not mad?"

How could he be mad when he wanted to take her into his arms? There was a radiance of happiness about her that he would never want to dim, even if she did "do good" in spite of all that he had said.

Returning to the hotel by taxi, he solved the problem. Her mother wanted to return to the mainland. So he would pay their way and set them up for a year. He would talk with her mother alone and they would surprise Ming Toy.

That left the sampan, what to do with it. Well, there must be a dumping ground for old sampans, the same as for old autos in the States?

At the hotel he emptied his pockets. He had the $7,000 HK for the gold coins and also the $500 HK that was his share for rescuing the bride. He had not intended to keep it but in the excitement of the moment had stuck it in a pocket. And then there was a mysterious envelope that contained another $500 HK. That would be his share for whatever scam the police "no know." Now he was an accomplice to at least two crimes.

He was amused and furious, and would have been more so if all of this had not been overshadowed by the threat to her of the two thugs. At the dock he had repeated, "Play along with them. Set it up for me to talk with them. Don't do or say anything that will antagonize them."

He hoped she would follow his instructions. But with that quick temper...

Mac, Mac, whatever you have done, why did you do anything that would involve Ming Toy?

Chapter 17

A few minutes after he returned to the hotel, a phone call came from Felicia Yee. Immediately he recognized the soft, husky voice. His pulse beat a little harder. He had hoped against hope he would hear from her again, yet his treatment of her had not been all that kind.

"I have what you ordered. Are you free? For lunch?"

He said he was. She hurried on. "Would you take the Star Ferry and I'll meet you when you get off."

He said he would and that he would leave in about 10 minutes. She said, "I'm taking you to a favorite place of mine. I think you'll like it."

The morning had such a sheen to it that he decided to walk to the Star Ferry which connected Kowloon Peninsula on the mainland, where he was now, with Hong Kong island. He passed the Peninsula, the Y.M.C.A. and the Cricket Man. Across the street, on his left, rose the Planetarium, Space Age, and Cultural Center, an intellectual side of Hong Kong seldom noted in fiction or the movies. He passed a mob of double-decker buses with motors panting while waiting to take the next crowd of commuters from the Ferry to points in Kowloon. People queued up for them with the same ritual and decorum as in London.

Vendors squatted on the sidewalks beside layouts of English, American and Chinese newspapers and magazines. There were, too, illegal hawkers, without permits, who sold silk ties, sunglasses, calculators, etc. At sight of the police they scrambled to pick up their wares and run. If caught, they were warned, seldom arrested. The philosophy was, everyone has to make a living. Give them a chance.

At the ferry stile, he bought a first class ticket and passed through a turnstile. Far up a vast approach lined with advertisements, he came to 50 or 60 customers waiting for a red light to change to green and a bell to ring. A sign read: Beware of pickpockets. A crowd mobbed a poorly dressed man selling stuffed pandas. Then they were moving en masse to a well-worn gangplank where they boarded a fairly large ship with long wooden benches lined up across its width. Somehow the mass of humans moved as if choreographed, no toes stepped on, no bodies shaken.

In a couple of minutes, there was more clanging, and the rumbling of the gangplank being pulled up. The ferry plowed across a harbor that was rolling with high waves. They passed sampans looking as if they were about to be engulfed, lighters, a two-decker tour boat, a jetfoil barely skimming the surface water on its way to the gambling port of Macau, a barge loaded with construction equipment, a pristine white Arab yacht, and a junk with stained batwing sails flapping in the wind, possibly carrying pigs or grain from mainland China.

Disembarking eight minutes later, he found Felicia waiting in an area where the ricksha men assembled to trap tourists.

"Hi," she said, smiling broadly. "Or should I say, Jo sun. Gay ho ma?" She translated, "Good morning. How are you?"

He tried repeating, "Ho sin."

She laughed. "No, it's jo sun. How about trying another good morning? Nay sik-jaw faan may?"

"Have mercy."

"It means literally, 'Have you eaten yet?' We use it for just good morning."

She was in acid-washed jeans so tightly fitting that he thought she must have used a shoe horn. Her decorated blue shirt fell outside and temple bell earrings swung about saucily. She had a new pair of dark glasses with white rims. The scar was scarcely noticeable.

She noted that he was looking over the rickshas with their "buggies" and long shafts painted Chinese red. Bony and wrinkled-old men, worn like knotted trees by the ravages of work and time, sat idly by.

"Don't try to get them to take you any place," she said. "They're here for photographic purposes only. They won't solicit us since I'm Chinese and you're with me and they'll figure you're a local. But if you've got a camera and especially children, they'll follow you, pester you."

She added, "These are the last of the ricksha people and I'll be glad to see them go. I don't like the idea of human beings working as beasts of burden. Come on, I'm taking you to a land of pines and mountain air and quiet. Yes, quiet. You won't believe Lantau island. I need to get away. We catch the boat two piers over. I know Americans don't like walking but if we walk we'll be at the pier in ten minutes. If we take a taxi, maybe tomorrow."

He grinned. "I think I can make it."

"Here, take this." She handed him the shoe box she was carrying that had a strap wrapped around it. "It's loaded. I hope you don't use it. I hate guns. I'd never have one around."

Gingerly, he accepted it, wishing he hadn't asked for it. He hadn't had a gun since college days. He wondered about his accuracy. With a rifle, he had plugged targets in the 95 to 98 range. But that had been years ago.

He caught himself as he was about to ask where she had bought it. "How much do I owe you?"

"Nothing. I borrowed it from a friend for a week."

As they walked briskly along Connaught Road Central, through a sea of people, his mind raced over a bumpy road that he didn't want it to follow. From a friend? The friend had to be a very close one, indeed, for her or him to loan such a powerful weapon, and the very nature of the weapon would indicate the party might be involved in some kind of criminal activity — and this lovely girl beside him could be on the fringe of such activity if not actually engaged in it.

Yet this estimate went against the very fiber of his being. He had come to accept her as an outgoing, compassionate person. He could not explain the inescapable fact that she had vital information that somehow incriminated her. There had to be an explanation, he told himself, a simple one that he was constantly seeking that would exonerate her.

He was going up against all logic. He knew that. There was no question of the sexual magnet at work. He sensed she was well aware of that and perhaps modestly exploiting it.

Once they stopped before a sidewalk showing of paintings. The young artist stayed shyly in the background. Dave liked particularly a picture of a full moon framed by a temple door.

"See the girl in the moon?" Felicia asked.

"Girl?"

"Yes. You westerners got it all wrong. Haven't you heard about the lovers who quarreled and the young woman was banished forever to live on the moon? Every year we have a Moon Cake Festival and light lanterns and bake moon cakes to let her know we care for her."

At the Outlying Islands Ferry Pier they waited ten minutes before boarding. They sat on an open deck with a cool, soft wind toying with her shoulder-length satiny hair and a kind, warm sun lulling them. It was one of those dream days that nature rarely sets up. The panorama of the harbor, with ships from far places and ancient tramps close to death, slipped past them, and then they were in open sea.

She cupped her hands and lighted a cigarette. "Does the smoke bother you?"

"No — but it's doing more than bothering you — and that bothers me."

She laughed. "You Americans! You take all the joy out of life. You won't eat this and that. You shop with a calorie counter and pay a fortune for the latest diet. You gain a pound and become manic depressive. You talk incessantly about diseases and your telly shows horror pictures every night of surgeons operating and people dying — and how you could be next if you don't eat bran. Or is it something else this year?"

"Okay," he said. "I plead guilty on behalf of a nation of hypochondriacs."

She had a Tsingtao beer and he followed suit. The same as the day before, she sat close, her body lightly touching his.

"I wish I could see your eyes," he said. One's eyes communicated so much, at times more than words. He felt shut out when he was around persons hiding behind dark glasses.

"I've an eye problem," she answered. "If you're interested, they're a light brown. And this disfiguration on my cheek, an eight-year-old clobbered me with a sharp letter opener when I was a child. I cover it with pancake make-up when I go out socially but when I'm with close friends..."

"I thought you got it in a knife fight in a bar."

She looked up suddenly, sharply. He had struck a sensitive issue. Then she smiled to let him know she considered it banter. "Sounds romantic. I'll use that story some time."

The wind whipped up more strength and tossed her hair about.

She said quietly but not hesitantly, "I must ask for more compensation since I am delivering a tremendous amount of information."

He was taken by surprise. "How much?" He hadn't meant for the question to sound curt.

She wasn't fazed. "Eight hundred HK a day." He rapidly translated the sum into US dollars. About $100 US.

He brushed a strand of her hair out of his eyes. "I'll settle for that."

"Thank you. I have something to tell you. You were expecting a courier from the Mong Tai Liberation Army?"

Before he thought, he blurted out, "How did you know that?" Instantly he was sorry. "Forgive me, I didn't mean to ask. The answer is yes. What about it?"

"He arrived this morning. Passport detained him for two hours since he is on the list. He was granted a visa at the urgent request of the police. I imagine he will contact you later today or tomorrow."

"What does he want with me — if you know so much?"

"I thought you could answer that. They're in the drug business, as you know. The police will run a surveillance on him, and will know that he met you, and will be curious to know what you discussed.

She added, "And so will I. You've never been sure that I was being honest with you, and now...well, I was awake a good part of the night. I could not continue with a client who is involved with people who are providing the world with tons of opium...who are ruining lives..."

He moved so that he looked straight at her. "Listen, I wrote a series of newspaper articles some time ago about the Shan warlord, Khun Sa. I went to a small village near Mae Hong Son in northern Thailand, in the Golden Triangle area, and we talked. As a person I liked him. He has a certain charisma. And he liked me. We were adversaries and we both knew it — and my articles were not kind to him. I wrote what he was doing, objectively, the facts were heinous..."

He paused. "Yesterday they called my secretary in Los Angeles to know my whereabouts and I told her to give them the information. I have no idea what they want. Possibly publicity, another interview. I simply don't know."

She stubbed out the half-smoked cigarette. "I didn't know about the articles. You can understand my point of view. It didn't look right."

She didn't believe him anymore than he believed her story about the scar. And what about the courier? Her only source would be the police department, a friend inside. Or could it be that she was an informant for the police and had overheard? Still, no one in the department had known in advance about his rendezvous at the Bird Market. She might have several sources.

With an effort, she brightened. "Let's forget all of this business — and have a fun day."

They were coming into Silvermine Bay, a large cove with wooded hills set against a spectacular background of white clouds moving sluggishly across a pastel blue horizon.

"One more question and then we'll drop it."

"Yes?"

"The gun." He was lugging the box under his left arm. He wished he could park it somewhere.

She bristled. "What about it?"

"Can it be traced — if I use it and the police recover the bullet?"

She walked ahead of him to the gangplank, shoulders back, head high. "You're spoiling my day."

Her backside, the curves so tightly outlined, stirred other thoughts. "I'm with you," he said. "No more business. Definitely."

"Thank you." She turned with an impish smile. He realized she was as adept at playing with his thoughts and emotions as a rock star with an audience.

There were no cars about. Lantau, a mountainous island twice the size of Hong Kong island, permitted none, except for a few taxis and buses, and those owned by the residents. It was a scattered colony of 30,000 with homes recessed in the pines, a trendy resort not unlike some in California.

As they started up the hill to the Po Lin Monastery, they were conscious of the largest Buddha in all Asia looking out with peace-like countenance over a peace-like setting. This bronze Buddha was 110 feet tall, weighed 248 tons, and sat on a lotus-shaped concrete base.

Dave thought to himself, it doesn't matter what country or what faith or what era, somehow man believes his dedication will be measured by the size of the temples he builds, whether in the pyramids of ancient times or the great cathedrals of the middle ages, or today's Crystal Cathedral. God will be impressed by bigness, and the more gargantuan the better.

They were approaching the entrance to the monastery's grounds — a beautiful white arch picturing three Chinese temples across the top span — when Felicia stopped suddenly and turned about. She had the instinctive slow breath and concentration of a bird dog sensing prey.

A slightly built Chinese woman directly behind them came to an immediate halt, too, and took a step back in surprise. She was in a cheap, blue cotton dress, wore glasses and needed a hair styling. She was approaching her thirties.

She spoke quickly in Cantonese and Felicia answered her in short, terse sentences. The woman passed them. Felicia reported, "She asked if she might join us. She said she didn't know the way. I said no, that we had business to discuss."

"She's been following us," Dave said. "I saw her when I came off the Star Ferry and she stood behind you when you bought the tickets to Lantau and then followed directly behind us when we landed."

Felicia's face was anger set in concrete. His took a calmer, analytical stance. "She wants us to know she is following us."

It was the same old game he had encountered before. Someone places a "tight tail" on you with instructions to make the surveillance so obvious that you will be well aware of it. The purpose: (1) to let you know you are under surveillance and will worry about your guilt or innocence, and wonder how much someone else knows, or (2) to cause such disarray you will make a serious mistake in your operations and perhaps reveal more than a "loose" surveillance might disclose, or (3) if you are a weak person, you may go completely to pieces and suffer a nervous disorder that may eliminate you from the game, whatever that game might be.

"The police, perhaps?" he said.

"No. They play for keeps."

"Who then?"

"I'll check my sources." She spoke with finality. She would brook no further discussion.

"Look at the way the sun plays through the leaves." A soft wind gently moved the leaves and the sunshine playing on them created a phantasmagoria of beauty.

"You're a Buddhist?" he asked, looking up. The sun gave the enormous figure of Buddha an even more spiritual countenance than the sculptor had.

"A good try," she said, teasingly, and the episode of the gaunt woman vanished. "In Hong Kong I could be a Taoist or Confucianist or a half dozen other things."

She laughed softly. "At UCLA I studied world religions and found that I liked and loved your Jesus. He and Buddha taught much the same things, sometimes almost word for word, or so the scholars through the centuries would have us believe."

They came to the great temple, 60 feet high, considered one of the finest achievements in traditional Chinese architecture. They stood admiring it and later, the three Grand Buddhas inside.

"I'll always be a Buddhist," she continued, "because of my mother. I would never do anything to hurt her. As for my father, if he were alive, he would kill me if he knew I'd ever gone into a Christian church."

He wondered if he dared to probe. "I remember you said something about how you hated your father."

She turned to stare up at him. He wondered if behind the dark glasses the eyes were angry or contemplative, soft or calculating. "My father never lived by what Buddha taught."

Dave heard the gurgle of venom in her voice. "I tell myself I must forget — but there are some things you never forget."

She stubbed out the cigarette. "You never talk about yourself."

There was the faint clip of a camera shutter. The gaunt woman had come up from their blind side and now was casually sauntering away.

Felicia shouted something in Cantonese but there was no response. "I told her to come back and we'd pose and she could get a good picture."

He realized the snapshot meant nothing. It was only one more ploy in a well-laid-out campaign of harassment. He could not guess what that campaign was about.

"Forget her," Felicia said softly, the anger passing quickly. Her emotions, he knew by now, were a chameleon's. "She's not going to ruin a beautiful day."

They walked on, through a burst of flowers in neatly tended expanses, of every color, blues and whites and red, dog roses and azaleas and rhododendrons. The exotic smell of incense filled the air, too, and there was the soothing chanting of monks praying and the rhythmic clanging of gongs.

"I never knew my father," he said. "He died when I was six. There are times I feel sad I can't call to memory a picture of him. My mother worked as a real estate agent, and I remember the times when she sold something, and we would celebrate. I'd have a chocolate malt, a real treat, and she a sundae, and sometimes we'd rent a home video. I remember my favorite was 'Indiana Jones' and hers was 'Love Story'."

They entered the Protector Temple and after passing a white-jade Buddha, had lunch in a restaurant that looked like an assembly hall. Monks scurried about serving meals. She had already told him that for $15 US a night, he could rent a room and the monks would generously provide a board for him to sleep on. "Where can you get such a bargain in the States?" she asked.

He learned the meal was vegetarian. "We don't believe in killing any living thing," she said.

"I don't like vegetables," he protested. "I'm with President Bush on the broccoli issue."

She laughed. "You'll never get to nirvana."

He saw her pushing some vegetables to one side. "You're sorting out your vegetables," he said accusingly.

"Some are better than others."

"None is better than others."

She was amused and a little shocked. "I shop every morning for fresh vegetables. No respectable Chinese housewife would ever think of eating frozen foods or day-old lettuce. Some have big white beautiful fridges but they're for show purposes, like a Rolls Royce. Open one and all you'll find are bottles of soda the teenagers keep there."

Near them a Caucasian boy entered with a Chinese girl. Both were in their late teens and the boy an American judging by the cut of his clothes and hair. They were holding hands.

She turned serious. "I can never marry an American."

He was mildly surprised. "You're a racist?"

"Not me. Americans." She lit another cigarette.

"I wish you'd give up smoking."

"I didn't know you cared." Her tone thanked him for caring.

She continued, "You think I'm racist? Well, let me tell you a story, my story. I fell in love with the most wonderful boy at UCLA and I brought him home to meet my mother. That was a mistake. I took him to the temple. I thought he would understand. Instead he laughed at what he called the fat-bellied Buddha.

"We drove down Des Voeux Road Central, and they were building a skyscraper, and had the bamboo scaffolding up all the way to the top, and he said he didn't know we were still living in the Stone Age.

"I took him to a building on the same street and to get inside we walked down an alley to the entrance. I explained that the feng shui scholar had decided after weeks of study of the wind and other forces of nature that the entrance had to go there and not out on the main street. I explained that every building in Hong Kong, all of this jungle of skyscrapers, had been gone over by feng shui experts who had decided how the buildings would be placed on the lots, their entrances, and even where the desks would go in the offices. I explained that this was necessary to insure the prosperity and well-being of the people involved.

"He said, 'You're the third greatest financial center in the world — and you still believe in medicine men?'"

Dave remembered a news story he had read with amazement. A village called Pat Hueng (1,000) had become enraged when a construction company started work on a three-story, $6,400,000 US temple without the advice of feng shui scholars. The building would bring "bad luck," financial disaster and even death to everyone who lived there. One feng shui expert was quoted as saying that the half-finished temple was "like a tiger ready to eat us." Before that happened, the workers walked away from the project and it may never be finished.

"And then he learned about some of our gods," she continued, "Tin Hau, whom the water people worship, and Kwan Kung, one of our greatest deities. He lived centuries ago and was our Robinhood. He stands for gallantry and chivalry, and like your Robinhood, had a band of merry men who roamed the countryside defending the weak and women in general.

"But he's more than that. If you visit the Man Mo Temple where thousands go for spiritual help, you'll find two deities. One is Man Cheong, the God of Literature, and the other, Kwan Kung, known in this temple as Mo, the god of martial arts. We have celebrations twice a year at Man Mo and my mother and I never miss one. We take food and money and burn joss sticks. As for the money, the Tung Wah Group of Hospitals manages the temple, and spends what is needed for upkeep, and the balance — tens of thousands — goes to schools and other causes.

"I told my fiance all of this and he said, 'We've got temples all across America to Manny, Mo and something. The Pep Boys.'

"A week after he arrived, we broke up. I didn't ask him to accept my cultural background but merely to understand it. But you Americans are not used to clouds of incense and the beating of drums and gongs, any more than I am to churches as barren and cold as Hilton hotels."

They took the late afternoon boat back to Hong Kong Central. The gaunt woman sat opposite them, staring, occasionally making a note. They averted their eyes, pretending she did not exist.

They said little. His thoughts went scrimmaging about, on the events of the day, on this alluring creature beside him. Only a few hours ago he had been most suspicious of her. He had even considered the possibility that she was engaged in some criminal activity. He had been very careful in everything he said or did. She might be an informant. She might be setting him up for something fearsome beyond imagination.

How preposterous. He was paranoid.

But was he? Had the situation changed any beyond the fact he knew her better and he liked what he had learned? She was still privy to information that it would seem only someone close to a crime or criminal could possibly know. The most damning fact was that only the next morning after he had requested a .357 Magnum, she had supplied the weapon. Even someone in the shadowy world of guns and ammo might have difficulty in providing such a weapon, especially in Hong Kong.

He thought it likely that the same thoughts about him might be swirling about in her mind. She knew a courier was coming from the most notorious warlord in all Asia, one who controlled most of the world's supply of opium. Yet Dave would be shattered if she had doubts about him after three hours of walking and talking among the pines and flowers, a day radiant not only for the beauty of nature they had shared but for the revealment of themselves.

On landing, they parted. She thanked him and kissed him lightly. For a brief second, he felt the warmth of her body and there was the familiar haunting scent of her perfume. "Bi-bi," she said softly. "Goodbye."

She hailed a taxi and he walked to the Star Ferry. A time or two he looked back and the gaunt woman was there, only a few steps away. She may have deserted him at the Star Ferry. He couldn't find her after the boat left.

At the Regent he walked into stark reality. The luster of the day broke with a crash when the desk clerk handed him twelve messages from Mac's widow, Heather. She had called every ten minutes or so for the last two hours. On the last message was scribbled a note, "The caller requested that you phone immediately. She said it was a question of life or death."

Chapter 18

She answered on the first ring. "Dave Anderson here," he said.

"Thank you for returning my call." It was the same matter-of-fact, laconic voice he remembered. "Two men were here. They wrecked my apartment and threatened to kill me if I didn't come up with a staggering sum of money. I need your help, Mr. Anderson."

He couldn't fathom why there wasn't more of a sense of panic. "I offered it and you rejected it."

"I was confused. So much had happened. I know now Mac would have wanted me to ask your advice since Mac and you were such good friends."

"Someone tried to kill me before...you can't expect me...we might meet some place..."

"I daren't leave. If you came in the back way...no one would know. I'm sure Mac would want you..."

She drifted off, then continued, "I know I shouldn't mention your friendship with Mac...as if I were taking advantage..."

"Let me think this over." He regretted he sounded belligerent. He was more irked than angry. He simply did not understand this woman. Besides, he was not about to return to the place where he would have been slain if the gunman had had better aim.

She might be setting him up. He discarded the idea. She was strange but not one to entrap him, he didn't think.

"I'll call you back," he said.

"Thank you." For the first time, he detected an iota of emotion. Perhaps there was a deep well of it but she concealed it through some mistaken belief that only the meek showed feeling, or some such ridiculous idea. He had known people like that.

After hanging up, he sat for minutes as if in a coma, mulling over the situation. He would have it on his conscience forever if she were murdered. His conclusion was to consult with Inspector Yeung, a step he had sworn he would never take. He disliked the man's clever manipulations and his way of covering up his wiles with feigned graciousness. But Dave realized that this development was completely out of his experience.

He caught the Inspector as he was leaving the station for home and dinner. Yeung listened attentively, as if his wife and little son and two sub-teen daughters were not expecting him. "Thank you for ringing me up. Most thoughtful."

While Dave listened, the Inspector outlined the possibilities. If Dave were willing to return to her flat — and Yeung acknowledged that Dave would be showing considerable courage if he did — then Yeung would secretly cordon off the neighborhood with as many as 20 officers. They would "work" the area for an hour before Dave arrived.

"I can assure you," Yeung said, "that you will be taking no chance in going to the flat and coming out. However, there is one gap we cannot cover."

"Yes?"

"The woman. Has she a weapon?

Dave did not believe so and commented that he thought she was acting in good faith.

The Inspector had his doubts. "Give me an hour and a half. It's now thirty past seven. Tell her you'll be there at nine o'clock. Go in the front door. I don't like the idea of moving you around in the dark."

Dave was firm when he phoned her. "I'm coming only on one condition, that you will be frank and honest with me. I want to know where and when Mac died, and of what. I want to know what this deal is all about that supposedly produced millions in profits."

Her voice was low as though someone were listening. "I will tell you what I know. I promise."

To his analytical mind, that was not reassuring. The promise could be as evasive as before. Nor did the Inspector's conviction that he could protect Dave with certainty. From his years as a newspaperman, he knew full well that neither the FBI, the CIA, the Secret Service, nor any law enforcement agency could seal off a person. There was always a way a clever killer could get to his target.

He had been in casual clothes all day. Now he put on a suit. He needed a coat to cover the .357 Magnum he tucked in his belt. He debated about buttoning the coat. If he did, he feared there might be a telltale bulge. He decided to let the coat swing open. He reminded himself that he would have to take care the coat did not open too far and reveal the weapon.

As per arrangement, at precisely 15 minutes to nine a taxi pulled up to the hotel, chauffeured by the same police officer who had driven Dave to his first meeting with Ming Toy. Dave could not remember the officer's name.

"Sergeant Tang Shun-yan," the officer said. "Call me Sergeant

Tang. I understand, sir, you have a drink in your country by that name."

The same heavy traffic, the same landmarks, the same panorama unfolded as on that first night. All except the duck episode. Dave found himself breathing a little quicker, his hands not too steady. He took a tighter grip on himself. This time he had a gun.

When he left the taxi, he heard the police helicopter thrashing quite low above him. Its high-powered spotlight played circles around him but never shone directly on him. He was conscious, too, that the foot traffic of three nights ago was lighter. The police were holding pedestrians each way by a few minutes.

As instructed, he walked as he usually did, not too fast, not too slow. Approaching her flat, he noted the geranium pot turned upside down, the pot smashed, the dirt and plant on the ground.

At his first knock, the door opened. She was another woman from the Heather before, her blonde hair tousled, her make-up smeared, and those expensive diamond earrings he remembered so well, gone.

There had been no greeting before but this time, "Thank you for coming."

He nodded, walked silently past her to a door leading to a bedroom and bath, his right hand inside the coat on the Magnum. With her following him, he opened closet doors and checked under the bed.

She whispered nervously, "They're gone."

After looking over the kitchen and a lighted backdoor step, he returned to the living room.

"You can see..." She indicated the embroidered velvet sofa, completely torn up, the stuffing spilling out, the ebony elephant smashed, pieces scattered, a footstool with a long gash across its middle, the Monet and Gaugin copies on the floor, tossed there in a check for wall safes.

"Sit here." It was the same command.

She took over the conversation. "I must get out of Hong Kong, Mr. Anderson. They think I am hiding big sums of money. Several million dollars. It's ridiculous. They're crazy."

For the first time Dave spoke. "Who're they?"

"I don't know. I honestly don't."

"What was the deal Mac had?"

She was trembling. Her voice came in spurts. "I don't know the details. He borrowed to buy a ship, I know that, and it went down in the South China Sea. I don't know what happened. He wasn't much to talk about his business."

She shook herself and the words flooded out. "I've got a passport and a U.S. visa, and I need a ticket to Los Angeles on a plane leaving tomorrow morning. Will you buy it for me out of the $60,000 Mac sent you, and come with me to the airport? They will kill me if I go by myself. Could someone meet the plane at Los Angeles Airport and give me whatever you think I should have of the $60,000?"

Dave was shaken. He had no idea Heather or anyone knew about the $60,000. Obviously, after sending it in installments, Mac had advised her of the total. Or could it be that Heather had airmailed the currency, after Mac's death, to hide it and have it waiting for her should she need it, such as now?

She continued, "And buy me a ticket to a town in Idaho named McCall? Mac bought a cabin near there. We were going to retire there."

Dave broke in. "Hold it right there, Mrs. Dunleavy. Let's back up and talk about Mac."

"What do you want to know?" she asked sharply.

"What happened to him? What caused his death? Was he ill a long time? All of that."

She ran a hand through her hair. "I must look a sight. I haven't had time —"

Dave raised his voice. "What did he die of?"

She took a deep breath. "Leukemia, I think."

"You think? Don't you know?"

Her gaze darted about the room. "Yes, he had leukemia. He was very sick when he went to China and then I got the message he was dead."

"Where in China?"

"A little fishing village near Lufeng, not far from Guanzhou."

"Why did he go there?"

"I'm not sure. I think he had a business matter to discuss with a man from Guanzhou."

Dave got up, paced about. "You're forcing me to cross-examine you. Can't you just quietly tell me everything the way people do when a relative or friend dies?"

She rose. "I'm not myself. It's been rough."

"I think you are yourself," Dave said. "I'm told you are a brilliant business woman. You worked with Mac in the export / import business. You married him."

She sank back in the chair. She was barely audible. "Yes, we were married but it was not romance, not love."

She hesitated, then proceeded quietly, calling up memories. "We went to work every morning at 9 o'clock, and used each other's brains all day — and at 9 o'clock every night, we went to bed and used each other's bodies hours on end to satisfy our needs. We —"

Dave exploded. "Dammit, let's get back to Guanzhou. Mac died suddenly, I assume. Who called you? Where's he buried? When did he die? I don't know why you're being evasive, what you've got to hide. You want my help, yet you won't open up with me."

He started for the door. "To hell with you!"

She grabbed him by the arm. "Please, don't desert me."

She held him tightly. "Yes, he died suddenly. I got a call from Sir James Mahoney. He was the Brit Mac went to see. Don't ask me his address. All I know he was staying at the White Dove Hotel in Guanzhou. They met in the fishing village because Sir James did not want Beijing to know he had a deal with Mac to import tractors. It was Sir James who phoned me. He said there would be complications and take weeks, maybe months, if we tried to move Mac's body to Hong Kong. He suggested sea burial and I went along with it since Mac loved the sea. He made all the arrangements and sent me Mac's ring and watch and some papers and a little carved elephant I'd given Mac one anniversary."

She squeezed Dave's hand. "Please, what else, Dave? I want to call you Dave. I'm closer to Mac when I do. I know I've been evasive. I'm just that kind of person. I keep everything to myself."

Dave pulled his hand away. "The deal," he said.

"Yes, the deal." She raced on breathlessly. "Mac borrowed millions from three parties to put down as an installment on the ship, the Mintoro. He loaded it with Lexus cars in Tokyo and it was bound for Kota Kinabalu and other ports in Borneo. It was only five days out when it sank. There was an explosion and fire. No one knows what caused it. Just after it cleared the Sulu Sea, miles from any port."

She moistened her lips. "Two of the parties Mac borrowed from were Triads. That's the Hong Kong Mafia, and they're after me, along with a bank in Northern Thailand. They think Mac made a lot of money from insurance they think he collected. But we haven't got a cent to date, and when I do, if ever, it won't be the big money they figure on."

She reached a hand up to an ear lobe. "They took my earrings. Mac paid $38,000 for them. I've got to get out of Hong Kong. They're going to kill me. They're not bluffing. The Triad doesn't bluff. They've given me until 10 tomorrow to come up with the money. I don't know why 10. You will help me, won't you, Dave? For Mac's sake. He said once I could always turn to you — when he was sick and knew he was dying..."

Dave said softly, "I owed him one."

"I don't understand."

"Just an expression. I'll get you a first class ticket on the first plane out in the morning and my secretary will meet you in L.A. What are the names of the Triads?"

"I thought you would want to know." She handed him a list of seven names. One possibly, would be the Chrysanthemum Man. Felicia might know which one.

"You did call the police, didn't you?"

The question, so unexpected, stunned him momentarily.

"You don't need to tell me," she continued. "It's none of my business."

"I've a friend over in Wanchai who runs a small shop," she continued. "I thought I'd go there tonight. I must get away from here. Will you go with me?"

He hesitated, not because he didn't want to go but because she had cleverly arranged for the police to escort them. By asking if he had called the police — and learning he had — and by mentioning the Triad and suggesting they would be moving in on her before 10 tomorrow, she knew the police would continue a tight surveillance of her.

While she hastily packed two bags of personal articles, Dave phoned to set up reservations on a 9:40 a.m. flight to Los Angeles. He promised to call in movers to crate her possessions and ship them at a later date.

When she was ready, he went to the curb to flag down a taxi. Sergeant Tang promptly brought the cab up. Again, the police helicopter flew low and foot traffic was briefly blocked. If she heard the 'copter, she showed no sign.

They took the Cross Harbour tunnel and within 20 minutes were in the Wanchai district. Even at this hour, the little back lanes were crowded. Hawkers were peddling herb medicines, Chinese crullers, dim sums, snakes, clothes, toys, and on one curb was a photocopier whose owner was doing a brisk business. Over the general din rose the clack, clack of maj jongh tiles.

Heather's friend, a Chinese woman about 40, in traditional black cotton garb, was waiting in front of her tiny shop that was closed for business. Inside, a weak yellow bulb cast shadows over shelves holding big medicine jars, bags of colored rice, candles, packages of chrysanthemum tea, bottles of moo-tai, paper lanterns, and cardboard cutouts of automobiles, television sets, airplanes, and assorted furniture. Calligraphy, recently inked, hung from the ceiling to dry.

The woman handed Heather a cutout of a Maserati. "For your husband," she said. Heather stepped outside, put a match to the paper car, and held it over a metal rubbish container while it burned.

Heather thanked her friend profusely. "Will bring my husband much joy," she said. It was an old custom to burn a replica of something the dead had enjoyed. A piano for pianist, TV set for an actor, a typewriter for a writer, a cart for a coolie, clothes for a woman. It was somewhat the same as flowers or placing a memento on a grave in western countries.

The woman handed Heather a soap stone "chop" which Heather presented to Dave. "A short time before Mac died, he had this made for you. It has your name on it and you press it into hot wax when you seal important mail."

Shortly afterwards, Dave left. He would return at 7 a.m. to escort Heather to the plane.

At that hour he was sitting in the hotel lobby for Sergeant Tang to pick him up when he was summoned to a phone.

Inspector Yeung was on the line. "Our subject has just checked into Cathay Airlines for a plane leaving in a half hour for Kuala Lumpur."

"Where?" Dave asked, not believing he had heard correctly.

"Kuala Lumpur in Malaysia. There's nothing we can do. She has committed no crime we know about and no complaint has been filed against her. She holds a valid passport."

"You've got to stop her," Dave said angrily.

He could hear Inspector Yeung take a deep, weary breath. "In Hong Kong we respect a citizen's rights. She can travel any place she pleases."

Dave raised his voice, then brought it under control. "What if she murdered Mac? In the United States...you could bring her back."

"You are not the first to bring up the possibility of murder. We considered it — and our informant in the Triad advised that the Triad was pursuing that premise. But we don't have the slightest bit of evidence. Nothing to go on."

Dave had seldom known such anger. From the beginning this woman had played him for a fool. And now, through him, she had maneuvered the Hong Kong police into giving her protection step by step throughout the night, even to escorting her to the airport.

Chapter 19

Marge called from Los Angeles in late morning. Two American oil companies and one Dutch had requested economic surveys and a rundown on politics and the stability of the governments of Kazakhstan, Tajikistan and Kyrgyzstan, former Soviet republics. Dave instructed her to advise the clients that such reports would take 60 days, and to order Ramie Stevenson to those countries when she had finished her report on the Kurds.

"That's asking a lot of a 25-year-old," Marge commented.

"Age has nothing to do with it. Some individuals at 25 have it — and others never will."

Marge said, "You're being investigated."

"What!"

"Your bank called. They have had inquiries from a San Francisco bank with close ties to Hong Kong."

That would be a Triad bank, the one in San Francisco. The Triads operated, he knew, in Los Angeles, San Francisco, Chicago and New York.

"Don't give it a thought," he said.

But he did.

He met Inspector Yeung at the Inspector's "invitation," for lunch in the Regent Restaurant.

Between where they sat and the water was an esplanade where the tai chi people had worked out that morning. Now they had been supplanted by two young men rehearsing the front and rear ends of a colorful, ferocious-looking Chinese dragon. It was supposed to undulate in the middle, and that was the problem. A covey of young kibitzers, in the sub-12 age, were offering unsolicited advice.

The Inspector looked over the menu. "My children highly recommend hamburgers. I have never had one."

"Onions?" the pretty young Chinese waitress asked.

The Inspector looked puzzled. "The works," Dave volunteered.

"The works," she repeated, laughing.

"Our young people," the Inspector said, "get along very well with the American language."

After Dave ordered French onion soup, the Inspector said, "I thank you for ringing me up last night."

There he went again. The old "graciousness" bit.

"If you don't mind, I have a few matters I would like to clear up. Might I ask, had Mrs. Dunleavy ever mentioned Kuala Lumpur to you? Or Mr. Dunleavy?"

"Never." Dave found himself tightening up.

"Did you ever get a letter postmarked from anywhere in Asia from either of them?"

Dave shook his head and said curtly, "I never even knew his wife existed and as I told you before, the only contacts I have had with Mac Dunleavy in the last four or five years were Christmas cards. That was it, period."

"Yes, yes, I remember now, you did tell me."

The waitress brought a container of catsup with the hamburger. The Inspector examined the catsup gingerly as if it might jump out at him.

"You can put the catsup on the hamburger, if you want to," Dave said, "but you don't have to. Some Americans do and some don't."

"Probably I should. My children will interrogate me tonight and I don't want them to think I only went half way. You know, of course, that Mrs. Dunleavy is traveling under your name?"

Dave almost came out of his seat. "What?" he shouted.

"I did not mean to startle you," the Inspector said slowly, treading ground lightly. "Yes, there it was on the ticket, Mrs. David Anderson. The travelers checks were also made out in your name."

"Travelers checks?" Dave was floored.

"Two for $500 US each. American Express. Mrs. David Anderson. Surely you knew?"

Dave pushed the soup aside. "I did not!" He brought his voice level down. At other tables heads were turning. "Why would I give her travelers checks?"

"I agree, Mr. Anderson. Why would you?"

Dave took a deep breath. "I can see I have become a prime suspect in a matter I know nothing about."

The Inspector spoke up quickly. "I would never put it that way. There are questions and I am sure there are answers. We will find them, and we must find them before others do."

He rubbed his eyes and drew another deep breath. "My asthma. Keeps getting worse. I just came from Mrs. Dunleavy's flat. My men went through everything. Found nothing personal, no clues. The building's manager will store the furniture until he hears from her — which I don't think he ever will.

“As for the seven names she gave you, we have nothing on them. She likely took them from a newspaper or some directory.”

He cleared a cough away. “You might like to know that we have identified the assassin who attempted to kill you. I regret to say we have no evidence and cannot arrest him. He has four friends who will testify that he was having dinner with them at the time in question and a maitre d’ who informs us that he was at the restaurant the entire time. They are all members of the same Triad society. You may have had some dealings with the Triads...I mean, of course, professionally, as a journalist.”

The inference was clear. “They are your Mafia,” Dave said.

“That is what Americans and Europeans think. No, not at all. The Mafia is a family affair, a godfather, all of that. The Triads are a lodge, a union, a workman’s organization, a religion — and many of them exist financially on drugs, prostitution, smuggling, gambling, and every crime you can name, including torture and murder.”

He finished the hamburger. “My children will be proud of me. My next step toward leaving the barbarism of Chinese food and become a civilized person will be to partake of pizza, and I hope that experience will be more palatable than this one was.”

He smiled but Dave was not in the mood for his sly humor.

The Inspector continued, “We have hundreds of Triad societies in Hong Kong. One has 80,000 members and another 100,000. Anywhere you go in the world, into a Chinese community, you will find a Triad. They just spring up and one society has nothing to do with another unless they are dividing up the territory.”

He was talking to fill the time while he was thinking his way through the immediate situation. “Did you know that the Triads under one name or another have been around since 200 years B.C.? They started out as a patriotic organization. Dr. Sun Yat-Sen was a Triad member — and so was Chiang Kai-Shek who fought the Communists.”

A girl of about 16 in a white blouse and dark blue swirling skirt came up. “Mr. Anderson?” Dave nodded. She handed him a small envelope and was gone.

The Inspector watched as Dave opened it to read: YOUR SUIT IS READY AND MUST BE DELIVERED <u>IMMEDIATELY</u>. TAKE STAR FERRY, ASK TAXI FOR LADDER STREET. SUIT WILL BE DELIVERED AT CURB. PLEASE DO NOT DELAY. URGENT.

The writing was Felicia Yee’s.

Dave pocketed the note. “A suit I ordered is ready.”

The Inspector nodded and Dave asked the waitress for the check.

The Inspector continued, “You can understand how difficult it is to investigate a case in which the Triad has had a part. They swear by one another. Anyone who betrays them is signing his own death warrant."

He rose to leave and hesitated. "I might add this. If the Triads entered into a deal with Mr. Dunleavy and are now demanding their money — they may have spread their investment around among two or more societies — each may be taking separate actions to collect, and that would account for your assassin being under orders by his organization to eliminate you and the man you met in the Bird Market under orders from another Triad to negotiate. The one may not know or care what the other is doing. An interesting speculation, no?"

He started away, then turned back. "Your assassin is free to carry out his orders. I would strongly recommend that you let us pick up the suit."

He was gone before Dave could react. The man was not only a detective. He was a psychic.

Dave could scarcely contain himself as he took long strides to the Star Ferry. He was fearful of what Felicia would report. Something had happened, something horrendous, something he must know immediately.

At Ladder Street, a narrow, dark alley that climbed step by step past little shops, the cab driver pulled alongside a curb where two teenage boys waited. One paid the driver while Dave protested. The other grabbed his hand. "Come, please. Hurry! Hurry!"

Momentarily, Dave resisted, stunned by the unexpected urgency. Then the boy was dashing ahead and Dave was following the best he could, darting in between a thickening stream of people, entering a jade shop, rushing through, out a back door, up a corridor, more steps, into a smoke-filled room where four workmen sat at a table bare except for their rice bowls, never glancing up, using chopsticks. A small Buddha sat in a corner niche, incense burning, a strong fish smell, then out into another room, and then into a space little more than a closet, filled with easels and artwork and the strong odor of paint.

Felicia was waiting, standing beside a small window that looked out on a plaster wall. The boy disappeared. Dave saw a Felicia he had never known. Her shoulders sagged, her lips trembled. There was no life where there had been so much.

"I thought you'd never come," she whispered.

She took a deep breath, gasping for air and courage. "The people who are after you — they haven't been sure of you. Some thought you were what you said you were. A friend of Mr. Dunleavy's. But this morning when you worked it so, with police protection, this woman could escape —"

"I had no idea."

"They're certain she took cash in her bags, the money Mr. Dunleavy owed them. They plan to intercept her bags and kidnap her...torture her into confessing."

"Felicia, please..."

"I'm crying inside. They're holding a meeting this hour to decide what to do about you. They won't kill you until they get the money but they'll torture you if you hold out on them...and no police protection will help you. They are a law unto themselves. You may succeed in stalling them...but in the end..."

She broke, suffocated by fear.

"Let me explain what happened," he said. "She made a fool of me...of the police."

Her thoughts leaped elsewhere. "I know you have doubts about me. You think I must be one of the...because how could I know all of this if I weren't. And it hurts. I woke up crying this morning because I love you. Not in a romantic way...but as a friend. By all that's holy in the teachings of my Lord Buddha, I tell you that I am a purveyor of information, nothing more."

He was shaken. He couldn't come up with a quick answer.

"You don't believe me. You do have doubts."

"Wait," he said. "Everything's happening too fast. You know I'd be lying if I said I didn't have doubts. But I keep telling myself...I believe you. But at the same time I realize what you're thinking. Don't tell me you don't have doubts about me...my relationship with Mac...and his wife...and Khun Sa of the Golden Triangle. If I were you I'd wonder how I could explain this away...oh, the hell with it. You know what I'm trying to say."

For a moment they were quiet, then she said as much to herself as to him, "I think the time will come, Dave, when we believe in each other. If we can only now believe in each other when we don't believe in each other...and carry on as if we each are what we are supposed to be."

He thought that over, then broke the tension. "You should have been a lawyer. I've never heard a more obfuscated statement in my life."

She smiled. "When I was a child I saw an old American movie with Gary Cooper. It was 'High Noon'...and I prayed that night I would never grow up...because if I did I might have to shoot it out with Gary Cooper. Funny what children think...but here I am and it's high noon and I'm on a street in the hot sun and there's Gary Cooper waiting for me, hand on his six shooter..."

She continued, "And then I grew up and there were more old American movies...with the romance and love a young girl craves...and more years passed and there were more American films...and the romance was gone and there were killings and people dying...and blood all over everything...and romance was a couple wrecking a bed."

He wondered why she was telling him this. He didn't know what to say.

She continued dreamily, "Some day I will find my Chinese Clark Gable...and we won't kiss like guppies...or act like wrestlers...and I won't moan like I was on a torture rack...and he won't pound me like I was a cheap pick-up. We'll be passionate but gentle and kind and loving."

She lit a cigarette. "I'm talking like this because I want you to know that there is another side to your criminal suspect."

He took her in his arms. "I believe you."

She pulled away. "In time...if one of us doesn't die first."

She went back into his arms, clinging for the reassurance the touch of his body brought. She kissed him on the cheek. "Be careful. I've never felt toward anyone as deeply as I feel toward you."

She broke away, shook out her hair, smoothed her dress, and took a long drag on the cigarette. She was her old self.

"I've earned my money today. Pay me."

Chapter 20

A taxi was waiting for him at the foot of Ladder Street. Sergeant Tang hopped out to open the door.

Dave's personal flares went rocketing off.

"You followed me here?" Dave snapped.

"No, sir."

"Someone else did!"

The Sergeant got behind the wheel. "I could not say, sir."

"Stop calling me sir!"

Dave got hold of himself. What was, was. On the way back to the hotel, he reached two firm decisions. He had come to Hong Kong for only one purpose, to look after the welfare of Ming Toy. Not Mac's deals. As long as Ming Toy and her mother remained in Hong Kong, they were in grave danger. They might know about Mac's deals and they might not.

Tomorrow he would put the sampan up for sale. He would give them a one-way air ticket to mainland China and money sufficient to take care of them for six months. He would escort them personally to the airport, partly for their protection and partly to make sure they did leave Hong Kong. That would take two days.

As for his own safety, he reasoned that neither the Triads nor anyone else would murder him. On the contrary, they would do everything possible to keep him alive, on the premise he had information about "millions of dollars."

And then an evil thought strolled in. Inspector Yeung might have ordered surveillance on him to Ladder Street. Felicia might have kept the Inspector posted.

Dave thought, how could I possibly think that? I am so blasted suspicious. It's the newspaper experience. You start out as a cub reporter with naivete and idealism, and then the politicians lie or steal or get caught in sex scandals...the mayor has figured out a legal way to steal the city blind...half the celebrities have mistresses...the minister runs off with the church's secretary...the apartment house the supervisor owns burns down and 11 die because he refused to put in sprinklers...the lawyers bilk their clients out of thousands with exorbitant fees...your peers take joy in digging up old scandals that wreck lives...or under the premise of "in depth" and "objective" reporting slant stories that would make Mother Teresa look like a hooker.

However, at that point, idealism was not yet dead and you write stories about good people doing good things, and the editors throw them back. They said no one wants to read about Jimmy Carter helping the poor build homes, that kind of sentimental hogwash.

Cynicism followed, which was self-destructing in any profession, and especially in journalism. The saying went that you wouldn't trust your own mother.

Dave squared his shoulders. Culture aside, Felicia Yee was a woman he could love, in another time, in another place. She was much like Laurie.

Back in his room, he thought that over. Quickly, he got out his diary, to write a warning to himself. An admonition on paper would temper his thinking and actions. "I've got to put up barriers. I must take my time with Felicia, and as long as there is the slightest doubt, wait until that doubt has been removed. I know it's going to be hard. Nature has given the male animal such a strong, fierce sex desire and drive that the compulsion to satisfy it — under the guise of love — when it isn't love at all — can wreck a life. Laurie, Laurie, why did you leave me? We knew who we were...our thoughts, our feelings..."

Shortly afterward he took a phone call from Alfred Kwan's secretary. Mr. Kwan was interested in subscribing to World Coverage. Could Dave come to his office for tea at four o'clock?

Mr. Kwan was leaving the next day for Tokyo and most anxious to discuss a matter with Dave.

Dave could. With Alfred Kwan as a client, it was very likely that World Coverage would attract a number of Hong Kong financiers and industrialists. Still, a snake-like thought crept in, to wit: Alfred Kwan might have other matters to discuss.

At four o'clock promptly, Dave walked into an elegant but modern office where four secretaries were working at computer stations, answering telephones, and running fax machines. A well-dressed, beautifully coifed woman rose from a far desk to welcome him. "We thank you for coming on such short notice." She spoke impeccable English.

At the same time a door opened to Alfred Kwan's inner office, a woman who obviously had been in tears came out with him following. Even though she was speaking Cantonese, it was evident she was thanking him profusely.

Dave stepped into an office that, amazingly, was Swedish modern.

A large desk sat at a triangle in a far corner. In the foreground was a low table with several chairs. Only on the walls was the décor different. One had a mural of the Muffin Mountains of Kweilin and the Li River, and on the wall opposite, Dr. Sun Yat-Sen. On the blond desk was a picture of Kwan's wife and three children and neatly arranged papers. In a small, nearby niche was a gold-washed image of Buddha.

Kwan said to his secretary, "Tell Nicole we are ready." To Dave, he said, "Thank you for coming. We'll sit at the table for our tea. You may be wondering about the woman who just left. She is a gatekeeper at my ship yard, a most responsible employee. She borrowed quite a sum from a relative, that she cannot pay back. She has nine children and he demanded her 14-year-old boy to settle the debt. It is an old Chinese custom that is fast disappearing. If you cannot pay a debt, you are obliged to give up a child. I told her I would take care of the debt."

"Awfully good of you," Dave commented.

"No, not good in that sense. Good business. She will work hard and be loyal to me. You cannot purchase loyalty with pay raises. You buy loyalty by being loyal to others when they are in trouble."

Nicole wheeled in a trolley with a silver tea setting surrounded with small bamboo baskets containing dim sum (snacks).

"Har gau," she said. He translated, "Shrimp dumplings."

"Cha sin bao."

"Barbecued pork bun."

"Siu mai."

"Pork and shrimp dumplings."

And so it went, chicken with banana, steamed mashed mud carp, jelly fish, marinated baby octopus, preserved gizzards. Kwan said, "Canton cuisine. Been around for a thousand years."

When Dave chose the shrimp dumplings and chicken with banana, Kwan laughed. "You Americans never appreciate truly good Chinese food, the octopus, the gizzards."

Nicole poured hot tea. "Earl of Greystone," Kwan said. "May we talk while we have our tea?"

Kwan turned brisk. "In addition to subscribing to World Coverage, I want you personally to prepare a special paper for me. As you know, the island of Borneo is split in half. Indonesia owns the bottom and Malaysia the top. I need a research paper on the Malaysian part that would cover the economy, the ports, the Skull House out of Kuching, and I want to list other specific points. Can you do this?"

Dave hesitated. His mind searched out a quick answer to the question: Why does Alfred Kwan want a report on such an out-of-the-way land? Now if he had been asking for one on Japan...

"I would need some time," Dave said.

"How much?" Kwan put a silver lighter to a cigarette.

"You know why I'm here. I must sell the sampan and..."

"I'll put my assistant, Chen, on the sampan. No problem. Maybe day, two. If you want or need an assistant on this special assignment, I would recommend someone who is doing research for you already — and for me. Felicia Yee. A very fine young woman. Extremely capable. There is talk she is a Lesbian. Would that bother you?"

Dave stiffened his body to keep from betraying shock. "Not at all. But I won't need an assistant."

"I will speak to Miss Yee about it."

Before Dave could protest, Kwan plunged on. "Have you learned anything more about the tragic death of your friend...what was the name?"

"Mac Dunleavy." Dave hesitated. Should he tell him about Heather? Wouldn't he learn anyway?

"His widow left this morning for Kuala Lumpur."

Now it was Kwan's turn to be surprised. "I did not know. I thought she would stay, settle up his affairs. When you hear from her, please do warn her that she may be in considerable danger."

Dave bored in. "Why would she?"

Kwan stubbed out the cigarette, rose. "Chen will call you tomorrow about the sampan. You will prepare me a statement about the cost of the special assignment and give it to him. Thank you for coming, Mr. Anderson. It has been a pleasure. I look forward to a good relationship."

Dave said, "I'll get a cost sheet to you in a couple of days. As for Miss Yee, while I respect her capabilities, I never use anyone except a staff member. I make no exceptions."

Kwan said, "We'll see."

Chapter 21

At the hotel, the desk clerk handed him a small parcel wrapped in a dirty newspaper. Not thinking, Dave opened it and a flock of Hong Kong bills fell out across the counter and to the floor. The clerk picked them up. His sharp eyes said the obvious. A payoff.

Dave crumpled the contents in his arms and fell into a nearby leather lounge. He noted writing along the white edge of the newspaper. "Dear Mister Anderson — Daughter asked take you money. Business good today." It was unsigned.

He counted the bills: $4,800 HK. He didn't need a calculator to tell him that in no conceivable way could she have earned that much. She had been busy "doing good." He glanced up quickly, expecting to see Inspector Yeung staring accusingly at him.

Another thought dashed wildly about. If he didn't hurry, she would be in jail before he could get her out of Hong Kong.

He remembered she rose at dawn. He would be there tomorrow the moment the sun shot its sheen across the waters.

Even though it had been several years, he recognized the husky, carefree, bantering voice over the phone.

"Hi, old friend. Barney here. Remember me? Khun Sa's PR man."

Dave's pulse quickened. "How could I forget you? Where are you?"'

Barney was pleased. "In the big city for a day. Could we powwow? Lots to talk about. The boss sends his best."

"Any time. You set it."

"Tonight too soon? Eleven o'clock? That big nightclub over on — you know. Got to have fun with work."

Dave agreed. Barney signed off with, "They tell me they've got some of the prettiest bimbos in all Asia."

Dave paced about the room. He was like Hollywood characters he had known. He thought better when he was in motion.

The diplomats stayed at the Peninsula in Hong Kong, the Raffles in Singapore, the Plaza in New York, and the Mayflower in Washington, D.C. However, like Barney, the hired help wanted the expense account to include more than prestige and elegant rooms. They set up meetings in bars, nightclubs, restaurants, and on golf courses. He had conferred with them in such spots the world over.

His contacts had invariably "rented" him girls who spoke little or no English and he found it difficult to get across to them that he was definitely, most definitely, refusing the services for which they had been paid. Some thought he was gay, others impotent, an occasional one would not take "no" without hurt feelings.

But refuse he had, although in this age of promiscuity he never wanted his friends or associates to know. It was the "in" thing to "sleep around." They wouldn't understand that it wasn't a matter of morals, although that was part of it. They wouldn't understand that his love for his mother had been so great that he would never do anything that would hurt her. And then later there had been Laurie, and in places as far remote as Buenos Aires he felt a sense of loyalty to her.

Not that the temptation had not been great. Not when you sit with acquaintances in a nightclub across from a stunning-looking girl who rested her bare breasts on the table and said that if her G-string bothered you, she would take it off.

His thoughts were never far from the "tea" with Alfred Kwan. Felicia Yee, a Lesbian? Hadn't she taken his arm a time or two as they wandered about Lantau and kissed him lightly as they parted? Of course, these could have been friendly gestures on the part of anyone, regardless of sexual preference. But she didn't look like a Lesbian. How did a Lesbian look? He chided himself. Now he was into fictional stereotypes. He had known three or four Lesbians and they were women the same as women everywhere.

Then he remembered Felicia telling him about breaking up with a Los Angeles boyfriend after he had visited Hong Kong and ridiculed her culture. Still, it could be that she wanted for social or business reasons to marry a heterosexual. Dave had had two good friends, the guy a Gay and the girl a Lesbian, who for years had been the perfect married couple for the same reasons. They did like each other and were compatible but lived separately in different parts of their home. In the beginning, they had tried sex. "It was a living hell," the man told Dave.

Dave dialed, her mother answered, and then Felicia was on the phone, surprise in her voice.

He told her about the conference coming up. "I need an escort."

"There'll be plenty of escorts where you're going," she said teasingly.

"That's what I'm afraid of."

"You mean, they're expensive — and I'll settle for a beer? She laughed, and accepted a little too readily. He could see the wheels going around. She wouldn't pass up a chance to meet Khun Sa's representative and gather information for other clients. He realized that. He had thought the minuses and pluses through carefully. She would learn little she didn't know already from other sources, On his part, she would provide the protection he wanted in case Barney did offer a "house girl." He might find out if she were a Lesbian — and learn more about Alfred Kwan and where he fit in the puzzle, and she with him.

He was deceiving himself. This was only so much rationalization. The truth was he wanted to be with her.

Chapter 22

As the taxi pulled up in front of the Holiday Inn, Felicia was waiting. She was in a Chinese red cheongsam split above the knee and he caught a flash of bare leg. She had red shoes to match. She gave him a "Hi," and a smile that sent an exciting feeling stirring through him. She wore the same dark glasses but he was certain her eyes were sparkling. The red slash mark seemed more prominent, though, but offsetting this negative, was the way her shoulder-length hair and earrings in the shape of pagodas danced.

Once underway she whispered, "I have something to tell you...on the sidewalk...before we go up."

She sat close to him, her thigh touching his. He put his hand on hers and there was no pulling away.

A big neon sign stretched far out over the street. GIRLS, GIRLS, GIRLS. While Dave paid the driver, who surprisingly enough was not Sergeant Tang, she walked toward a shadowy part of the street, away from the entrance.

"What is it?" he asked, joining her.

She took a few steps to the curb. "Everything depends on tonight. They let the 48-hour deadline the Chrysanthemum Man gave you — and the threat to the sampan woman — go by to see what the Shan man gets out of you. They have every confidence in him. He's their top negotiator."

"Barney?" Dave asked in amazement.

"Let's go in. I don't want to stand out here."

They took a small, trembling, dirty elevator to the second floor, and stepped out into a warehouse-size setting. Their hearing was assailed by a five-piece band at the far end, struggling with an old American number. Overhead crepe streamers in all colors moved slowly in the breeze stirred up by couples on a postage-stamp dance floor. Immediately to their right was a long bar from which emanated a babble of voices. Sitting at the bar were hostesses in G-strings and a suggestion of bras, others in evening gowns cut low, and one or two in body tight street clothes. The men appeared professionals, lawyers, accountants, doctors, etc.

A maitre d' or a bouncer — in some clubs you couldn't tell the difference — waddled up and said roughly to Felicia in Cantonese, "You got reservations?"

That minute Barney appeared, waving. "Dave," he called out above the hubbub. "Come on in." He had put on some weight since Dave had seen him and his hair was cut shorter.

Barney's face soured at seeing Felicia. He hadn't anticipated Dave would bring anyone. Dave introduced her, "She's a student at Chinese University and has been helping me get around in Hong Kong."

Barney took a physical assessment and apparently decided he approved. He led them to a table where two hostesses were waiting, each in an evening dress cut so low there was no concealment.

"Sorry, honey," he said to one. "We won't be needing you."

The young woman who remained looked far too tired and hardened for her age which was somewhere around 21. Yet in acknowledging the introductions,, a refinement and graciousness showed through from far back. In deference to Felicia, she adjusted her gown so that it covered her breasts.

"You don't have to talk fast," Barney said. "I've got her for the night. Haven't I, honey?"

She nodded demurely. At the booths around them, the hostesses had small timers, much the same as used in sports events. The "guest" paid according to how long he talked with her, or otherwise took her time.

The waitresses wore boots and little else. Barney ordered bourbon and the hostess followed suit, although Dave knew she would get a Shirley Temple bourbon. He and Felicia asked for white wine. She and the hostess lit cigarettes.

Barney felt good. He had already had two drinks. "How's everything in California? Man, I wish I could get back there. Had some great times there."

He rambled on, the drinks were served. Like Laurie, Felicia fitted in. What was it that Laurie had said? "It's fun watching the animals perform."

Out of the corner of his eye, Dave saw the bouncer signaling to Barney who rose quickly. "If you ladies will please pardon us, Dave and I have a little business to talk over. We won't be long."

Dave hesitated. Felicia whispered, "I'll be all right." She would be, he knew. Any place, any time, she could look after herself.

He followed the bouncer and Barney to a back room some distance away, a room that was an office of sorts, in complete disarray.

Barney said, "You lucky stiff. You've got quite a broad there. Nice lines. I like nice lines. I don't go for big tits, big hips."

He settled in at the battle-scarred table and Dave took a chair on the other side.

He straightened up, all business, his voice authoritative. "Well, old friend, I figured if we put all of this on the table, we could work it out. First, I want you to know I'm with you all the way. We're two fellow Americans and we're not going to let these Chinks get away with anything. Right?"

He didn't pause for an answer. "I'll go first. I'm not representing Khun Sa but the First International Bank of Mae Hong Son. Isn't that something? Me, a banker.

"To get down to brass tacks. The bank loaned Mac Dunleavy $1,240,000 US. That's the bank's loan, at 20 percent interest. Doesn't include what two Triad societies put out. A lot of money. Right?"

He took a deep breath, hurried on. "My bank wants an accounting. Reasonable? Right. This Dunleavy guy said he bought a tramp ship that went down in the South China Sea. We don't know whether he ever bought a ship or if it went down out there. We don't know whether he died, was murdered, or he's out there somewhere laughing at us. Personally, I'd like to find someone who saw a body."

He stared hard at Dave. "We need some answers — and some money. The loan was due two months ago. So, I've put it right on the table. Your turn now."

Dave was prepared. He said quietly, "I understand that opium was part of the deal with Mac Dunleavy." He was bluffing.

"Where'd you get that?" Barney was on the defensive, where Dave wanted him.

"I understand that the tramp ship was a cover-up for one of the biggest opium deals ever."

"I don't know anything about that," Barney shouted. "I don't know any details. I'm here to demand an accounting, and I'm going to get one — or someone's going to be dead before the night's over."

He hit the table hard with a fist, then yanked himself back under control. Dave could see the tight grip in the jaw set hard, the body tensed, the breath quickened.

Barney said, "I didn't mean you, my friend. Never. But someone involved in this will pay. Not by me. I hate violence. I saw this film, 'Terminator.' We get all the latest pictures flown in...and I couldn't stomach it and half way through I told the guy running it to turn it off."

He was stalling. He was rambling deliberately.

Dave picked up the lance. "I know you do big business with Hong Kong."

"You're damn right we do. Everyone knows that. We've got a big deal going now with the Sun Yee On society. The most powerful

Triad in Hong Kong. We're bigger than General Motors if you count the street value of our product."

He laughed. "And we don't have to offer rebates to get business."

Dave massaged his neck. The muscles had tightened into a painful grip. "I don't understand something."

"Shoot."

"Why would anyone lend Mac Dunleavy all that cash without requiring him to post assets as collateral?"

"You don't understand how you do business with the Triads. This guy Dunleavy, from what I hear, started small. He put through some good deals with the Triads and they kept getting bigger, and he got a reputation for honesty, responsibility, following orders, loyal to the Triads and the men in high places. We don't go much for written contracts and security and all of that. The Triad does business with men they trust — and executes the traitors. It's that simple."

He continued, "Look at it from the Triad point of view. Only one of three people has Mac's money or knows what became of it or where it is. You as his closest friend. His widow who has disappeared —"

Dave interrupted. "She's in Malaysia."

"No, she never got off the plane in Kuala Lumpur, and the only other stop was Bangkok. The Triad in Thailand will track her down. Make no mistake about that. And the third is the sampan woman. No one in the Triad thinks she knows anything. Just a poor tanka. But I'm not so sure about that. I've seen my share of murder mysteries. No one ever suspects the butler. Right?"

He was wound up. "If Dunleavy didn't buy a ship, then he could've banked the money in Luxembourg, moved it a week later under another corporation name to Switzerland, and then a few days afterwards transferred it to a Triad bank in the United States, then shunted it here to Hong Kong. By then the trail would be difficult to follow. Almost impossible. But we'll do it if we have to. But I don't think we'll have to because you're a decent, fair man, Dave.

"I'll tell you this in confidence. Khun Sa would like to invite you back for another interview, take you up to his home in the mountains to meet his wife and children. It'd be a great story. He knows you'd sock it to him but if you ran a picture with him and his wife and children — well, that humanizes him and people will think he can't be all that bad. Besides, he wants you to break a story about an offer he is making to the United States about ending the opium trade. So he'd be willing for you to take a hundred thousand off Mac's debt for yourself, as negotiator, and turn over what remains to him. How's that for a fantastic deal, my friend?"

Dave rose slowly. "That does it, my dear old friend." The sarcasm told on Barney. "I'm not for sale. Not at any price. I do want to make one point before I walk out of here. I swear before God, and may He strike me dead, I don't know anything about Mac Dunleavy's business. I don't know anything about any money he may have left, if any, about any purchase of a tramp ship, about any loans, about any business with the Triads."

He headed for the door a few steps away. By now Barney was on his feet, "Hold it there. We can talk this out."

Dave turned, "And when you see Khun Sa, tell him for me, go to blazes and rot on a field of poppies."

Without running, he took long, quick steps. At the table he pulled a surprised Felicia to her feet. "We've got to get out of here."

He had her by the hand and was pulling her along. As they neared the door, Barney called out from behind the bouncer to stop him. The bouncer took a step to block them but was unprepared for the hard fist that smashed into his soft belly. He staggered backward and fell and was out.

All the way down the elevator Dave was shouting at it to hurry. "We can't wait downstairs for a taxi," he told Felicia. "We'll make a run for the next street and get one there."

Now they were out of the building and at one o'clock the street still had a heavy flow of people. They ducked in and out, his hand in hers, propelling her.

They turned at the next corner and immediately flagged down a cab. "Do you know a restaurant where we can talk — and be safe?"

She did.

Chapter 23

He never knew the name of the restaurant but it was packed. "Where'd all these people come from?"

She smiled. "I could ask the same question about the Los Angeles freeway at night."

They found a corner table for two and while he struggled to quiet the pounding inside him, the trolley ladies came by, old women pushing little rolling carts loaded with baskets or plates of food. They called out in voices near dead what they had to offer. With effort, they moved feet that time had mangled.

Felicia suggested shrimp, and mechanically, his mind still back there swinging at the bouncer, he took a basket from the shrimp lady.

Felicia ordered tea. "It'll help." She put a hand on his. "Why don't we wait a few minutes until...your hand. It's swollen."

"It's nothing."

"It could be broken."

He agreed he would see a doctor.

She continued, "You won't need chop sticks with shrimp."

He couldn't help but smile. He had tried faithfully to master the use of chop sticks but his fingers would not obey.

She took over the conversation. "Barney's young woman was a surprise. We got to talking, and she said she was a village school teacher, and a man from Hong Kong came one day and told her how much money she could make as a hostess. She doesn't regret going with him but she isn't happy either. She can't get used to men mauling her and some actually hurt her. She's going to work another year and then buy a shop in the village, maybe the bakery."

The tea instilled new life. As he recounted in detail his conversation with Barney, the muscles in her face tightened.

"They'll put a death notice out on you," she whispered, frightened, "and maybe the sampan woman. You've got to get out of here, Dave."

"In two days, three at the most."

"No, Dave, no! Tonight. Don't even go back to the hotel. Take the next plane out, no matter where it goes."

"I can't."

"Why not?"

"I'll be careful."

"No matter. You think you can lose yourself in the crowds — but some time they'll find an opening. Somehow. They always do. The police find a body, stripped, no identification..."

She was near panic. "If you have to stay, talk it over with Inspector Yeung. I know you don't like him but let me tell you about him."

A shadow crossed them and she jumped a little. It was another trolley lady, this time offering roast duck.

She continued, "You say Barney mentioned the Sun Yee On Triad. It's the most powerful in Hong Kong. They have about 40,000 members and 200-some street gangs. They're everywhere. In the police department. Maybe 200 or 300 there. You can't do business anywhere without finding them."

She hurried on. "I don't mean all 40,000 are criminals. Most join because they need jobs. You see all of the hawkers on the street, and the tourists come and think how wonderful it is, small capitalists making a living. And that's what they are but to become one they have to get a license and then the authorities give them a space. If they belong to a Triad they do well."

Dave interrupted. "The Inspector?"

"Yes. A few years ago he infiltrated into the Sun Yee On, and got evidence that sent a hundred of them to prison. He became a hero and the Triads don't dare touch him right now because of public reaction, but in time..."

She fumbled in her purse for a pencil and a scrap of paper. "Here's his phone at home. Call him tonight. He won't mind. Tell him I asked you to. If he's not there, tell his wife. She's a remarkable woman."

She added, "Promise?"

He nodded. At the same time he wondered how she would have the Inspector's home phone number and how did she know him and his wife so well that they would not mind being awakened in the middle of the night, if her name were mentioned.

"I'd better be getting home — and let you call the Inspector."

"Just a couple of minutes." Dave hesitated, thinking his way through.

Instantly she read him. Something unpleasant was coming up. "I'm listening."

He said slowly, "Alfred Kwan invited me to his office for tea this afternoon to ask if my firm would do a report on Borneo for him. I thought it odd that he would be interested in such a remote country."

He waited for a reaction. There was none.

"He insisted that if I did take this project on, he wanted me to employ you as my research assistant."

She said sharply, "I don't discuss one client with another. You know that."

"I need advice about whether to go ahead with the report. I thought you might have suggestions."

"I've told you, my service does not include advice. Is that clear?"

"He said the rumor was that you were a Lesbian."

There, he had it out. He had expected an emotional response. He got none.

"So?"

"He asked me if that would be a problem about employing you."

"So?" She didn't even flinch.

"I told him no."

She nodded. It was as if he were talking to a computer.

He was irritated. He tried not to show it. He had one question burning him, and he had to get it out.

"Are you a member of a Triad? You seem to know so much —"

She dropped her ivory chop sticks and one clattered to the floor.

"I don't understand how you could..." She was about to cry.

He said quickly, "I meant...I was only curious..."

She stiffened. "I've never known anyone I was so fond of one moment — and hated so much the next."

"Please, I didn't mean anything..."

She broke in, her voice rising. "You seem affectionate — and then if you'd slapped me, you couldn't have hurt me more."

He tried to get a word in.

Her voice rose higher. "You don't trust me! You never have! You never will! You think I'm setting you up — when I'm sitting here risking my life talking with you."

"Please..."

"I can't take this roller coaster any more!"

She was getting up, shoving the table into him, knocking her chair over. "You damn, no-good American! Take your fine clothes and your money and your superior race and get out of my life! And stay out!"

She was on her feet, running.

He sat stunned. A flustered waiter shoved the stubs the trolley lady had written. Dave took out a handful of dollar bills and put them on the table, and headed for the door on the run.

Outside he looked in vain.

Chapter 24

Women! You couldn't be honest with them. You had to think every word you spoke. One word, just one word, could set them off. They were quick to misconstrue your meaning...if your tone was not right, if you did not look right. They were too sensitive. Or acted like they were.

That was it. Usually it was a performance worthy of an Oscar.

He was angry, sitting there in his room at 3 in the morning. He felt guilty. He felt put upon. He wanted to call her. He didn't want to call her, ever.

Weariness eventually calmed him. The view across the waters to the shadow buildings rising high against cardboard mountains and the quiet of a moonlit night was a soothing narcotic.

He had asked only one simple question. Was she a member of a Triad? Hadn't she herself said that most members belonged to get better jobs or promotions? He had not implied that she was in a Triad for criminal purposes. No sensible person could possibly have misconstrued the question.

Back on Ladder Street, they had admitted they had doubts about each other, hadn't they? Tonight, though, he hadn't expressed even a doubt. He was being objective, factual.

Of course, before that question, he had mentioned she might be a Lesbian. Was that anything to get excited about? He had not implied she was. He had merely quoted Alfred Kwan.

If someone had asked him if he were gay, he would have taken it in stride. He would have put it down to curiosity. That was all. Well, maybe he would have been a little upset. His sexual preferences were no one's business, an invasion of privacy. Thinking it over, he granted that he might have been a little angry. Perhaps more than a little.

He spotted the trouble. He had asked in rapid-fire order too many questions Felicia might have found objectionable but no one else would.

He conceded she had a point, not a good one but one he could understand. He blamed the whole mishap on his journalistic training. In his newspaper days he had had to ask questions, often harsh ones, to find the truth under all the muck the power brokers shoveled out.

He remembered a lecture he had heard during his University of Arizona days from a visiting Harvard professor, something to the effect we are living in a Communications era. The computer companies shout it, the telephone companies advertise it, everybody stands in awe of how fast and effectively we communicate. You put a letter in a fax machine and before you can return to your desk, it's in Tokyo. Never before in all history, etc., etc...

"However," the speaker continued, "there has been little improvement in inter-personal relations. We still shout and scream at each other, from Washington down to the home. Our technology far outstrips the communications that mean the most, that start wars, that cause divorces, that result in business failures.

"We send students out from our high schools and universities who have little conception of how to talk with a boss when they disagree with him...how to handle jobs they don't like...how to discuss vital matters when others confront them...and most importantly, how to handle your wife and children when they want to take a vacation to visit Aunt Susie when you damn well don't want to see Aunt Susie ever...how to spread some of that love you felt during the early years of marriage into your partnership today.

"You need to understand the language you use every day, how some words are emotionally charged, are dynamite and poisonous. 'Words are loaded pistols,' Jean-Paul Sartre once wrote.

"Every high school and university should have courses in personal communications that are as well researched as the computers, the lasers and the other wonders of this age. We need the same marvels in our daily living."

Dave was sleepy but thinking clearly. He had erred. Thoughtlessly he had set up a confrontation. He should have started by saying, "I don't believe any of this, and it hurts me to repeat it but I thought for your information I should tell you..."

He was jarred wide-awake by the phone. The voice on the other end was muffled, as though the party were using the amateurish device of speaking through a piece of paper held over the mouthpiece.

Tonight it successfully masqueraded the speaker, a woman.

She was in a state of panic. "They are sending two men out to Aberdeen...to kill her if they don't get anything out of her. They..."

The voice went dead and a moment afterwards, the phone. It was as if someone had caught her in the act.

Quickly, while he dressed, his mind analyzed the voice. It bore no resemblance to Felicia's — but it had to be hers.

It was evident. Barney had reported failure in negotiations.

The Triad was moving.

Chapter 25

He was thinking smoothly. In a crisis he always had. It was in retrospect that he panicked, debating whether he had made the right decision.

He put on a jacket to cover the .357 Magnum. He found he had misplaced Inspector Yeung's home number Felicia had given him. He phoned the police at the Crime Hotline number, 5-277177. He talked rapidly but in short, terse sentences, covering the anonymous phone call and advising he was leaving at once for Aberdeen.

He added, "Inspector Yeung knows me. Knows about this case."

The young woman was bilingual. As he talked, she repeated his words in Chinese and he heard her typing out a message on the computer. "The address of the victim, please?" she asked.

He had no idea. He had always gone to the Jumbo dock, and when a tanka came by, told her, and soon Ming Toy appeared.

The young woman said firmly, "Stay where you are. We may need more information and must know where to find you."

He had no intention of following her instructions. He ran through the lobby to the doorman outside, asked for a taxi. The driver spoke little English. But money was easily interpreted. Dave handed him two $100 HK bills. "Hurry," he said. The driver understood the word, "Hurry," and shot the cab forward at a speed and in a wild weaving pattern that was as dizzying as a too-fast pan in a home video.

He recalled a buoy marked 3 about 100 feet distant from Ming Toy's sampan. But it would be too dark to see the 3. There were ladder-like steps nearby leading to an upper land level. Nearby was a sampan covered with green canvas. Her mother's was blue-striped. On Ming Toy's sampan was a shredded tire on the prow that she had remarked needed replacing. The night he had gone there, the mother had laundry drying on a rope stretched across the top of the covering.

The driver cut 12 minutes off the usual trip. Dave gave him an extra $100 HK. The driver offered to wait. Dave motioned him on.

He stood on the dock very much alone. There was a three-quarter moon barely lighting a shadowy, mysterious world of nothingness, without anything having definite shape, a world that invited exploration but at the same time was threatening.

He started off along a little path that bordered the water. He had gone only a few feet when out of the mist a sampan took shape. An old, weather-beaten woman was bringing a young couple from the skyscraper concrete jungle at the far side of the harbor. As the couple left, Dave dropped into the boat. "Miss Chan?" The tanka shook her head. "Ming Toy?" She nodded enthusiastically, smiled. "Take me." She shrugged her sagging shoulders. "No know."

He took out a pencil, placed part of it in the water, held up three fingers. "Mark three?" She accelerated the motor and they rode the waves. In a few minutes, buoy 3 took shape. He could barely make out the ladder steps, pointed to them, and she brought the sampan into a vacant slip.

On the walk, he was barely conscious of a man passing by, someone on the way to work or returning from a night job. In the distance, a haunting Chinese tune was barely audible, coming from a radio. He smelled breakfast. The sampan people were coming alive.

He heard low voices from the mother's sampan. He dared not stop for fear a pause might alert someone. The voices were men's and threatening. The covering was open, about a foot above the sampan's structure, for air to circulate.

He never stopped his pace but bent low, almost doubled up. He could see little more than forms. One man was astride the mother, pinning her legs with his and her arms with his hands. Next to him was another man...the picture blurred.

He walked on, then retraced his steps. This time, from a different angle, he saw the second man astride Ming Toy. Her nightdress was pulled down exposing a breast and there was a knife there, at the bottom of the breast, positioned to slice upward.

The sight shocked him momentarily, then he gained control. He was still walking. Any second he might be too late. He had to surprise both men. Somehow he had to attack both at the same moment or the mother or Ming Toy or both would be dead.

In the distance, on the mainland, about a block away, he saw under a streetlight, officers leaving two police cars. He could run and lead them back. But that would take minutes and he might not have that much time. His gut instinct told him that any second the man with the knife might mangle Ming Toy, a final move to get information out of her.

In seconds, he was walking the rim of the hull of an adjoining boat passing a father and mother and three youngsters all asleep. He took a long step over to the prow of the mother's sampan. The boat rocked, the voices stilled. Oh, God, he prayed, don't let them look out to investigate.

Then the voices continued, a little louder, more threatening. He slipped quietly to the stern and lifted the covering. In a flash, before they knew what was happening, he let out an old Apache war cry he had learned from an Apache friend at the University of Arizona, and lunged his body in one powerful forward movement. He hit the first man hard who collapsed on top of the mother. In the same second, Dave shot his arm forward to grab the second man's wrist, holding the knife, and turned the wrist so hard that he heard it crack.

There was a shot. He didn't know where it came from or whom it hit, if anyone. He took another lunge, hit the second man hard, who reeled backwards, but brought up a gun. Dave fired straight at the attacker. The powerful Magnum sent him reeling and Dave followed up with a push that knocked him into the water. He swung about to find the mother wrestling with the second man. She was struggling for the weapon he held. Dave swung the Magnum and pistol-whipped him. The man dropped his own weapon and was trying to pull away from the mother when the officers stormed the sampan. In that second, before the officers had a good view, Dave tossed the Magnum into the water.

Ming Toy was bleeding profusely, blood running over her body. The officers put in an emergency call for an ambulance, then they searched her and her mother for gunshot wounds. They found none. Others were recovering the man's body from the shallow waters.

"You kill him?" a detective asked. Dave just stared at him. He pretended to be in shock. "Must've been a neighbor."

Two officers had handcuffed and were leading away the mother's attacker who had his head bent, as if to avoid identification.

By now a score of neighbors had gathered, talking as if someone close to them had died, not believing this could happen to one of them, especially to gentle ones like Ming Toy and her mother. They were orderly, respecting authority, anxious to see but not if it meant interfering.

Ming Toy was crying, calling out pitifully for her mother who dropped to the floor by her, kissed her and cradled her in her arms. An officer shouted for a first aid kit and when it arrived from a police car, applied a crude dressing to her breast in an attempt to stop the flow.

She quieted then and looked up at Dave. "I hurt, Mister Dave. I hurt. I die, no?"

He assured her she would be all right, an ambulance was coming.

"I tell men to see you. Like you said. I say know nothing. See you. I love you, Mister David. You good. Like Mister Mac. I no die."

Gently, Dave carried her a block to the ambulance, her blood soaking his clothes, her body crumpled in his arms as if all life were draining from her. His heart was pounding.

By the time the aides placed her on a gurney and pushed it into the ambulance, she was unconscious. En route, with Dave and her mother at her side, the aides gave plasma and frequently checked her pulse. Her breathing was so silent that it seemed she was fast slipping away.

Nurses were waiting at Grantham Hospital on Wong Chuk Hang Road, and as she was wheeled into emergency, they asked Dave and her mother to wait outside. Except for shock and bruises, her mother was unhurt.

As they waited, officers asked questions, quietly, gently, but persistently. Dave said the attackers were from a Triad. That was difficult for them to believe. What kind of a relationship could a sampan girl have with a Triad that would infuriate them to this extent? What could she possibly know that would be important to a Triad?

They drifted away, and the two were alone. Ming Toy's mother held his hand tightly. She was breathing heavily.

Dave's memory went back to that night he first met Ming Toy..."Hello, Mister American," she had called...the sparkle in her eyes...her joyousness in being alive...her determination to "do good"...her charm even when she was feisty and telling him off...the simple ways of a simple young woman who loved people and her sampan and the sea...

He prayed she would be all right. He prayed to his God and hoped Buddha was eavesdropping...

Her mother was whispering, "You saved us...until now. If no come, we both die. I know my daughter live. I go temple tomorrow. Thank Lord Buddha and pray blessing on you."

He squeezed her hand.

"If my daughter live, they come back. They try again. Next time...please, Mr. David..."

"She's tough," he said. "She'll be all right."

Her mother continued, "Please Mr. David, she worshipped Mr. Mac. She do what he say. Never break promise. Please, Mr. David, tell her must break promise. Mr. Mac not want her hurt. Must tell where hide money. Must. Please, Mr. David."

Chapter 26

From the start, he had suspected Ming Toy possessed more information than she was divulging. At no time, however, had he considered that Mac had given her money to hide. That was the primary reason, he reasoned now, that Mac wanted her protected. He had turned to an old friend whom he could trust to look after her. An old friend who "owed him one," who would keep the secret as hidden as the money if he should learn about it inadvertently from Ming Toy.

Now he understood why Ming Toy panicked when approached the first time by the Triad. "They kill Ming Toy," she had said flatly. But did the Triad know that she had hidden the money for Mac — or were they on a fishing expedition, desperate to explore every possibility?

Now they sat alone, her mother and Dave, on a little island remote from the rest of this busy, restless, emotion-charged hospital. Quickly, he analyzed the situation. The chance this area was bugged was negligible. Still, a listening cone could be focused on them from an unseen location. That, too was unlikely but possible.

Barely above a whisper, he asked, "Where is the money?"

She took time to answer, ransacked by turmoil. "I no know. She not tell. I no ask. I no want know. She frightened."

"Did your daughter hide the money or did Mr. Mac?"

"Say he gave one night. She hid same night."

"Somewhere around the harbor?"

"Think maybe. Not sure. She gone little time."

"When was this?"

"Five weeks past. Maybe six. Getting old. Not remember good."

He cautioned himself to approach the matter easily. He continued gently, "How much?"

"Could buy all sampans."

"One hundred thousand? A million?"

"No know. But much money. You tell her, Mr. David, if she keep, they kill her. They come again. Come soon."

She was near hysteria. He took both her hands, icy cold, without circulation, as if she were near death. An unseen force hit him hard in the guts.

He said slowly, "This will never happen again. I promise. I will work it out — with the help of the police — that she will be under watch all of the time."

Her tongue was thick with desperation. "You no promise she tell where money is?"

"Look, we will work it out with Ming Toy. We will do whatever she thinks is best. Please, I beg of you, do not say anything until we talk with her. You and I. As soon as she recovers. Please, do this for me, for her. If you tell others..."

"You no promise," she whispered — and dropped to the floor.

He called to a passing nurse, and soon others were about. They moved her to a room, and a doctor was there within minutes.

Dave returned to the waiting area, his insides torn up. He sat a long time in limbo. No one came by to report on Ming Toy or her mother.

If Ming Toy led the Triad to the money, would they not kill her? They would want no witness to testify later about who had the money. With her dead, they could divide it among themselves and no one would ever know.

Eventually Inspector Yeung came by. Without any chit chat, he began a stern, business-like cross-examination. "I want you to tell me, step by step, what you did after you phoned us. Do not leave out anything."

Slowly, Dave answered. Slowly, since he needed to think through exactly what he said, how it would sound in a courtroom, if it came to that. He edited nothing out until he reached the climax. "He was lunging for me and I gave him a push. He lost his equilibrium and fell into the water. I then grabbed the other man who was trying to free himself of the woman who was fighting like a wild cat."

"The shots," the Inspector said. "You killed him before you shoved him overboard?"

"I heard shots. I don't know where they came from. I didn't have a gun. That would be illegal."

The Inspector shook his head in disbelief. "I admire your great respect for the law. Am I to assume that if you had had a weapon, you would have stood bravely and let him kill you?"

Dave offered no answer. He had been clobbered so viciously in the last few hours that his mind was in slow gear. He cautioned himself again. Silence on his part would reflect guilt. On the other hand, silence might protect him from future repercussions.

The Inspector said matter-of-factly, "I will put down what you said in my report. I will keep to myself my suspicions. I am not the best detective. Often I don't report the indisputable facts if they would embarrass a good citizen. I confine my embarrassments to criminals."

He paused. "When we find the weapon, whom should I return it to?"

"How would I know?" Dave countered.

"The examining officer reported that the wound looked as if a Magnum had been used."

"Yes?" Dave countered.

"We have few such weapons in Hong Kong and can trace it to its owner which will be the party who loaned it to the user this morning. Am I boring you, Mr. Anderson?"

"You are a brilliant detective."

"Thank you. When it comes to the Triad, I would hope so. My goal in life is to wipe them off the face of the earth. I will go to any ends to do that. You understand, Mr. Anderson?"

Dave nodded. His pulse had shot up to full speed. This hunting dog was moving in for a kill. "If I can help...I feel as strongly as you do."

"You can help. What information did Ming Toy have that brought the Triad down on her?"

"So help me, I don't know."

"By all logic, I must assume she either has certain funds of Mr. Dunleavy's hidden away — or knows where they are."

"She has never said anything to me to indicate that."

"But you have thought along the same line."

"I've had no reason to. I came here solely —"

The Inspector interrupted. "You have told me the story several times. You need not repeat it. One more question. How did you know the Triad was here?"

"I had an anonymous phone call."

"Didn't you recognize the voice?"

"No, I didn't."

"Could it have been an informant? Someone you have been paying?"

Dave sucked in his breath. "I said, I don't know the identity of the caller."

The Inspector rose. "Thank you for phoning us. You have been most gracious."

He walked away briskly. Dave was left knowing that the Inspector by now, if not before, had him listed as an active participant in a most puzzling crime.

The surgeon was tall and slender, in his forties and still sweating profusely. He had the no-nonsense look of a military person. "Are you a member of her family?"

A sudden feeling of affection, a love of sorts, touched Dave. He nodded.

The surgeon smiled. "Interesting. A Caucasian Chinese."

"I own the sampan and think of her as a relative."

"No matter. It took nine stitches to repair her breast. The stitch line won't show once it is healed. She had twelve lacerations, four extensive, some knife cuts, and was badly beaten about the head. Suffered two concussions. In addition, I can't estimate how much of a traumatic shock she went through. There may be brain damage but we won't know for several days."

"Oh, God," Dave said, his voice breaking. "Are you telling me she may not make it?"

The surgeon thought through his words. "I would like to report that she has a strong, healthy body and seemingly a will to live, which is important, and that she will come through very well. I believe this but I can't tell you she will survive. No one knows for sure in a case of this kind. She went through so much, was beaten up badly, maybe far worse than we can tell at this time."

The old anger, fanned when Dave first looked in the sampan, came surging back. He had never thought he was a violent person, or ever could become one but at this moment he wished he had the Magnum back.

"Can I see her?"

"Tomorrow. She's heavily sedated."

"Her mother?" Dave asked.

"She'll be all right. Needs rest."

The surgeon gone, Dave fell into a nearby chair. He picked up a magazine but did not read. He remembered bits of happy memories with Ming Toy. She was an unheralded saint, as so many are who cross our paths. She made life better for everyone about her with her pixie smile and quiet laughter and an outgoing sense that all was right with her world, because it was a world peopled by ones she loved.

He could never send her and her mother back to China...deprive them of the happiness they had created in this sweaty, impoverished sea of sampans. Happiness was not all material possessions. Happiness here was the caring and love of those about you, the sun coming up, the waves rolling, the ocean growling, loaning and borrowing food, the pride of succeeding by earning a few dollars in a place where dollars were scarce, the fireworks in time of death, the soft praying in a Buddhist temple, living as Confucius would have you, all of that.

A nurse awakened him. There was a call for him at the nearest station.

He recognized Felicia's voice but before he could speak, she said,

"This is your Lesbian member of the Triad, Mr. Anderson. I have information. A speedboat will pick you up at the Jumbo dock in exactly 30 minutes."

She hung up abruptly. He wished he could have said something. He brightened, realizing he would see her soon, and set everything right with her.

She was still angry. She had called him, "Mr. Anderson."

Chapter 27

Dave looked in on Ming Toy's mother who would be discharged shortly. She had suffered a fainting spell, nothing more. The doctor said, "Everyone has a right to faint once or twice in a lifetime." Dave could only hope she would keep her secret.

He kept his cool on leaving the hospital. He paused at the door to survey the territory, a cougar on the prowl. He spotted Sergeant Tang and asked if he would take him to the dock.

En route the Sergeant talked incessantly. Dave heard only a voice turned too low to be understood. He struggled to line up his thoughts. He wanted in the worst way to reach a rapprochement with Felicia without compromising his conviction that he had been justified in questioning her. His approach, he would admit, had been too blunt and aggressive. He admitted to himself he had a fondness for her and a fierce longing for her to return the fondness.

Ming Toy had one virtue Felicia would never have. She was outspoken, honest. You knew where she stood, what she felt down to bare, raw emotions. She was a fighter. She was out there every day in a world that offered no concessions, a harsh, cruel world. Yet somehow she had retained a refreshing, primeval innocence. She was one of those rare people who created her own happiness while others about her were bemoaning their fates.

The speedboat, glistening white in the hot sun, was waiting, motor throbbing. The pilot was young, not more than 17, in the usual jeans and a T-shirt with a hungry, ferocious-looking dragon emblazoned on the back. Sitting at the wheel, he raised a hand in signal.

Dave stepped in, and before he had his equilibrium, the pilot gunned the speedboat. Dave fell into a polyethylene seat and grabbed hold. Never had he had a ride like this. The boat bounced the waves with the gusto of a motorcycle in rough country. It mounted each wave with a rush, then at the crest, dropped off with a wallop that Dave could feel up his entire spine. At each bump, the young man would come to his feet with a shout, and laughing, swing about to learn how his lone passenger was faring.

Dave yelled, "Where are we going?"

The boy shouted back, "No English!"

That had to be a lie. In Hong Kong every child was taught English as a second language. If you were to become an entrepreneur and sell to the Brits, Americans, Canadians, Australians and even some Asians, you had to know English.

"Go to hell," Dave yelled.

The boy reacted quickly, raising a fist high in the air and shaking it. He knew some English.

They were out of Aberdeen harbor and into the open sea. The boy played Russian roulette with sampans and other light craft, weaving around them so closely that Dave thought a crash was imminent. He even took on a big yacht, shooting across the prow, missing by a few feet, and then whirling the speedboat about and returning for another heart-stopper.

On the left was Lamma island, and the main town, Yung Shue Wan, came into view.

Dave was becoming ever more apprehensive. Thoughts streaked in and out that he would not admit even to himself.

She said she had information. How could she have? The nightmare was over, concluded. Obviously, the Triads would try again. That was not new information.

In about 20 minutes they came to deep-water Victoria Harbour where great ships of all nations put down anchor to pick up fuel and supplies before venturing out into the Pacific, the South China Sea and other distant waters.

The speedboat idled while it wove its way past British, American, Scandinavian, African and other ships from places with the exotic names adventurers in another century had given them. At times the boy had to throttle the boat down for a long wait since there were so many tugboats, lighters and small cargo ships blocking the waterway. They passed a reefer and a bumboat carrying shipments to nearby godowns (warehouses).

The more time that passed, the more fearful Dave became. Had Felicia planned passage for him out of Hong Kong, certain he would be killed if he stayed? Or was there possibly a Triad assassin lurking in ambush? He was gambling his life that no matter how furious she was with him, he was still her "client" and under as much protection as she could give.

Then Dave caught sight of an old, wizened Chinese on the prow of a cargo boat. Imperceptibly he raised a hand, and the boy brought their craft up to the dock where many coolies were unloading boxes from the cargo ship, taking them down a walkway a hundred feet, and up a gangplank into the hold of a Portuguese vessel.

The boy indicated Dave was to get off and go up the ramp to the cargo ship which had its name painted on in bold letters, TIEN SUNG WING, LTD.

Dave was starting up the beaten-up wooden ramp that swayed under the many feet of the coolies when Felicia materialized at the top. She stood very straight and proper, her faced marked with severity. She was in old, torn jeans and a tattered, paint-stained shirt. Except for the glasses and the knife mark, she looked nothing like the Felicia he had last seen.

"Thank you for coming, Mr. Anderson," she said evenly. "I was in the garden working when I heard the news."

They were in the midst of pandemonium. Not only were coolies brushing by but also crew members and others associated with the cargo business.

A smart-looking Chinese in his thirties, expensively suited, came up. "This is my cousin, Tien." she said. "Mr. Anderson. Tien was kind enough to loan us his office."

Tien offered a strong handshake. "I have many good American customers." His English was excellent. He shouted something in Cantonese to a workman who nodded and scurried away. He continued, "I am most happy to have you aboard, Mr. Anderson. Come, I will show you the way."

Down one hatch, he opened the door to an office papered over with documents, invoices, bills of lading, and letters. There was not a smidge of bare space anywhere. He scooped up a paper load from two chairs. "Felicia has promised she will come and organize me when school is out."

When he left, she took an office-type chair by the desk which was as old as the ship. He sat a few feet away.

"Felicia," he began.

She broke in. "Tien owns this boat. He runs supplies to ships that put in here from all parts of the world. Some are restricted and the sailors can't come on land, and he supplies them with everything from toothbrushes to clothes."

She was filling space. "He speaks nine languages and deals in the currencies of a score or more."

"Felicia," he said again.

She interrupted. "I would prefer that you call me Miss Yee. We Chinese are formal when we do business, especially with a foreigner."

"Let me talk," he said brusquely. "I know I was heavy-handed —"

She broke in. "I do not desire to discuss the situation with you, Mr. Anderson. Not now. Not ever. You are a client of mine. A good client and I appreciate your business. That is all, Mr. Anderson."

She handed him a shoe box tied up with string. "I am a good Buddhist, Mr. Anderson, and we do not believe in any kind of violence."

She paused while he opened the box that contained a Smith and Wesson 9-mm, an eight-round semiautomatic. She lit a cigarette and continued, "But there are times when evil people commit a violence so horrible that they should be put away. I could not find another Magnum and thought you should have protection."

"Thank you," he said quietly. His mind raced along in the same groove. Where had she gotten the 9-mm? How could she have found one so fast? Her source of weapons was unbelievable. If he asked for a howitzer, he was certain she could deliver one within 12 hours.

"Let me explain —"

"Please, Mr. Anderson, I'll do the talking. They will try again with the sampan woman, if she lives. I understand there is some doubt about that."

He interrupted, "Thank you for phoning me."

"About what?"

He was floored. "Why, the Triad..."

"You are mistaken."

"I don't think so."

Her face reddened. "You Americans are so sure of yourselves. You and the Japanese think you run the world."

She bit her lips. "Now to continue, as you may know, you have been the target for some time of one Triad society but it was a kind of a haphazard affair. The other society involved wanted to negotiate with you on the premise that they would locate more money by the soft approach. But both are united now. They voted this morning to assassinate you immediately and then to search for the money. You are marked anywhere you go. Even while you are sitting here. Someone may burst in with a machine gun and wipe out both of us."

"I wish," he said in a tone that came from the heart, "that you were doing all of this because you are fond of me as well as because I am a client."

She reached for a roll of toilet paper nearby, tore off a few feet, and dabbed it to her face. It was a hot day, growing hotter. "Our Kleenex," she explained. "I have more information."

Her lower lip was quivering. She tightened the muscles by will power alone and brought it under control.

"When you arrived here, you were assisted by a young detective assigned by Inspector Yeung to meet you and then run surveillance. He followed you to Mrs. Dunleavy's flat. When you came out and the killer opened fire, he was standing in bushes across from him and returned the fire."

He broke in. "Why would the police run surveillance on me? I'd just arrived. They didn't know me."

"Mr. Dunleavy's widow told the police you were coming to take over Mr. Dunleavy's affairs. The police had already opened a fraud case on Mr. Dunleavy. They did the usual, checking banks for accounts in his name, finding none, doing a detailed rundown on his activities in recent months, all of that. The Inspector still doesn't understand why Mr. Dunleavy's widow would set you up for an investigation — unless, of course, you did plan to take over his business."

By now he didn't care what Mac's wife had or hadn't done. There Felicia Yee sat, not more than three feet away, in her torn jeans and stained shirt, her physical being a magnet, strong, healthy, shoulders back, breasts jutting forth. Lesbian or not, he wanted to take her in his arms. She had to care deeply for him, if not romantically, then as a friend. Why otherwise would she have produced the weapon, perhaps risked her life to find and deliver it?

She was saying, "Incidentally, the woman who followed us at Lantau was hired by the Chrysanthemum Man. A rather amateurish attempt to frighten you. One more thing. My mother called you. Not I."

She continued, "The boy will take you back to the hotel where Sergeant Tang will meet you. The Inspector has assigned him to stay with you night and day."

"Thank you, Miss Yee." He wanted to change the name to Felicia but held back. It would do no good.

"You are welcome, Mr. Anderson."

Into the diary: "I was never very good in that Psychology 107 class but I do remember now that challenging anger begets anger. If I bide my time..."

After some minutes, he returned to the diary, "I said a prayer tonight. It's been a long time since the last one. For Ming Toy, and yes, Felicia. And me. I remember my mother saying, whenever she prayed aloud, 'God guide that I may think of others and do for them.' My mother saw a little girl crying her heart out once. She had lost a dime. My mother asked God to help the little girl with her problem — and then my mother asked God for some help that she herself needed. My mother. Because of her, I am what I am."

Chapter 28

About 6 a.m., the telephone rang, awakening Dave out of a half-sleep, half-awake situation, one that he had dreaded since childhood. All kinds of devils would charge through his consciousness, then he would roll over and wake up to a certainty that they forecast a day fraught with disaster.

A woman's voice said, "This is the hotel operator, Mr. Anderson. We are advising our guests that we have received a One warning signal — a state of alert — for a tropical typhoon moving in from 800 kilometers away. You may want to change your activities for the day. You can get further details from the English channel or by phoning 3-692-255."

He hung up to hear a drenching rain pounding the pavement outside. There, under an overhang, sat a police officer, ensconced in a black world. Not a harbor light shown.

By the time he called for breakfast in his room, the number Eight signal had been broadcast, warning that a storm blowing between 63 and 117 km/h was coming in, and gusts could exceed 180 km/h. "Violent squalls could occur. Take all necessary precautions. Windows and doors should be bolted and shuttered. Secure all loose objects, particularly on balconies and rooftops...If the winds increase, stay indoors to avoid flying debris...but if you must go out, avoid overhead wires. All schools and courts will be closed. Ferries will stop running."

In the midst of breakfast, he took two phone calls in rapid succession. One was from Ming Toy's mother who was near hysteria. He must come as soon as possible. They must talk with her daughter. He promised he would if he could reach Aberdeen through the storm.

The other was from Felicia's mother. She had a low cultured voice. Did he know where Felicia might be? She had not returned from meeting him at the cargo ship. She had rung up her mother in the evening to report a crisis had developed that she must take care of immediately. But there had been no word since.

When Dave said no, he had no idea, her mother said hastily, "Pardon me for taking your time. She stayed over with a friend. I just remembered." Before he could question her, she bid him good day.

He was frightened. Felicia and her mother were close. She would never fail to keep her mother posted, unless there was a reason she absolutely could not.

"All boats must take shelter in the typhoon anchorages."

The report said the Nine signal, the all-green one, had been hoisted. The storm was expected to increase significantly in strength, from 181 km/h to 220 km/h.

He was so wrought up about Felicia that he only half heard a spokesman for the Observatory explaining over the radio, "The 'eye' at the center of a tropical typhoon is fairly calm...the winds blow in a tight band around the 'eye'."

Sergeant Tang was adamant. There was no way he would venture forth into the typhoon. Dave was equally insistent. If he failed to reach the hospital, Ming Toy's mother might talk too much, and place Ming Toy in a far more dangerous situation than she was already in.

Eventually Sergeant Tang reluctantly agreed to take him. With the drenching rain a curtain that sealed off all vision except for a few yards ahead, the car rolled slowly through a deserted city. The tradespeople had shuttered their shops. A cat so soaked he looked as if he had been shaved to the skin ran across a street. A little boy jumped shallow pools. An old man with a cane took his time. A couple of subteen schoolgirls laughed their way through what to them was an adventure. A delivery boy on a bicycle shot by as though there was no storm. A police officer huddled in a store corner, his yellow raincoat hiding all but the eyes.

Now and then they skirted a sign that lay fluttering on the street. Once they were brought to a sudden stop when the furious wind, sweeping the pavement cleaner than that of a Dutch housewife, plastered a newspaper across the windshield. And always there was the growling of the monster.

Ungraciously, the Sergeant delivered Dave at the hospital entrance. "Thank you," Dave said. There was no answer.

Inside Dave almost collided with Ming Toy's surgeon.

"Ah!" said the surgeon. "Miss Chan's blood relative. The Caucasian Chinese." He turned sober. "She is doing better than expected. Five minutes. You understand? Five minutes. Not a minute more."

A spit-and-polish young officer sat outside Ming Toy's door, and as Dave entered he spotted another officer just beyond an outside window. Ming Toy was slightly raised in bed, her head more bandages than skin. Still, the sparkle was there in her eyes as they switched to him. Her mother sat at the bedside and her face lighted up.

Ming Toy tried to speak but her voice was as thin as her body. He pulled a chair up on the other side from the mother. He wanted to kiss Ming Toy on the forehead but perhaps that would violate Chinese custom.

En route, he had considered that Ming Toy's hospital room might be bugged. He concluded, though, that no one from the Triad would have had a chance. The police might but this was a risk he had to take. Anyway, anything vital that came out of his conversation with her he would report in time to the police. Only they could follow through and protect her.

He started out by engaging in small talk. He was wondering how he could break out of the pleasantries when she did that for him. She was not one to delay or hedge.

"Mum wrong." She squeezed her mother's hand. "Mum no understand."

"No, no," her mother said firmly. "Remember that night, Mr. Mac come, you go with him, you tell me when come back..."

"I joke." Outside the typhoon let go with an elephant roar and shook the building.

Dave said slowly, "I know you promised Mr. Mac..."

Ming Toy raised her voice. "Love Mister Mac. Never say anything hurt him."

"You must tell the police," Dave said. "They will protect you. Those men will come back."

"No tell police. They make much trouble. No like police."

"You must," her mother put in, half sobbing. "They will do awful things to you."

Dave hesitated before continuing. He was fearful the conversation might hurt her recovery. At that moment he was called to the phone. An aide to Alfred Kwan said Mr. Kwan must see Dave at once, that the matter was of great urgency.

When Dave said he could not leave immediately, the aide ordered him to do so in no uncertain language. Dave said, "Tell Mr. Kwan I'll damn well get there when I can." He hung up. The events and the long days were telling on him.

Her mother was saying, "Mr. David right."

Dave added, "They will torture you. Maybe kill you."

"I get knife. Next time I cut where men make babies."

"Please listen," Dave pleaded. "Mr. Mac is dead. Things have changed. He wouldn't want to see you tortured. He would say forget the promise."

Ming Toy raised herself up on her elbows. "Me honorable woman.

Mister Mac know. Never break promise. Mister Mac dead. No matter. Love Mister Mac."

Dave rose. He had stayed his five minutes. "They will torture your mother if they can't get you to talk."

It was a telling blow. She hesitated. "I kill man who come for Mum."

"They will kill your mother when you are not around."

"Tell you. Not police."

He nodded.

She fell back into the bed. "Hurt much. You come back. We talk. But think, never break promise. Mister Mac dead. No matter. Think go pray to Tin Hau. Ask what say? No? You good man. Like Mister Mac. Love you, Mister David."

He walked in a daze back to Sergeant Tang. The rain fell with a fury he had never known. But he scarcely was aware of its anger. How did you deal with one who had no sense of reason. Only tenderness and devotion and a loyalty few ever have. She was a saint in the rough. A saint who was going to die.

Chapter 29

In his room, the message light was flashing. The operator reported receipt of an urgent ring up from Alfred Kwan. "Mr. Kwan will see you immediately in his office." Mr. Kwan was too important to call on others. They called on him, typhoon or no typhoon.

Marge had left a message. She was concerned. If he were all right, he needn't return her call.

He phoned Felicia's flat. The operator advised that "we cannot connect you with the number you are calling." The same was true when he put in a call to the cargo ship. He wanted to ask Tien Sung Wing if he knew where Felicia was going.

The phone rang. Inspector Yeung was at Reception. Would Dave meet him in a basement storage room? "This noise," he said, "is worse than when the neighborhood teenagers get together at my home."

When Dave walked into the storage room, a 20-foot dragon hanging from the ceiling leered and wriggled its spine as if about to pounce. Stacked along a far wall were colorful banners, costumes and other trappings, dominated by Chinese red, for Tet, the Chinese New Year when old quarrels were forgotten, sins forgiven, often debts wiped off the books, a time of compassion and meditation as well as riotous celebration.

The Inspector stood there drenched. He began without even a hello. "You met Miss Yee at ten minutes after three o'clock yesterday afternoon aboard a cargo boat?"

Dave tightened his jaw muscles, ready to counterattack if the Inspector intended to cross-examine. "So?"

"What was the purpose of the meeting?"

Dave hesitated, knowing full well he was being pulled smoothly into a trap. "She was concerned about my safety. She had heard rumors that a certain Triad planned to assassinate me."

"Rumors, nothing more?" The Inspector was moving in for a kill.

Dave asked sharply, "What are you getting at?"

"Did she not say a vote had been taken and an order issued?"

"She may have."

"I question why she made a trip to Victoria Harbour to tell you that? Why didn't she phone or meet you in Kowloon?"

"Why do we do many things, Inspector? We are all creatures of impulse."

"Don't give me that behaviorism talk." He bit the words off sharply. "Did she deliver something to you? Is that why she met you aboard a boat a relative owned?"

"I don't follow you."

"Have you talked with Miss Yee since — either in person or by phone?"

Dave shook his head.

"Answer the question."

"No. Her mother called me." Dave repeated the brief conversation. "Has something happened to her?"

"We don't know." The Inspector took his time lighting a cigarette. "Her employer at Chester, Ltd. was found murdered in a back room — by a bullet fired from a .38 Colt. Both the weapon and Miss Yee are missing."

Dave's heart beat like a tom-tom. Thoughts raced in and out of his mind, only to be discarded.

"You surely don't suspect her?"

The Inspector's diamond-cut eyes focused on his. He said slowly, as if counting the words, "I never suspect anyone unless I have evidence. In America, you rush into print with your speculation — and ruin lives." He took a long drag on the cigarette, blew the smoke upward. "It has come to my attention that you two had differences, yet she sets up a meeting."

"She wouldn't kill a fly."

"I am not talking about flies. About differences."

"I asked too many questions. She's very sensitive."

The Inspector dropped his severe manner. "My wife is, too. Many women are — and Miss Yee is all woman. Very much a woman. Don't ever doubt that."

He is telling me something, Dave thought.

The Inspector continued, "I won't search you or your room. I would not want to embarrass a friend. However, if you do have a weapon, place it in a plain envelope and leave it with the concierge, and one of my men will come by in an hour or so to collect it."

Dave looked away. It was obvious the Inspector had run a surveillance on her yesterday. Maybe for many yesterdays.

The Inspector put the cigarette out. He was cutting down on his smoking. His quota was half a cigarette at a time. "If you talk with her, ask her to ring me up — and don't use the word, suspect. She had every reason to murder her employer — but I would not consider her a suspect."

As if debatable, he repeated, "I would not."

The questioning seemed at an end, yet the Inspector lingered. He paced absent-mindedly about. Once he thumped the dragon, and the head swung about, jaws open, on the attack. He had something more to say and he was editing the material. Few people, Dave thought, ever edit.

He stopped a few feet away from Dave who sat on a goods box. "My wife — a brilliant woman — you would like her — met Miss Yee at Chinese University where they were helping Chinese-Americans who had come to Hong Kong to adjust to our ways. Both liked each other immensely."

He took a deep breath. "I am bone weary. An Americanism, no? Miss Yee needed someone to talk to and she told my wife she was working for a sadist who screamed obscenities at her and tormented her and threatened to kill her — and she did not know how long she could take it. But she needed money.

"Something she said — I don't remember what it was — prompted me to post a constable to look into this man — and eventually we found he was the unknown power behind the scenes of the Sun Yee On Triad, one of the most corrupt in Hong Kong. Later, I was shocked to learn that Miss Yee had not reported this to us, as any good citizen should."

Dave tried to interrupt but the Inspector waved him down. "My wife had told me what a fine young woman she was — and intelligent — and I interviewed her one day at the university, to ask her to turn informant. In this business, as you know, these so-called informants look and act like some of the slimy creatures you put in your cinema. They lie to us, double-cross us, and set us up for hired killers if they can get a better deal. But Miss Yee was a woman of culture and character."

The Inspector hesitated. "I soon learned she doesn't like to be called an informant. She said she would sell me data. I had the impression she had done this before — and then I learned that you are a client."

He swung about and asked unexpectedly, "Have you been satisfied with her?"

Dave hoped he didn't look as surprised as he felt. He took his time. "To answer that question, Inspector, would be self-incriminating." He smiled, to soften the impact of the statement.

The Inspector raised his voice. "You Americans! Always falling back on technicalities. That is why you don't have justice. Too many barristers looking for crickets in the cracks."

He continued, "As far as I know, she has been honest with us. Honest but not productive. She knows more than she reports. There is something inside of me — maybe it is the detective — we are all paranoid — that informs me she is too smooth, too skilled, too honest...and now this murder."

Dave started to break in. The Inspector said firmly, "No questions." He paused, then, "I am telling you this when I should not — but a wee bit of paranoia is not all bad."

He was at the door. "I hope I have not inconvenienced you."

Dave sat stunned. Felicia was a member of this Triad. She worked for and with the Triad. She sold him and the police information but gave very little, and in return kept the Triad posted on what each was doing and thinking.

Yet she had delivered a .357 Magnum and a 9 mm Smith and Wesson.

"...a wee bit of paranoia is not all bad."

Chapter 30

The unseen force that had turned on the typhoon, just as quickly switched it off. Once again crowds swarmed the streets, the double-tiered buses were groaning and rumbling, the ferries plowing water, and cars clogged every thoroughfare. The sun was hot and brilliant. The little cat in the street box awakened, found he was hungry and set forth to forage. Overhead the police 'copter resumed its search for criminals.

Alfred Kwan hurried around his desk to welcome Dave. He asked how Dave had fared in the storm. He offered sympathy about Ming Toy, and was there anything he could do? He was in a tailored, gray suit, a white silk shirt, and an expensive gray tie, highlighted by a tie pin that held a sizable diamond. His hair, cut short, matched his suit, and his cologne was properly faint. He was a suave version of a taipan of old.

Once seated in front of the massive Swedish desk, he said quietly, "I need to expand my request for the Borneo coverage. It is a matter of great urgency and I will explain that shortly. It will make an even better report for you to do, the kind the *New York Times* or *London Times* would like to print. But then I will own it. It will be mine, is that not right? No one else will have access to it?"

Dave assured him. "Absolutely. We take pride in the confidentiality of our work."

Kwan took his time putting an expensive lighter to a cigarette. "I know that this report will be only the beginning of many assignments from my friends when they hear about it. I daresay I could bring in for you — if I get on the telephone — and I am not speculating — I am a dreadful conservative — a quarter million dollars US. We are among the ten largest companies in all of Asia. We do business from Seoul and Taipai to Singapore and Sydney."

Dave nodded absently. His dark thoughts were far away, in turmoil.

Kwan spoke rapidly, "Although there is urgency about your report, I must first give you a bit of background. You will recall that

I represent Lloyd's of London in Asia in certain key cases."

Dave was restless. He kept shifting his body. Vaguely he remembered Kwan mentioning the famous insurance firm at their first meeting.

"The policy on the Mintoro," he said, "was for 40 million HK, about 4.8 US."

"The Mintoro?"

"The ship Mr. Dunleavy owned that sank in the South China Sea. He owned it through a phantom company based in Manila, The Great Asian Trading Company. A tramp ship, 42 years old, suffering from metal fatigue, wood rotting, paint gone. But it was worth 70 percent more than the policy. Anything that floats these days brings a good price."

He referred to a small leather book bearing his initials. "The date was October 4, 1997. It sank shortly after leaving the Sulu Sea and crossing Balabac Straights. About 100 miles north of Kota Kinabalu in Borneo."

Dave was fascinated. He pulled his thoughts away from Felicia and Ming Toy.

Kwan stated the facts briefly, concisely. "The Mintoro had docked at Zamboanga, a sizable port city in the southern Philippines, and crossed the Sulu Sea without reporting any problems. In fact, the ship never did radio that it was in trouble. Several eyewitnesses on a nearby ship, the Jahore, out of Singapore, reported that it looked like an explosion had taken place a few minutes before the Mintoro sank. The Jahore circled a wide area of flotsam but found no survivors."

Again, his intense, brown eyes studied Dave. He was a veteran salesman sizing up a prospect to determine how well the message was being received.

"An attorney in Manila handled the claim. After Lloyd's investigative staff had checked the facts, they negotiated a settlement for 30 million HK. At this point, Lloyd's in Manila should have been suspicious. Most policyholders would have held out for the full amount. This was a clear loss — no question at the time that the ship had gone down — yet their Manila attorney was quick to accept our initial offer."

Dave shifted uneasily. He was desperately anxious for Alfred Kwan to come to the point.

Kwan continued, "We learned later, after Lloyd's in London paid the 30 million into a bank account for The Great Asian Trading Company, that the money was being withdrawn in a procedure commonly used by money launderers. I should add that I knew nothing about this policy, since Manila handled everything until Manila discovered that one Mr. Mac Dunleavy, an American who lived in Hong

Kong, was treasurer of The Great American Asian Trading Company, as well as president."

Dave broke in. "I know nothing about my friend's business dealings."

"I know, you only got a card from him every Christmas." He rose, paced about. "Shortly afterwards, we learned that The Great Asian Trading Company had taken out a duplicate policy with our competitor, Munich Re, and they, too, had paid off."

He explained that both Lloyd's and Munich Re were re-insurers. That is, the policies were written by other companies, and they, to protect themselves against a catastrophic loss, re-insured the policies with Lloyd's or Munich Re. Munich Re, Kwan said, was a fierce competitor, founded in 1880 with offices in a marble palace off the Englisher Garten in Munich, Germany.

"Pardon me," Dave said. "I've got to go. I've got a crisis breaking."

Kwan heard nothing. He was completely wrapped up in his narrative. "I have never believed Mrs. Dunleavy's account of her husband dying in that Chinese fishing village. These little settlements keep no records, of course, but our investigator did learn from an old headman that a Caucasian visitor had died suddenly and they had buried him at sea. He didn't know why the Caucasian had been in the fishing village but said that he, the headman, had sent the dead man's possessions off somewhere. Our investigator couldn't verify that another Caucasian, a Brit, had been with the party who died. I have to admit that the man who died could have been Mr. Dunleavy — although it could have been a happenstance and was an unknown Caucasian."

He sat down, leaned forward toward Dave. "Mr. Dunleavy bought the Mintoro in Kota Kinabalu and it docked there from time to time. The crew was mostly from there. I want you to go there and see what you can learn while you are roaming about as a journalist doing an article. I will pay you $10,000 US for the article, and guarantee you a quarter million in the future from friends who will want to subscribe to World Coverage.

"In addition, if you should locate the millions hidden away, I will pay you five percent of the amount you recover."

Dave straightened. "I'm not a detective."

"In World War II," Kwan said slowly, "John Edgar Hoover recruited 38 journalists as counter-intelligence agents in the belief that newspaper men and spies operate much the same. Each goes out to get information and then must report it back, the journalist to his editor, the spy to his spy master."

"It's not my field," Dave said flatly.

"You are a respected foreign correspondent. You can get information that a private investigator never could. I am certain that as a foreign correspondent there have been times when you have been a detective, ferreting out a hidden story, going from sources criminal to those high in government or business."

Dave said, "No. Absolutely not. I cannot...I will not walk out on Ming Toy."

Kwan answered in a confidential tone. "I anticipated that. You are too much the gentleman to desert her. But listen, I have talked with the two Triads interested — through my liaison man with the Triads — every major firm and financial institution in Hong Kong has a go-between — and he has reached an agreement that they will not harm Miss Chan, whom you call Ming Toy, as long as you are on assignment for me."

Dave kept his voice low. "They gave their word? Forget it!"

"Look, Mr. Anderson, the Triads are interested primarily in getting their investment back, with a fair return, and so is Khun Sa of the Golden Triangle. They don't care about a poor sampan woman — and if she has some money — or knows where there is some — well, we will negotiate with her later. We are convinced — I and the Triads — that the millions are out there somewhere and what Ming Toy may have secreted is negligible. No one with the criminal intelligence of Mac Dunleavy is going to leave several million with a sampan woman."

He took a deep breath. "I give you my word, Mr. Anderson, before your God and the Lord Buddha, that she will not be harmed. On the contrary, by taking this assignment you will be protecting her. Otherwise, one of the Triads — and it doesn't matter what strategies you or the police use — will move in."

Dave said slowly, "It's more than Ming Toy. I learned only a few hours ago — but you know it..."

"...that Miss Yee has disappeared. That her employer was shot to death?"

"Yes, you must understand..."

"— that you have fondness for Miss Yee and —"

"— as a close friend, I cannot stand idly by. It's not romance. You yourself —"

"— hinted she was a Lesbian." Kwan smiled slyly. "I tell all Americans that to protect our Chinese women. I read the newspapers, watch television, see American films."

Dave looked at him in disbelief. "You think American men are all rapists?"

"Not at all. But you know yourself, Americans have no morals, they are promiscuous, and as an amateur historian, I would say they are at the period the Roman Empire was in when it started breaking up, because of the orgies. I apologize if I have offended you."

Dave started to counter him but Kwan raised his voice to override him. "Miss Yee is in no danger. She is waiting for you at the Tanjung Aru Beach Hotel in Kota Kinabalu. I put her on a plane before the storm came in."

Dave was rocked for a moment. "What is she doing there?"

In a flash, Dave saw the set-up. "You mean she will be reporting on me...every move I make?"

"Exactly. Every day." Kwan hurried on. "Let me recapitulate. You cannot refuse me. You will be paid well, you will have many future assignments from all over Asia, you will have the assurance the sampan woman will be protected, you will be working alongside a lady you admire, you will be covering a story that when I give my release could become a world wide sensation — and you will have proved yourself."

"Proved myself?"

"I regret to inform you that some of my associates have had difficulty in accepting your account that you came here on behalf of an old friend to look after a sampan 'tanka'. They think you are here to look after Mr. Dunleavy's financial interests, cover up for him, launder money. I have never believed this. I have never considered that anyone as intelligent and respected as you are would come up with such a ridiculous story — unless it were true."

Dave ignored that. "Will she be representing the Triads as well as Lloyd's?"

Kwan shook his head. "I knew her grandfather well. On her mother's side. A fine old gentleman whose word was all that anyone needed. Miss Yee is of the same stock. I have known her since she was a child."

He continued, "There is considerable urgency. One of our investigators interviewed a party in Kota Kinabalu who had seen the widow — or wife — anyway, Mrs Dunleavy — only two days ago."

He added, "Your plane leaves in five hours. Someone from Thomas Cook Travel will meet you at Cathay Pacific Airlines with the tickets and other papers."

Chapter 31

Alfred Kwan interrupted the session to take a call from his wife. "I am in conference with that pleasant young American I was telling you about." A pause. "Of course, we will have him to dinner but this is not quite the proper time. I will explain tonight at the opera."

A long pause, then he put a hand over the receiver and said to Dave, "My third daughter would like to know if the Apache Indians are still a problem."

Dave smiled, "Tell her the Apaches got all of the scalps they could use and now they are farmers, lawyers, secretaries, and even a few are politicians."

Much of Asia believed, and others who knew better *wanted* to believe that the Old West was still a rugged land of desert and high mountains...Indian raiding parties...John Waynes leading the cavalry...creaking and rumbling wagon trains forming a circle to fight off Indian hordes...tall, broad-shouldered, gun-toting men saving damsels in distress...and panting crinolines whose cloying sweetness and proper manners belied any lust they may have had. After all of these years, Zane Grey sold widely. For many, his novels were scripture.

Dave slumped, thinking his way through this sudden, complicated turn of events. He had been the target of the Triads. Now, for what might be a brief time, he would be doing their work as well as Lloyd's of London's. If he failed, or covered up what he discovered, once more he would be marked for assassination.

The break relaxed him. He straightened up when Alfred Kwan rejoined him after the phone call.

"I am most fortunate to have a wonderful family — and it all started at Berkeley. There were only five of us Chinese students then and I read the other day that we Asians will soon outnumber everyone at the University of California. Imagine!"

With pride he added, "We work hard."

That summed it up, Dave believed. In every Oriental country, to survive, the people had to work hard. And when they migrated to the

United States they brought the work ethic with them.

Kwan shifted to his low, crisp, all-business voice. "Someone is sitting on millions of dollars in cash...in U.S. money...in one of the most remarkable frauds in recent history.

"It took a mastermind, a genius in detail to work out the disbursement of a huge sum of money without anyone learning about it in financial circles. It had to be Mac Dunleavy. If he didn't die — and as I told you, I have my doubts about that — he may be the one sitting on that pot of gold. If not, probably it is his widow...unless someone has moved in on her."

Kwan lighted another cigarette, pulled the ashtray closer. "I want you to know every detail of what our people have done. Our accountants have traveled the world following a fabulous paper trail. This is how Mr. Dunleavy worked it.

"Lloyd's paid off in dollars in London, depositing about three million, seven hundred and fifty thousand (roughly 30 million HK) in a bank specified by a legal firm retained by The Great Asian Trading Company. This legal firm then wrote checks for $370,000 US, more or less, for deposit in ten banks, one each in Paris, Dusseldorf, Geneva, Milan, Madrid, the Cayman Islands, Penang, Manila, Singapore and Kota Kinabalu.

"Then other attorneys in those cities handled the disbursement of checks for $100,000 US and $70,000 US to banks in more than 20 cities around the world — except for the one in Kota Kinabalu. The deposit there remains en toto to this day.

"The procedure was repeated with deposits in these 20-some banks, and repeated again, until there was no deposit anywhere of more than $20,000 and in most cases, not more than $10,000. In your country, a bank must report to the government any withdrawal exceeding $10,000, and the deposits there ranged between $5,000 and $10,000.

"At this point it was a simple matter for Mr. Dunleavy to travel from bank to bank withdrawing the deposits. If they had been large, say a half million or so, then a request for payment in U.S. dollars would have attracted attention and suspicion. Banks would have thought that drugs or a major embezzlement or theft was involved. Besides, U.S. dollars in that amount would be difficult to come by.

"He was not greedy, as most criminals are. We estimate he paid out about 30 percent in legal fees involved in moving the big sums at the beginning, in bank charges and taxes.

"The risk he took was small. He defrauded the Triads and Khun Sa but he fled Hong Kong before the scam was discovered. He left his wife behind to wind up business matters but no evidence was ever produced to implicate her. He defrauded Lloyd's — and Munich Re — but only if it could be proved that the ship had not gone down. I should add that Munich Re — we were advised after the fact — had paid out about the same sum. Hence, you can multiply the figures I have given you by two. The total would be 7.5 million US."

He rose and walked about. The adrenalin was pumping hard. He could sit only so long. "Since he was clever in handling the insurance payout, I have been wondering if the Mintoro ever sank. The flotsam could have been dumped from a small, fast ship, and an explosion staged that the seamen on the Jahore saw. I suppose this is all fantasy...but I wonder."

And then Kwan came up with information that would put a zinger into the story.

"I am all the more suspicious," he continued, "since the Mintoro was carrying 94 Lexus cars for delivery in Singapore — at least that was what the manifest said. The Great Asian Trading Company put in a claim for the cars, over a million dollars, which Lloyd's paid."

He sat back down. He was breathing heavily. "This was all routine until about a week ago when one of those cars surfaced in Manila. It came to the attention of the police when a thief stole it, the police recovered it, and in checking the serial number, found it matched with a car loaded on the Mintoro in Japan."

His throat was husky. He had about talked himself out. "Our London people have informed me that they have had two cases recently where a ship secretly unloaded a valuable cargo, usually at night, and then a few days later the ship would sink, and the owners would put in a claim not only for the vessel but for the cargo. In the meantime, the freight they had unloaded would be shipped within hours aboard another tramp and then sold in another port."

His secretary looked in and asked how long he would be, there was an urgent matter he needed to handle. He asked if he could have 20 minutes. She nodded and left.

"We have two investigators, accountants actually, who are watching the Kota Kinabalu bank. Dunleavy, if he is still alive, or the wife may tap into the deposit.

"Might I be presumptuous if I suggested what I would like you to do? Such as talking with the harbor people in Kota Kinabalu about the purchase of the Mintoro, how many times the ship docked there...what they have to say about the vessel and Mac Dunleavy...look in on the pubs frequented by the seamen...ask around about Heather Dunleavy. I have a list of more suggestions."

He handed a page with his ideas written out in English, the penmanship excellent, that of a meticulous person who knew what he wanted and set it forth concisely. "I ask your pardon for even mentioning all of this. You are a brilliant journalist and I should not be intruding."

He added, as if by way of an excuse, "I am under dreadful pressure. Lloyd's has suffered its worst losses in its 304 years — almost four billion US — and its twenty-two some thousand investors are angry."

Dave asked questions. Kwan answered them honestly, frankly. Dave had no reservations about Alfred Kwan. He did have about Felicia Yee.

Kwan said, "If you get any leads or locate the money or learn the whereabouts of Heather Dunleavy, ring me up at once and I will notify the Triads. If they think you are keeping anything from them, they will kidnap and torture you until they break you. They will have someone tracking you — day after day."

"Will Felicia know them — spot them?" Dave asked.

"She might."

As Dave was about to leave, Kwan said, "You will have dinner with us? The weekend after you return? My wife will ask me if I set up a date. My third daughter, too, will want to know more about the Apaches."

Dave said he would. His thoughts, though, were far from a dinner party.

He might not return.

Chapter 32

The flight attendants on the Cathay Pacific airliner brought hot towels before the lunch and afterwards. They spoke Cantonese and English and a few, Japanese. English was universal, having taken over from the French of another generation.

Before he left the hotel, he placed the 9-mm Smith and Wesson in an envelope and left the package with the concierge, as he had been ordered by the Inspector. Under other circumstances he would have refused. But he had enlisted the Inspector's assistance in providing round-the-clock protection for Ming Toy. To make double sure, he had employed a private security firm to watch over her until he returned. By leaving, he was "buying time" for her — and for himself. When he returned, if he failed in his mission, then he and Ming Toy would be marked again for death. Not even Alfred Kwan would be able to stop the Triads from moving, if Alfred Kwan wished to do so.

He told himself he was going on this insane trip for Ming Toy. When he was honest with himself, however, he knew that a good part of the motivation was that he was still very much the newspaperman and always would be. He had a compulsion to know "the rest of the story."

There was something more than myth or legend to the old chestnut about newspapering "being in the blood." He had been hooked since that first day when, a cub reporter, he had walked into a police station on his first assignment.

The roar of the 747 engines was muted as the pilot dropped elevation and prepared to bring the craft in for a landing. Below was Kota Kinabalu, called KK by the natives, a neatly laid-out, concrete city of a quarter million people, known under British rule as Jesselton, famous during World War II when the citizens destroyed their city before the advancing Japanese.

This was Borneo, the stuff of his boyhood dreams, reading the National Geographic, knowing he could never afford to travel there.

And now he was going there with all expenses paid on possibly a very dangerous assignment.

This was the "Land Below The Wind," or the "Land of the Hornbills" (a bird). And he knew from reading in his teen years, that KK and the other harbor towns stretching southward were only a cosmetic facade. Behind them lay the land of the Kazadans, the long houses, the headhunters of a half century ago, the skull collectors, the jungles and rain forests and rubber plantations and green padi fields, and Orang Utans (the wild men of Borneo).

Now there came into sharp focus, under a blistering, merciless sun, the gold dome of the State Mosque...the towering round, silver Sabah Foundation...the islands dotting South Sulu waters...and sandy beaches with palms standing tall.

His heart quickened. He hadn't known that his boyhood was only below the surface.

A dark-complexioned girl, possibly 18, approached him as he headed for Immigration. She had flouncing black hair falling to her shoulders, a simple, print dress, and was in native sandals. What captivated him was the smile, unaffected, outgoing, almost a trademark on South Sea islands.

"Welcome to Sabah," she said. Her voice was girlish, enthusiastic.

Sabah was one of two Malaysian states that formed the northern half of Borneo. The southern half belonged to Indonesia. Sabah and Sarawak were 400 miles distant from the Malaysian capital of Kuala Lumpur, separated by the South China sea.

"May I help you?" she asked, reaching for his attache case. Rudely, he shifted it beyond her hand. All too well he remembered the young Chinese at the Hong Kong airport.

She led him to the head of the line where Immigration quickly stamped his passport, which she waved before a Customs official, calling, "American!", and then he was in the airport proper.

She was from a travel service. Would he like to book a trip to a water village, or Sandakan to visit the Orang Utan Rehabilitation Center, or might he like to climb Mt Kinabalu (13,455 feet)?

No, he would not. He thanked her and headed for the taxi exit.

Another time he would have paid her to sit and talk for a couple of hours. He had landed "cold" in many cities the world over, without contacts, and seized on the first person he met, a bellman or taxi driver or anyone who knew the "lay of the land." From that first meeting he would establish a chain of contacts.

A rumpled, long-haired young taxi driver, who called him "Old Man" (Dave could have killed him), drove him to the Tanjung Aru Beach Hotel on Jalan Aru, 10 minutes from the airport. The vast lobby had no sides, and a soft wind was chasing away the heat of the day. He was assigned Room 448. Yes, Miss Felicia Yee had arrived and was in 352. He decided to wait until morning to call her.

He was weary deep down. He performed better in a tense situation when he was rested. And meeting Felicia might be a tense one.

From his room, he placed two phone calls, one to the Aberdeen Hospital where he was told Ming Toy was "doing as well as could be expected." He hung up infuriated. Even the Chinese hospitals gave you the same line that American ones did. Maybe the medical profession had it copyrighted.

Next he called Marge. He got only the answering machine. He told the blasted thing where he was.

He rose early. No matter how late he stayed up, his built-in alarm sounded at 6. He put on the same light blue suit he had worn the day before, a tie to match, and a clean white shirt.

As he was slipping into the jacket, he heard a faint rustle of paper in the left pocket. He pulled out a note on coarse wrapping paper folded four ways. The message was in big block, black letters, inconsistent and awkward in size, as if someone had deliberately fashioned them that way to avoid recognition.

He read: YOU ARE INTO SOMETHING YOU KNOW NOTHING ABOUT. GET OUT BEFORE YOU GET HURT. TAKE THE NEXT FLIGHT TO THE STATES. WISH YOU LONG LIFE BUT YOU DECIDE.

YOU DECIDE...

The fear he might have experienced emotionally at one time was only a mental jolting. In these last few days he had undergone one shock after another until fear was an accepted factor in his daily living.

He turned analytical. The WISH YOU LONG LIFE sounded Chinese but the rest of the contents could have been Anglo, penned by anyone who knew English. The threat was there but it was an oblique, soft one, as if thought out by a woman rather than a professional killer. And who had slipped it into his pocket? The girl who met him? The taxi driver? He had been jostled a time or two after leaving the plane and he preferred to think it was an unknown person. Really, did the identity matter? He slipped the note into his jacket's inside right pocket.

Slowly he walked into the Kasturi Terrace for breakfast. Carefully he chose a table for two in a corner where his back was to a wall and he could scan the other early risers. The air was invigorating with a scent of its own. He looked out on palm trees rustling in the breeze. In the distance, beyond the palms, was the South China Sea, a vast surface of water with a few islands nearby and a ship anchored not too far away. Some 100 miles to the northwest was the spot where the Mintoro went down.

He caught the Shalimar scent, rose quickly and turned abruptly about. Felicia stood motionless, her dark glasses fixed on him, her mouth a penciled, thin dash. The scar was as evident as ever.

"Good morning, Mr. Anderson," she said politely, the way a young person might address an elder she scarcely knew.

He pulled a chair out and she thanked him. Back in the States these days he scarcely knew what the response might be to such an arcane bit of chivalry — a pleasant thank you, or a glower from a feminist which said she was perfectly capable of handling her own seating.

"What would you like?" he asked, meeting tone for tone.

She took her time ordering, finally decided on a fruit plate of coconut, pineapple, papaya and bananas. She was ill at ease, sitting a little straighter, toying with a spoon. "I am in a most uncomfortable position," she began.

He broke in. "You don't have to tell me anything you don't want to. We need to plan for the day, get some logistics settled..."

An Arab sauntered by, sizing them up, a paunchy belly threatening to break the elastic belt on his swim trunks.

Dave continued, "I've got to be honest. I'm not happy about this arrangement. I'm doing a story — and you're representing Lloyd's. I'll give you living space — and I'll expect the same from you."

The day was hot, already in the late 80's, but her words came from the deep freeze. "Whether you want to hear it or not, Mr. Anderson, I have certain facts you should know before we start our work together."

She emphasized *work together*. He shuddered. He knew it would be this way.

She said matter-of-factly, "First, I am not a fugitive. I was not in the office when my employer was shot. At that time Mr. Kwan was putting me on the plane for here. It was all so sudden. He had entered into an agreement with the Triads, and he moved fast, the way he does. I tried to ring up my mother but she was not home, I tried again when I reached the hotel and we had a long talk. She told me she had called you..."

She erased a cigarette, lit another. Her hands trembled. "As you can see, I am nervous...upset...so much has been happening."

He wished he could console her. She was a wounded deer. He could not understand his feelings. One moment he disliked her, the next he wanted her. He was not experienced in a love/hate relationship and he was confused, frustrated, and bewildered.

When he started talking, she held up a hand to silence him. "Let me finish. After I spoke with my mother, I rang up Inspector Yeung to let him know where I was. He had the usual questions. Who had seen my boss in the last few days? Did I have reason to suspect anyone? I informed him I would return if Mr. Kwan instructed me to do so. I have known Mr. Kwan since I was a child and he and the Inspector are fully aware that I am opposed to all violence."

She slumped. "If you have questions..."

He hesitated. He noted she had never referred to the victim by name. Was his name one that Dave would recognize?

He decided not to pursue the point. No matter what he asked, she would disclose no more than she wanted him to know.

He said, "I'm concerned about Ming Toy's safety. Mr. Kwan swore by Buddha...but I keep having nagging thoughts that Mr. Kwan may not have that much influence."

She was quick to answer. "In his business he has to work closely with the Triads. He contributes generously to their charitable causes."

Dave exploded. "Charitable causes!"

"You don't understand since you are not Chinese. The Triads have many sides, the same as —"

He finished the sentence. "— same as all of us?"

She took a deep, exasperated breath. "I didn't mean that personally."

"I'm sure you didn't. Let's get down to specifics...what we're going to do today, Felicia. I'm going to call you Felicia even if you parboil me."

The glasses only stared. His anger rose. How could you talk with someone who hid behind dark glasses? Were her eyes sparkling, cold, mad, amused, happy?

"And take off those damn binoculars!" He half shouted.

She spoke quietly, plaintively, "If you only knew why I wear them. And do not raise your voice at me...ever...ever."

He collapsed. "Sorry."

There was an embarrassing lull before he picked up the conversation. "Since we are at each other's throats, I want you to know that I will be expecting to read the reports you phone in each night. I have every right —"

"The hell you do!" she snapped. "I'm working exclusively for Lloyd's. You're my client only in Hong Kong."

He struggled to subdue his fury. "You mean if I'm going to be killed, you won't warn me?"

"Don't be asinine!"

She added, "If you permit me to come along with you I will be cooperative and accurate. If I have to follow you, I may not be."

He cooled somewhat. "I'll introduce you as my research assistant."

"Make it a fellow editor."

"My heavens, you're pushy."

"For your information — and I do not understand why I am telling you this — the Triads are running a surveillance on us. Do not ask me how I know. You usually do ask — and it is not in keeping with a distinguished journalist who once was threatened with prison if he did not reveal his sources. And he did not."

He took the note from his inside jacket pocket and handed it to her. "We've been put on notice."

Spreading it out on the table, she read it. "We expected it, didn't we?" she said without emotion. "Someone in Hong Kong talked and the Dunleavy people knew we were coming before we even arrived."

With minimal discussion, they agreed they had to move cautiously. Every word they uttered might be overheard — or recorded. Every step they took, every room they entered, they had to estimate the possibility of an ambush.

They settled down to planning the day. By the time they finished, an hour later, they had fallen into the old pattern of feeling comfortable with each other.

She said, "I hope we can find time to do something on our own."

"Like Lantau?"

She smiled wanly. "Like Lantau."

The girl brought the check saying, "If you're interested, there's a class in blowpipe starting in a couple of hours."

They looked baffled. The girl said, "You know, a blowpipe. That is what my ancestors used to kill their enemies."

An arrow was dipped in poison and "fired" from a long pipe, often made out of bamboo, by a marksman blowing into the pipe.

Dave asked if he could buy one. Marge's daughter would like one to hang up in her room.

Somehow the subject of the murder came up. "I am most relieved," she said slowly. "He deserved to die."

Dave couldn't hold back. "Who was he?"

"Not someone you would know. He was a cruel man. But my mother and I had to have the money. It was a job I could not walk away from."

He started a question. She interrupted. "Please do not expect me to discuss this further. One day I will tell you all about it — but not now. It is too painful."

Her voice broke. He expected tears to follow. But she was of sterner make-up.

Chapter 33

Felicia never looked lovelier or more sensuous as she entered the Semporna Grill in downtown KK with Dave. Her yellow billowing skirt bounced with every movement of her lithe body, as did the long gold temple earrings. Her lips took shape in a little mock smile that suggested she reveled in all of this.

The Semporna was a madhouse with executives and professionals brushing shoulders as they came and went. The Semporna was Borneo's fast food place. The sign read, "Lunch is complimentary if it is not served within an hour!"

At the taxi stand, they hired a car for the day. The driver was in his late teens, well-mannered, short hair, in a T shirt with a tiger leaping out, and Levis not acid-aged but aged by wear.

"What's your name?" Dave asked.

"What name you want? Got many. English, Chinese, Malaysian."

"Doesn't matter."

"Good name. Doesunmat. Got new name. Doesunmat."

First they chose the *Borneo Mail*, an English-language daily. Wherever he went, Dave dropped by the local newspaper. Seldom had he drawn a blank. Editors and reporters enjoyed meeting someone from the United States. If he caught them in a quiet time, after the paper had gone to press, they would sit and talk about the news they could not print and the citizens they could not expose. Within an hour he would know far more than their readers.

At the *Mail* they met Borneo's top reporter, Alam Koding. He was in his fifties, shaped out of blocks, his square head resting on a square torso. He peered at them out of thick bifocals. He had the bushy hair of a native, which he was, of Kadastan stock, well-educated, with a love of the English language, spoken everywhere in this former British colony. He was reserved, slow to talk with strangers, yet obviously impressed that an American correspondent would take the time and interest to come by. Dave invited him to lunch. Once out of the office, he might become more talkative.

At the restaurant, they sat in a far corner. Dave had read a couple of Koding's stories in *The Mail* and congratulated him on the writing and perception. Koding smiled in appreciation. He accepted them. They were "in." Americans had a tarnished reputation but this one was all right.

They ordered hamburgers. Koding was pleased with the choice, Felicia not too happy, and Dave with utter disdain. Never abroad had he found a hamburger that tasted like one. In Tibet they were made of ground yak and in the Russian republics of horse, dog or cat meat.

While Felicia listened patiently, the two discussed the economy, what the Japanese were doing in Borneo (they were cutting swathes through the jungle and shipping the timber back home), where Borneo was headed, and other like issues. Then Dave brought up the sinking of the Mintoro.

"It was a big story here," Koding said, "since this was the ship's home port. We broke it first when a crew member came in on another tramp and then Reuters News Service got busy piecing together reports from Zamboanga and Singapore and by radio phone with the crewmen who had witnessed the explosion from another ship."

He waited until the waitress served dessert. "Around the paper we thought it suspicious everyone had survived the explosion. Not a single casualty. We couldn't do much investigation since the ship went down so far out from here and not near any other inhabited place. We did have one good lead."

He paused, noting that Felicia's eyes were signaling Dave. She nodded toward three tables away.

Dave stared, blanched.

"Someone you know?" asked Koding.

Dave's throat had gone dry. "Yes."

Sitting by himself, looking their way, was Barney, Khun Sa's PR man. He raised a hand in greeting.

Dave switched back to Koding. "Sorry about the interruption. You said something about a lead."

"The Captain of the Mintoro lives here. Out near the Lee Man Bookstore in the Bukit Padang area. I almost got killed trying to interview him. He would not talk and pulled a gun on me and fired a shot as I was running for my car."

Dave suggested the three of them might corner the Captain, preferably in a public place. He glanced at Felicia. She nodded in the affirmative. Koding agreed, and as he left, they set up a date and place.

As soon as he was gone, Barney tore over and grabbed a chair. "Hi, glamorpuss," he said to Felicia. "If you ever get tired of this old man, I'll be waiting."

He belched out a laugh. Dave's anger reached the boiling point.

"What the blazes are you doing here?" After the blow-up at the nightclub, this slime was acting as if nothing had happened.

"Same thing you are. Got a deal for you."

"Get out of here! I don't want to see your dog face ever again!"

"A deal. A sweet deal."

Felicia raised her voice. "You heard him. Brush off."

Barney leaned across the table. "If I find the pot of gold and that swine, I'll let you know right off. If you find them, you let me know. That way we cover for each other — and the Triad can take a walk."

Felicia said in a no-nonsense tone, "I represent Lloyd's of London and we're in this for our share of the money."

He laughed. "You Chink broads —"

In a flash, Dave rose, swung a haymaker that connected with Barney's jaw, a blow that knocked Barney and the chair backwards, both hitting the floor hard. Barney thrashed about like a fish plopping on a boat deck.

He struggled to his feet, put a handkerchief to the cut lip but failed to stem the blood.

"What'd I say? What'd I say? She's a Chink and she's a broad."

Felicia grabbed Dave's arm as he swung again.

Barney was halfway to the door when he yelled back, "I was going to tell you where you could find that Heather bitch — but go to hell."

All eyes were on him as he made it to the exit, blood dripping along the way.

Dave sat stunned.

At the police station, they encountered a roadblock. The officer was gruff and in a hurry. They showed him photos of Mac and Heather. He had no knowledge of either. "I'd like to help you but we have no extradition papers filed...no report that either has been charged with a crime. I will request information from Interpol."

They fared better at the old English bank, The Caliber, where London reported the entire sum of $370,000 was on deposit. The managing director was an elderly Chinese with cropped graying hair, a pair of glasses lodged precariously halfway down his nose, and quick dark eyes.

He was courteous in the old Chinese way. He offered tea. Felicia accepted. Dave thanked him. The tea would be strong enough to hold up a drunk horse.

"You are the third one to inquire about the account," he said, fondling a neatly trimmed goatee. "I must offer sincere regrets. We are not a Swiss bank sworn to secrecy. However, we hold the same standards as your banks in the States do. We cannot divulge facts about an account unless we are authorized to do so by the depositor or unless the authorities serve legal papers on us with specific demands."

He had repeated the same admonition a month before, he said, to a Lloyd's of London investigator and recently to an English-speaking lady who was in her forties and offered an "official" letter from The Great Asian Trading Company instructing The Caliber Bank to provide information about the account and authorizing her to withdraw any sum she wished.

He continued, "We seldom receive a blank endorsement for a withdrawal and I excused myself while I faxed the Manila Bank that had made the original deposit. They faxed me within ten minutes that she was an imposter and no one had authority over the account except the investment company's president or their solicitor (attorney)."

He fumbled through an assortment of papers on the ancient desk and came up with the name of the president, Mac Dunleavy, and the solicitor, Joseph Z. Kurup of Kuching, a Borneo city south of KK.

"The lady was furious but then I have been a banker for 32 years and no one scares me — except my grandchildren."

Felicia placed a photo of Heather Dunleavy before him, and he nodded in recognition. He shook his head when presented with a picture of Mac.

He and Felicia talked in Cantonese for a half hour. Dave was baffled. Twice he rose to leave but each time she tugged him back down.

The old gentleman scribbled briefly on a note pad and excused himself. Dave asked what that was all about. Felicia stepped to the desk, picked up the note, read it and returned it to the exact position it had been in. She gestured for Dave to keep quiet.

The banker returned and they said their goodbyes. He was overwhelmed with regrets and offered a thousand apologies.

Outside, on the busy street, they took their time walking to the car a block away. She hugged his arm tightly and leaned over to whisper. "We had a talk about Confucius and how the young people today have no understanding of the great principles he taught...and how the schools should include Confucius in their curriculum...and they have just begun to teach the Shih Shu — the Four Books — in Singapore."

A truck thundered by, blocking out all sound.

Dave was frustrated. "How the blazes did Confucius get into this?"

"We talked and I told him my mother had taught me to live by the principles of Confucius...and we talked...and talked...and at last he knows I am an honorable person. He leaves the room so I may read the note. It is an ancient Chinese custom. When an honorable person cannot reveal openly the truth to another honorable person..."

She trailed off as they were caught up in a swarm of youngsters just out of school.

"Is there a point to all of this?" he asked bluntly.

She took a deep breath. "The bank was authorized two days ago by the solicitor in Kuching to pay out $30,000 US to one Aka Harum, the captain of the Mintoro."

Dave wanted a "back up" for when they met Captain Aka Harum. For Felicia he had to interpret the term. "You haven't seen many American police movies."

"I hate them. I thought all America was like that when I went to California. Brutality and sex."

She suggested the City Market. By accident, they parked in front of the furniture section, a long row with little pagoda roofs over each stall. It was mostly open air and their gaze went to four young guys who looked about 20. They were gathered around a Singer Sewing machine. No matter where he had gone in Third World countries, even in deepest Africa, Dave had found ancient Singers.

The young man seated behind the old treadle machine was in torn jeans, supported by a cracked leather belt, cinched by a silver buckle that would have been the envy of any cowboy. He had a colorful headband holding back a hill of hair that flounced every which way.

At the sight of the two, he was on his feet, running. "Make suit cheap. Fast. Take size. Come back two hours. Get suit...look like Mister Brook." Translated, that meant Brooks Brothers.

The other three joined in, plugging for him. "Good tailor. How much want pay? Get cheap price. Good cloth."

They were the kind of hard sell salesmen one encountered in most native markets. But good natured, all smiles.

When Dave explained that he needed bodyguards, not suits, they were gung ho. They had seen Hong Kong's karate movies and they demonstrated how good they were with karate chops. Dave offered $5 US each and the deal was made.

En route to the Harbor, the two plotted how they would "interview" Captain Harum, how he might react, how they would counter. "Keep back quite a way," he admonished her. "You can't help and I don't want you hurt."

He was to recall later she had offered no comment.

They talked with caution. Both feared that Doesunmat, at the wheel now, driving very carefully, might be a "plant."

They liked Doesunmat. He was a "yes, sir" and "no, ma'am" kid who hurried to open doors, rushed to get a pack of cigarettes if Felicia merely mentioned it, and grabbed everything they carried whether they wanted him to or not.

Dave was surprised that Felicia, even more than he, was wary. He was learning that she trusted few which suggested she had come from a background he knew nothing about. She was quiet now, her features set firmly, as if she might be contemplating what was ahead, a fistfight that might result in injuries, or worse, in which there might be gunplay.

In an effort to produce a smile, he congratulated her on her clever ploy of talking about Confucius. He recalled that in his crime reporting days with the *Los Angeles Times*, there was a judge who was obsessed with Abraham Lincoln. If you listened to him recount his research into Lincoln's life, you would get any news break you wanted. Never before or since had *The Times* had so many reporters versed in Lincoln's life.

"Historians differ," she was saying, "about why Confucius plays such a part in our lives today since he lived about 2,500 years ago. The cynics argue that it's because Confucius advocated reverence for one's parents and respect for the government. Generations of parents and governments liked that — and you might say, promoted Confucius. In China today, you'll find in almost every village some kind of memorial to him in the plaza, and the whole community gathers on his birthday to honor him."

Alam Koding was already in the Harbor Master's office when they walked in. The office was a neat arrangement of papers on the desk, maps and charts on the white walls.

Koding introduced them, very proper. The Master had the sharp looks, the personality, and the glibness that would have fitted him into any Rotary Club in the States.

"I know the States well," he said, his English accented with a British flavor. "I studied at the University of Chicago. Great days they were."

Quickly he turned away from the opportunity to reminisce. "Captain Harum is down there. Comes by at this time of the evening every day. Looks for a job but spends most of his time talking with the officers and crews of any ship docked here."

They were on the second floor and through a narrow window they saw the figure of a man moving in the distance, down near the water.

The Harbor Master laughed. "The seamen think he is a direct descendant of Captain Bligh, and I wouldn't be surprised. Advance with caution and keep your rear open."

They took old, crumbling cement stairs down. The military and other security officers were maintaining a tight cordon about the entrance to the Harbor. The scene was one of organized pandemonium. An officer approached to escort them through the pedestrian gate. They had left the four Singers, as they called them, on the sidewalk and Felicia and Dave motioned to them.

Dave said to Felicia at the gate, “Stay here. You can’t help and it may get nasty.”

She backed up a few feet. The arrangement was for Koding and Dave to lead the way with the four “bodyguards” following by about ten feet. When they were a short distance ahead, Felicia surreptitiously followed.

The distance to where the Captain stood talking with a ship’s officer in uniform was about two city blocks. They passed a ship from Serbia that was under repair. All kinds of machinery littered the ground. At this time of evening everyone was gone. This was a pleasant hour, with the sun low on the horizon and a gentle breeze cooling the lingering heat of the day.

She was a lonely figure walking through this wide-open space. She had anticipated Dave would spot and order her back but he was too engrossed in the upcoming clash of wills to check on her.

As they advanced, Captain Harum took shape, a giant of a man, well over six feet, broad shoulders, muscle-bound, hips narrow, hair a bushy black, a heavy black beard, and penetrating eyes. He was in a sweat shirt that looked smelly and khaki trousers held up by a ship’s rope.

Koding said, “Captain, this is Mr. David Anderson, the famous American correspondent.”

The Captain stared at Dave as if he would eat him, bones and all. “You bringing a whole damn army?” He indicated the bodyguards. “I know them guys. One cough out of me and they’ll run for their lives.”

He advanced a couple of steps. They stood their ground. It was deadly quiet.

“Five seconds,” he bellowed. “Five seconds — and I will fill your asses with shot.” He pulled a gun from his rope belt. It was clean, shiny and menacing. From far off, a ship’s horn sounded.

Koding said quietly, firmly, “If you want to go up for murder...”

The Captain was jarred briefly, then he brought the Glock 17 straight up, on Koding. “I told you yesterday...you don’t hear good...I’m thinking about spilling your guts right now...here on the pavement.”

Dave cut in, “I don’t know what this is all about. I came here to interview one of the great captains of the Far East...pictures...everything.”

The Captain thought that over, then anger swelled into rage. “You are out to get me along with this sewer hole. But Allah tells me, kill the infidels.” His voice rose. “Kill the infidels! Allah has spoken.”

His finger was slowly pulling the trip hammer.

A woman’s scream petrified him.

“Hold it!” Felicia cried. She pushed her way roughly through the Singers and past Dave and Koding. Dave shouted, “No! No!”

She came to a standstill about ten feet away. The Captain stared down at her in amazement, baffled, as if he were looking at an alien. She had stripped herself of all jewelry, loosened her hair until it cascaded below her shoulders and covered part of her face. She had a gun.

She said, "One shot out of you and I'll kill you. You may kill me — but I will bring you down with me."

Slowly his hand dropped. "Who are you?" he roared. "What do you want?"

Dave was yelling, "Get out of here. You're committing suicide."

She resumed a normal voice. "Shut up and listen to me."

The Captain stared in disbelief. A female? With a gun? Challenging him? He could not kill a woman. Even if she were an infidel.

She continued in a steady tone, "I am your friend. A friend from out of nowhere...and you are going to need a friend. You are the captain of a ship that may or may not have sunk...that may have been blown up."

No one scarcely breathed, shocked by this sudden, bizarre turn of events.

Her voice never quivered. It was threatening without seeming so. "I represent Lloyd's of London, the great insurance company that has many detectives working this case. You are in dreadful danger, Captain, but I have a way out for you. Go home...and tonight send me an anonymous note to the Tanjung Aru Hotel. Tell me what took place. Do not identify yourself."

This was not the woman who had approached Dave in the hotel, blithely offering information for sale. This was not the woman dressed seductively for the nightclub. This was not the woman who seemingly had an arsenal. This was not the woman of a few minutes ago who looked so utterly feminine in a yellow billowing skirt.

She said, "If you are not arrested, you have lost nothing. If you are, you can deny everything — and I will deny receiving information from you...and I will stand up for you and plead for you with Lloyd's. Tell me everything and you will have a friend in court."

She slipped the weapon back into a skirt pocket. After a long tense moment, the Captain turned and walked slowly toward a ship in dock. Koding wanted to follow but Dave held him back. "There's always tomorrow," he said quietly.

Chapter 34

They sat in the hotel's Kenanga Lounge, the air warm and soft, with strange exotic music wafting their way, marked by a heavy, sensual drum beat and discordant string notes from an instrument neither knew. In the distance a fireball sun was slowly setting, painting a golden glow over the waters of the South China Sea. Out there were little islands of coral reef and iridescent fish of many hues and sizes, islands that KK had turned into national parks, with such names as Gaya and Sulung.

The deep down fury that had burned Dave's insides in the hours following the standoff were now only coals. He had ordered her to the rear for her own safety. She had placed them all in danger. They could have been wiped out.

She had sensed his anger. She, too, had fallen silent. No doubt, she thought, with her own fury.

Now he was under control, and after they ordered a piña colada, he said, "You could have been killed."

With effort, she smiled. "He was bluffing. He wouldn't have shot me before six witnesses."

"And you?"

She sucked on the coconut sliver that came with the drink. "The same."

"You were bluffing?"

"I wouldn't kill any living thing."

"You expect him to write a confession?"

Her voice tensed in her conviction. "He will have a compulsion to do something. His kind reacts. He can't just sit."

She took the tiny umbrella that came with the drink and placed it in her hair. Despite the ordeal, he thought she never looked lovelier, more alluring.

She put her drink down without a tremble, rose to full height. "Good night, Mr. Anderson."

She sounded more hurt than angry.

She walked away, her footsteps never faltering.

Back in his room, he paced about, troubled by his treatment of her. To get the problem out of his system, he wrote in the diary: "I don't think I'm a male chauvinist but then we're often not what we think we are. I've been around some that were domineering and uncaring, but most were thoughtless and never looked outside of themselves. You can't truly love someone unless that love reasons as well as soars."

They were about to leave for dinner — it was going on nine o'clock — when a small, scrawny boy scampered up in the lobby with a message, shoved it into her hands, and disappeared.

The note was typed on a white sheet of paper. Perfectly typed, with no mistakes. She read it slowly, her lips tightening.

> Miss Yee:
>
> You are one damn, brazen, gutsy bitch. But next time know what you are doing before you show off with a gun. I was fired as captain in Zamboanga before the Mintoro sailed for the South China Sea. Me and eight others. By the ship's owner, Mrs. David Anderson. Last time I heard she was up the river out of Kuching. Talk with her. But be careful. She is one mean slut.
>
> Aka Karum
> Captain

Without comment, she passed it to Dave. Before he finished, she asked, "Mrs. David Anderson?"

"Mac's wife. She's been using my name."

"You knew it?"

"Yeah."

He continued, "They paid him $30,000? For what? Payment to the crew so they'd keep their mouths shut? He's lying about being fired."

He scanned the note again. "He's trying to squirm out of it. He's establishing an alibi with us — with you since you represent Lloyd's. He wants us to go after Heather Dunleavy."

During dinner they decided they would leave for Kuching an hour plus by air the next day. They would set out from there, up the Sarawak River into jungle country. They could not conjecture why Heather Dunleavy would be hiding — if she were hiding — in such wild, rugged terrain of thick, matted growth, swamps, snakes, gibbon apes and other animals — and onetime headhunters.

It could be, of course, that the Captain had fabricated her whereabouts.

Chapter 35

The next morning Doesunmat was waiting for them in the lobby. His happy self had disappeared. He was all business. "You talk in car. I no listen. I no want hear but I hear. You want know about sinking big ship?"

Dave shot him a puzzled glance. "Yes?"

"I know man who saw crew after ship go down. I no know how much he know but I take you and you talk."

"Where?" Felicia asked.

"Not far. Live on beach. Go up, down. Every day. Find what people throw away. Food, small money. You call him —"

"Scavenger." Felicia volunteered.

"No say. Word too hard."

They returned to their rooms for a change into old clothes. When Dave came for her a few minutes later, she asked him in. She took the 9mm Smith and Wesson from her purse and handed it to him.

"I'd feel better if you carried it."

He took a deep breath. He found it difficult to apologize for his reprimand of her for disobeying him the afternoon before. "You had the Captain pegged right. He was bluffing."

"Sometimes I guess right." She was making it easy for him.

He pushed the weapon inside his trouser belt, on the left side, covered by the jacket.

On the way out she said, "That wasn't much of an apology — but in time I think I can whip you into shape."

"Why you little...!"

She put a hand over his mouth. "It may take longer than I thought."

Suddenly, all was right with his world.

Doesunmat drove them two miles down the highway and then turned off on a sandy trail that ended at the South China Sea. "Walk little. Not far. You take off shoes?"

Felicia removed her high heels which sank in the sand with each step. She was wearing no hose. A few hundred yards away, along the beach, they came to a shack. The roof was rusty sheet metal wired to four poles and covered with palm fronds. At the sound of voices, a wizened man of not more than five feet emerged. He was little more than a skeleton with wispy, white hair, sunken suspicious eyes, trousers out at the knees, and a ripped sweatshirt. He was barefooted and bearded.

Doesunmat introduced them, translating from Bahasa Malay to English. The creature — he struck Dave as sub-human, what hominid man was like in ages past — neither nodded nor spoke.

Doesunmat continued talking. After a few minutes, Doesunmat said to them, "Want money. I say no money."

"How much?" Dave asked.

"Ten Malaysian dollars." That would be about $4 US.

Doesunmat added, "Not sure what he know. Maybe not much."

Dave nodded. "Okay." He produced $10 M.

The $10 M was a wind-up key on a toy. The creature turned human. He talked and gestured. Doesunmat had difficulty keeping up with the translation. The gist was that the little man was sleeping one night when awakened by many voices. He saw some distance away — he indicated about where on the coast line — many men — which he narrowed down under questioning to between eight and twelve — get off a high-powered speedboat that had anchored some yards off the beach.

It was a dark night and they had torches (flashlights). They gathered on the beach and a fair-skinned foreigner talked briefly in a foreign language which an older man interpreted. Each would receive $500 M every month provided no one talked about the sinking of the Mintoro. If anyone talked, the payments would stop. Everyone agreed by holding up his hand. They then disappeared into the night, all except the foreigner who returned to the speedboat. He was the skipper. He revved up the engines and took off.

Dave's attention was diverted by a flash in the distance, back the way they had come. A cardboard cut-out of a person stood there, too far away for Dave to discern the sex. Another brief flash, the sun on a reflector of some kind. Probably the cut-out was using binoculars. Dave saw no car. Perhaps the party had come on a motorcycle.

Dave turned back. Felicia was asking questions. He joined her. What kind of foreigner was he? Australian, the little man thought. He spoke English? Maybe, not sure. Never heard English. That is what we are speaking. Did he sound the same? Maybe, not sure. Was he a big, strapping man, more than six feet, with a booming voice? Yes, yes, big man, giant. Could he have been an American? Maybe, not sure. Never met an American. Dave said he was an American. Did he look and sound like me? Maybe, not sure.

Nighttime. Very dark.

Did he see name of speedboat? No, dark. How big was the boat. Very big.

And then one month later, maybe three months, maybe five or six, he could not be certain, he kept no calendar, one day same as next, he hears voices again, and there is the speedboat, and two men and the same skipper are loading a box shaped like a casket, a heavy box because there is much grunting and groaning. They get it on deck, then the skipper pays the men who leave, head toward the hotel, and the skipper takes off.

They exhausted their questions. The little man said he would think and would recall more if they wished to return. "Now tell truth," Doesunmat said. "One more $10 help memory much. He tell color eyes."

Later, Felicia and Dave agreed that the skipper of the speedboat could have been Mac Dunleavy. They had no idea what was in the box that the three had loaded onboard.

They had two more hours before they would board the plane for Kuching. Dave put in a call to Grantham hospital in Aberdeen and Ming Toy came on. She was her old, effervescent self. The happy sound of her upbeat voice lifted his spirits.

"Mister David!" she screamed with joy.

He asked how she was, and she said she would be returning home — to her mother's sampan — tomorrow. "But no can work," she said sadly. "Lose much money. You not mad, Mister David?"

He assured her he was not. She must take good care of herself, not return to work too soon.

"Lose much money," she repeated. "Ming Toy no forget. Work two days before trouble. Pay you soon. Miss you, Mister David. No happy, no see you. Come soon?"

"In a few days," he assured her. "I miss you, too, Ming Toy. You are the happy part of my life."

"When go to work, do no good. Like promise. Do no more good."

She continued, "I no talk, Mister David. Mum no talk. Wait for you. I no take money, Mister Mac gave me. I no work for money. You take all. I love you, Mister David."

When he hung up, he sat a short spell. How much money had she hidden for Mac? And where?

Probably Mac intended for her to keep it all. Mac was generous. Dave remembered once, when Mac read a news story about a teenage girl who would die before the week was over if she didn't have an operation. He had drained his checking account.

While Felicia packed, he sat in the bar with a beer, deep in thought. The old Pygmalion idea haunted and challenged him. In Los Angeles, he would hire a tutor to teach Ming Toy and her mother English. He would look up an old girlfriend from his university days who would show Ming Toy how to dress and walk and the niceties that an aging and anemic civilization demanded. And then there would be classes in all kinds of subjects. As for her mother, she should fit in well with others who had fled Hong Kong for the Los Angeles satellite town of Monterey Park.

He could visualize Ming Toy now, standing straight and slender, speaking English in that soft, alluring voice, saying the right things at one of his parties.

Marry her? Of course not. Although she would be loving and understanding and compassionate to the end of her days, and he would revel in having her call him in that low, enchanting voice, "Mister David." She would make someone a wonderful wife.

Well, why not him? No, he didn't think so. But then...

Felicia surprised him. "What are you looking guilty about?"

He was so shocked that he could think of no retort.

Chapter 36

In KK's open-air airport, Felicia and Dave still had a half hour to wait for the plane to Kuching. They were conscious that most likely they were under surveillance by several "trackers": One from the Triads, or possibly two, another from Barney and his Golden Triangle bank, and one or more from Mac Dunleavy's Great Asian Trading Company. It mattered not whether Mac Dunleavy was alive. If not, someone in the company would be protecting the millions.

Felicia thought it probable that Lloyd's also might have a "spotter" following her and Dave, as a precaution that neither would betray Lloyd's.

They talked softly, comparing notes about the passengers they guessed might be their "shadows." There was the attractive tall woman in her twenties, beautifully dressed and coiffed, possibly English, who appeared directly behind Dave when he checked the bags in. While he talked with the airline clerk, she surreptitiously read the tags on the luggage.

And then there was the little old Chinese lady with the frayed bag, a peasant in appearance, who shuffled along after them, shoes too tight. Once they moved to another part of the waiting area and she followed.

Finally, there was the Muslim woman in the long full, drab skirt popular with women of her faith in this part of the world, with a turban-like headdress and a shawl concealing the lower part of her face. Perhaps it was her intense, dark, fierce eyes that drew Dave to her.

The eyes were those of Heather Dunleavy. He could swear they were, yet he had only the briefest glance.

Instantly he was on his feet, advancing towards her, thinking that if he could hear her voice he would know for certain. She was too quick. She melted into a mob of passengers.

A short time later, Felicia saw the woman entering a restroom and started that way. Dave grabbed Felicia's arm. "Don't," he said. "You don't want to be alone with her."

In Kuching, a compact, picturesque town of 300,000, once a pirate lair, they checked into a Holiday Inn of a breed seldom found in the States. The floor was of marble, and enormous bouquets, including orchids, added to the glamour of the reception quarters. Outside flowed the Sarawak River, in the direction of one of the world's oldest rain forests, 150 million years, give a few million one way or another. Back there tribal peoples still foraged for food in dense jungles populated with insects, birds, and animals that could trace their genealogy thousands of years. In the interior, too, were Deer Cave, 93 miles long, and the Sarawak Chamber, the largest cave in the world, that could hold four or five football stadiums.

Back there, also, hidden away in the jungle, were the longhouses, the original condominiums, a string of apartments built high on stilts, that might run for a mile or so, with a common "boardwalk" of bamboo in front of the homes. A hundred families, more or less, were bound together. In the old days, they had been headhunters, and most still had a Skull house where they showed off skulls collected as recently as a half century ago. Sometimes, it seemed, with pride. They were Christians today, they told you, or Muslims or Buddhists but on Gawai Dayak festival day (June 1st), many turned out to worship their old god, Betara. Today they worked as farmers, weavers, hunters, fishermen, and on plantations, and some traveled miles into Kuching where they were taxi drivers, even accountants, teachers, and solicitors. But a longhouse was still home to most of them. "Who will take care of me when I am old and sick?"

By the time they checked in, night had come. They had dinner in the Orchid Garden Room. Outside, native long boats, looking somewhat like the craft college crews use for sculling, glided by on the Sarawak River, some with sheet iron roofs. Their occupants could scarcely be made out, a fisherman, a family with two boys, a grandmother who handled the oars as well as any man. On the river's edge stood a great fan that nature had sculpted from a palm tree, and nearby were azaleas and camellias in bloom.

They planned the next day. They would put subterfuges aside. They would state that they were old friends of the Dunleavys, that they just happened to be here and heard that they were, too. It would mean so much to see them again and reminisce.

They would "cover" all of the hotels, the tourist places, the city offices. They debated whether to call on the solicitor, Joseph Z. Kurup, who had authorized the payment of $30,000 to Captain Aka Harum. Felicia thought they would be tipping their hand. Dave pointed out that the solicitor would know they were in Kuching to find the Dunleavys. "He may say something, give himself away, that could be valuable to us. If you get someone to talking..."

They were working together in harmony. She recognized this was his field. He had had experience in questioning people and interpreting what they said, even when they were lying. Through their proximity they had developed a fondness for the other that was building into a sexual longing.

She said unexpectedly, "Please don't look at me that way."

He was jolted. "What d'ya mean?"

She smiled. She could do more with a smile than anyone he had ever known. She said, "We have our differences...but I feel about you the way you feel about me. We've got to break it off."

"What are you trying to tell me?" he asked, knowing perfectly well what she was saying. But he was on the defensive. Those blasted dark glasses. He inevitably blamed his problems on them.

She said softly, "I want to marry my Clark Gable and have two boys and two girls — and I want them all Chinese. They can't be half-Chinese and half-Caucasian. My people would not accept them and neither would yours. They would be flotsam floating around in a bitter, unhappy world."

He raised his voice slightly. "You sound like a racist. You don't know what you're talking about — not about America. We —"

She hushed him. "I lived in your country for two years and I was treated with respect. I was one of you. But I wasn't half one thing and half another."

"You're crazy," he retorted. "At one time, yes, years ago, but not now."

He shook his head, then relaxed and slumped in the chair. "I don't know what we're talking about."

"You're a liar, Mr. David Anderson. All I'm saying is let's take it easy."

He rose, pushing the chair back with sound effects. "You're the most aggravating, frustrating woman I've ever met."

He stalked off, only to discover he was headed in the wrong direction, then shaking himself, found the right turn. In his room, he sat a long time thinking, brooding. Could you love a girl and at the same time, have doubts, nagging doubts that you try to shut out, not think about, but they keep charging in and out. They could drive him up against the wall, to use one of his mother's expressions.

He was the first down for breakfast. When she came a few minutes later, he said, "Mac's alive. And he's around here somewhere. Or was."

He handed her a copy of the *Sarawak Tribune* and pointed out a news story. She read:

> The Board of Trustees of the Land Dayak Children's Fund has announced that an American visitor to Kuching, who wishes to remain anonymous, has contributed $50,000 M ($20,000 US)...

She read on, another four paragraphs.

"But there's no name."

He interrupted. "You have to know Mac. He was always giving money to help kids. He gave $5,000 US to a fund I set up in memory of my fiancée. Do you know what this means to me?"

They agreed that their first call of the day would be at the Fund's office. An enthusiastic young Malay woman met them. She was sorry, she said, but she couldn't give out any information about the American contributor. Dave pleaded that he was a close friend of Mac Dunleavy. She was courteous but unbending. "We gave him our solemn word," she said.

Under questioning, she revealed that the Land Dayaks lived in the longhouses and the Sea Dayaks in homes on stilts along rivers. Had their contributor visited the Land Dayaks? She could not answer that. When did he visit Kuching? Was he in Kuching now? She did give away the fact that he had written a check two weeks ago for the full amount. Was he in Kuching at that time? She really could not answer that. But from her hesitancy, they surmised that he had been.

They thanked her and left. "What did we get out of that?" Dave asked himself as much as Felicia. "That Mac was interested in the Land Dayak children, and he had to visit the longhouses to get excited about their welfare to the extent of giving $50,000 M...that he had been in Kuching about two weeks ago...that he had written a check for the full amount which many people could or would not do...that the Malay woman liked and admired him personally, which fit in with Mac's profile."

They showed photos of Heather and Mac around at several hotels, and then at the Ferritel on the Kuching by-pass, just out of the city, a clerk recognized Mac. He had spent two nights, exactly one week ago, in one of the chalets. His signature was a scramble and the hotel had registered him as M.D. Levy. He had talked at length with the clerk about taking a pack trip to the Sarawak Chamber Cave. To do so, the clerk said, he would need a permit from the National Parks office.

At that office, a pleasant, middle-aged man searched the records to find that a permit had been issued to one Mac Levy for a trip beginning six days before. The applicant gave his age as 37, his height six feet two, his weight 180 and his eyes, blue. The description matched that of the Mac Dave had known. The clerk telephoned the park office at the Chamber Cave. No Mac Levy had signed in yet.

Their final call was at the office of Joseph Z. Kurup. The bright-eyed, anxious-to-please young secretary said, "Mr. Kurup is expecting you," which floored the two, and showed them into an inner office that was inundated with paper work. Books, magazines, and legal documents carpeted the floor, and stood in crazy stacks on a desk and table. They covered every inch of space. Out of this horrendous mass rose an equally horrendous man in his seventies and dressed in accordance with his surroundings. His papier-mache face was wrinkled but artistically so, as an artist might have painted him.

He was gracious in the manner of an old southern senator in the States, of another era. "Welcome to Kuching." He scooped up papers from two tattered sofa chairs. "I thought you might come. Mac and I had a long talk about you some months ago before his unfortunate death. He was most fond of you, Mr. Anderson." He turned to Felicia. "Did the lady know Mr. Dunleavy?" No, she did not, and she offered to step out if the two wished to discuss a matter in private.

"Why, my dear, of course not," the solicitor said. "We have no secrets and I welcome the presence of a beautiful lady."

Dave pretended ignorance. "I had hoped to find Mac here in Kuching and in good health."

"No, no. Most appalling. I had talked with him in this very office only two weeks before he took ill in some miserable village south of Canton and died the next day. May God rest his soul."

Dave questioned him about Mac's death but Mr. Kurup knew no more than Dave did, or so he said.

"Who is running the company now?" Dave asked.

"His widow wanted to but we told her to stuff the job, as Mac asked us to do. He sat in that very chair you are in, Miss Felicia, and we discussed how we would handle the situation if he should die suddenly. I think the dear boy had a premonition."

"So his widow didn't take over. Might I ask who did?"

"I felt badly that we had to ship her out but she was one of these broads, the way Mac told it, who was good in bed but a hellcat out. Pardon my language, please, Miss Felicia, but we solicitors see so much of life that we don't always use polite conversation."

He asked about Ming Toy, and Dave told him she missed Mac, and let it go at that.

"Nasty thing, that ship sinking, and Mac had worked so hard."

Dave quizzed him diplomatically about the Mintoro but if he knew any details he was not about to recall them.

Dave returned to Mac's death. "Did he leave everything to his widow?"

"Nothing. Not a farthing. Mac said she had stolen a fairly large sum and that was her inheritance. She came around here weeping and I gave her a couple thousand to get her out of town. A dreadful woman. She tried to proposition me and I informed her in terms that I cannot repeat, Miss Felicia, and warned her if she ever tried that again I would have her arrested."

He saw them to the door. "Thank you for coming around. It is like Mac was here again. He was truly one of God's noble creatures."

He added in an aside to Dave, "Be careful. We have many enemies."

Once outside Dave said, "He's a liar but he does it with such elan."

"I've known people like that." She kept a straight face.

He bopped her with a newspaper.

That evening they had dinner at the hawker stands in the Rex Cinema Centre. They sampled sweet-and-sour fish, sea cucumbers, shark's fin, jungle ferns, shrimp paste and chili on wafers, bird's nest soup (scraped from a nearby cave) and jungle rice. She was delighted, a happy gourmet overwhelmed by new delicacies.

He acted the slob. "I'm a McDonald's man."

Shortly after returning to the hotel, a bellman summoned Dave to a small room off the lobby and pointed to a microphone on a desk. "You have a radio communication coming through," he said, and then into the mike, "The party is standing by." In the background Dave heard the Mas orchestra playing softly for a dancing crowd in the Melati ballroom.

A girl's gentle voice came over the loudspeaker that constantly crackled.

"Mr. David Anderson?"

"Yes."

"I am calling for a person who refused to give you information. They have thought it over..."

There was a long pause. She had been speaking as though reading.

"I'm still here," he said.

"The party says that you will find answers to all of your questions at a longhouse up the river. A Dayak guide will call for you and your friend at the dock at 10 a.m. You will not be in any danger and will find the trip rewarding."

She went off the air quickly.

They sat on the Sarawak River bank debating what to do. It was an idyllic night, made for lovers, a half moon casting a ghostly light on a river running quietly, with an occasional long boat gliding past, trees and homes on the other side, distant conversation a pleasant murmur, a jungle bird far off sobbing. And in the distance, high up, was Fort Margherita wavering in the faint light, calling up memories of the White Rajahs, the English Brooke family who had ruled this land for a century, an incredible tale told and re-told by those who loved adventure. It started with "once upon a time," as all old stories begin, when in 1839 James Brooke, an officer with the East India Company landed in Borneo to learn that the Sultan of Brunei, Pengiran Mahkota, was under siege by the Bidayuh tribe. Brooke organized an army that defeated the Bidayuh, and as a reward the Sultan gave him the territory of Sarawak. Brooke established a government and one Brooke family after another ruled the country until the Japanese invaded in 1941.

The Brookes were diplomats. Instead of forbidding headhunting, they offered sizable bonuses each year to tribes that had not collected a single skull. Charles Brooke, who ruled for 49 years, built Fort Margherita which was never attacked until the Japanese tried to bomb it in World War II — and missed.

They sat so close they could hear each other's heart beat. He put his arm firmly about her but just as firmly she removed it. "Not now."

She thought Heather Dunleavy was waiting at the Longhouse to enlist their help in getting the money she thought she deserved. She might have information about where millions had been redeposited or cached.

Dave said, "I've got a strong feeling it's Mac. He wants to see me, make a deal, call up old memories by way of breaking me down."

She had strong doubts. Why would he expose himself, if he were still alive, and she didn't think he was. "Why would the solicitor lie? What purpose would he have?"

Simultaneously they both had the same thought. Barney, Khun Sa's PR man. Could he be setting a trap? But again, what would be the purpose? If she and Dave had located the money or had come across vital information, then Barney would make his move.

At length they discussed the possible danger of making the trip up the Sarawak. They could think of none. The longhouses were peaceful communities with virtually no crime. The two were drawn by an overwhelming compulsion to meet and talk with the party who had invited them. They went over all of their contacts that day but failed to pinpoint one who had openly refused to talk freely.

Still, Felicia, more than Dave, insisted on discussing with the Kuching police early the next day the danger factor, and moreover, they would hire at least two armed men from a detective agency to accompany them, along with the Dayak guide.

Chapter 37

Slowly, about half way through their talk on the river bank, Dave became conscious that Felicia was more subdued than usual, not at all herself. She was nervous, lighting one cigarette after another, even halting in her speech. They still sat so close he could feel the tremors running through her body.

"You all right?" he asked.

"No."

For a moment he was jolted. He started to ask what the problem was but she was ahead of him. She was breathing hard and the words were none too stable. "I have something to tell you. I have deceived you — and I'm sorry. Dreadfully sorry."

She pulled away as if she had no right to be near him. "I've wanted to tell you ever since you arrived from Hong Kong. But I couldn't. I don't think I can now. But I will try. I haven't slept. But I must get it out. Could we walk? I don't want to see your face."

She rose and he followed. "I don't care what it is," he said softly.

She continued, "I picked up a Hong Kong paper at the newsstand this morning, and there was this article on the front page. About the Hong Kong police arresting the killer of my employer. A member of the same Triad. The paper said the assassin had fired three shots into his head at close range. It said the murderer had killed him since my boss had ripped him off, out of a quarter million dollars. I believe it because my boss was a vicious man. You cannot know — unless you knew him — and I did — how evil he was."

Dave said quietly, "I thought you might have —"

"Never. I wanted to. Many times. But I would never bring such shame on my mother. I would never violate my faith."

She leaned against a palm tree, her focus on the river. "When my mother and I came back from Los Angeles, I wanted to continue with my studies and I needed a job badly but I couldn't find one. At first, Mother couldn't get work either and we were desperate. This man..." She said the word with utter contempt. "— offered me twice what was being paid, to work afternoons for his construction company. I had sworn I would never work for him. I knew what to expect. I was not naive."

"He abused you?" Dave asked, uncertain where the conversation was going.

"He never touched me. But you don't have to beat up someone to hurt them terribly. Verbal abuse can be as bad as physical. Maybe worse because it begins to rot your feelings, rot away at all that is fine and good. Very slowly, yes, slowly, you begin to poison yourself, to want revenge, to get even."

Her mouth was dry. She was finding it ever harder to talk. "I knew what he would do but I — we were desperate. So I took the abuse. Every afternoon. He would scream at me, call me horrible names. 'You damn whore...How many men are you sleeping with...You're going to get Aids...Do you use condoms?...How many abortions have you had?...You are nothing but a stupid little bitch...You're screwing everything around here.'

"And worse, he called me names I can't repeat. He accused me of doing things I can't repeat. Day after day. And it gets to you. And you get to thinking, I will fix him. I will make him suffer."

She paused a second, as if remembering exactly what transpired. "He was a power in a corrupt Triad, although no one ever heard of him. He was the one who mapped everything out. The strategist. He never showed up anywhere in person."

She started walking again. "I shouldn't have done it. But it came very gradually. Your hatred grows and grows and as I said, it poisons you. His office was directly behind mine. I sat at a little desk in the reception room. The wall was thin and I heard everything he said. I couldn't help it. He screamed and yelled at everyone. I knew what was going on, and my fantasies on sleepless nights gradually became realities. I would get even. I would fix him. I would let his victims know what was coming, what the Triad was going to do to them. I rang up several anonymously. You were my first paid client. I didn't intend to ask for money in the beginning. I talked myself into justifying what I was doing by selling information. But I was afraid someone from the Triad would recognize me. So I fixed my hair differently and wore these dark glasses..."

She removed them but it was too dark for Dave to see more than that her eyes were large and a little slanted.

She continued, "And I put a scar on my face with make-up."

She rubbed her cheek but the scar remained.

"In time I found I was cleansing my soul. I was getting revenge but it was a game and the hatred was not as intense.

"You wondered where I was getting the weapons. There was a third room, one behind his, and it was an arsenal. The Triads were always coming and going, taking out guns and returning them. No one kept records. I could have outfitted a hundred."

She barely whispered. "I fell in love with you that very first day. I have loved you ever since. I only wish I was an American girl and could ask you to marry me, which I understand girls in your country do now. But my mother wants grandchildren — and I will give her grandchildren. Chinese grandchildren."

He started to protest. She shushed him. "I haven't finished. You may understand better — and I want your forgiveness and understanding — when I tell you I lived with this man..."

Again, the utter contempt at mention of "this man." "— for twenty-eight years...and for twenty-eight years he made life hell for me and my mother, to the point where once I thought she was going insane.

"This man..." She hesitated as if hating to say it. "— was my father. Technically, my father...I told you and everyone, he was dead — and he was for me...and forever more, as in the past, he will be only a stranger whom I hated and despised and whom I was glad to see taken from this world...and I will go to my Buddhist temple when I get home and ask for forgiveness and try in some way to repent and forget him."

She added quickly, "We'd better get back to the hotel. It's getting late. But I wanted you to know before tomorrow...because none of us ever knows what may happen tomorrow."

"I'm glad you told me," he said, "and I understand — but there is nothing to forgive — only to forget."

Chapter 38

The day was overcast and a dark cloud mass loomed coastward. The waitress said a storm was coming in. Any other time Dave would have been depressed. He was a sun worshipper.

Today was different. He had difficulty taking his eyes from Felicia. Without dark glasses and the scar, she had the classic features of a Chinese lady from out of an old dynasty painting, a piece of fine sculpture. She had her hair pulled tightly back, pushing into bas relief a gentle-featured face.

She was ill at ease and he wanted to remedy that. "I feel as if I were with a different girl."

"For better or worse?"

"It couldn't be better. And now I know everything you're thinking."

"Not everything." She was back to teasing and whether the cloud coming in overhead would pass or not, her cloud would.

They hurried with breakfast, then they took the long way around to the Central Police station. They passed the General Post Office with its Corinthian columns, the work of some admirer of ancient Greece, and the Square Tower, a onetime fort and later a dance hall.

The police desk officer allayed their fears. "Check in with the Headman before you go anywhere. Tell him what the situation is. He'll take care of you. They are good people — since they quit collecting skulls." He laughed uproariously at his little joke.

"Not much different," Dave said, "from our American Indians collecting scalps."

Even the motivational factor was similar. No Dayak girl in "olden times" wanted to marry a young man who did not give her at least one skull. As the men grew older, they took pride in the number of skulls they had lined up in their homes, to show what macho males they were.

At the dock, the Dayak guide was waiting with a modern motorboat that looked insignificant alongside several ships that were carrying teakwood, sago flour, jungle rubber, cotton, coffee, sugar, tobacco, and spices (cinnamon, cloves, nutmeg).

The guide was young, tall and good-looking with jet black hair cut short and a wispy mustache. He was in a white shirt and dark blue trousers. He offered a smile and a handshake. He brought with him the comfortable feeling of being the next-door neighbor, not at all what they had expected.

Dave bore in with a question. "Where are we going and whom are we going to see?"

The guide didn't know. He took tourists two or three times a week to this Longhouse. He had had a telephone call the day before from a Kuching businessman who would pay for the trip.

"We want to see the Headman before we go anywhere," Dave said.

That was all right with the guide.

They had to wait a few minutes for a "couple of their friends" to show up. The Dayak may have been surprised that two more were coming but he merely shrugged. They sat in the open boat, sweltering. The storm clouds had dissipated. The heat was intense, the humidity devastating. Their clothes were drenched.

The "friends" arrived. They were two well-built Malays who could have played defense on any football team. Dave had requested Malays from the detective agency rather than native people. One Dayak was enough.

The guide started the motor with one spin and headed for midstream. Across the way was a jungle of trees lining the shore and Fort Margherita, now a police museum, rose impressively.

The scenery was as peaceful and varied as the people. This was a land of Malays, Chinese, Ibans, Bedayuhs, Milanaus, Kayans and Kenyahs. A land of Muslims, Buddhists, Christians and what some would call pagan gods. Somehow 23 ethnic groups lived in peace and respected how others dressed, worshipped, and thought.

They passed houses on stilts sitting on the water's edge, jungles of palm trees and mangroves, and then open stretches of high grasses or crops. The guide spotted a long-tailed macaque, a monitor lizard, a hornbill, a covey of probosis monkeys, a small rhinoceros, and a wildcat lapping up a drink. He talked of crocodiles and wild boars. They saw turtles and falcons and what he said were "barking deer" and "honey bears." There were the "gliding and flying things," bats and butterflies.

If they had been adventuresome tourists, they would have been thrilled. But they were not. They were walking into the unknown. They were concentrating on potential dangers and surprises, and setting up defenses and mapping possible offensive strategy. They were at a decided disadvantage. The enemy could choose the location and the timing for attack. They had no choice. The enemy could retreat or advance, but they could not plot exactly how to counter such moves.

By now, he wondered if they should have come, if this were a foolhardy mistake. Probably Felicia was thinking the same, although she was of tough mettle. Beautifully adorned mettle, he must say. He valued her greatly as a trusted partner whom he could count on if they were cornered.

He had hastily bought binoculars that morning and kept scanning the countryside and the river behind them. He held for minutes on a native long boat trailing them by a half mile or so, then passed the binoculars to Felicia. "The Muslim woman."

She took a long look. "There's another boat behind hers. Two men, I think."

The guide revved up the motor and slid their boat up on land over a mass of mud in a mangrove forest. He apologized for the mud which threatened to pull off their boots before they reached solid ground in a jungle of bamboo, palms, pitcher plants, wild orchids and other tropical growth. The guide hacked his way with a barbarous-looking knife through vine thickets, past enormous ferns and massive tree trunks covered with woody creepers. The trail, barely marked, was a thick, springy, wet mat of decaying plant life that smelled of death. With almost all energy sucked out of them, Felicia and Dave followed, with the Malays behind them.

Birds squawked obscenities and the bird radio sent messages far ahead. Once a six-foot-long snake went squirming across the path.

Then Dave held up a hand, and they were quiet and stood frame frozen. After a couple of minutes he signaled to continue. He thought he had heard thrashing on the trail behind them. He was certain he had.

Several hundred yards deep into this wild and thick growth which threatened, as in a horror tale, to tighten its hold and throttle all life from them, they came to the Longhouse. From ground level they could see only stilts stretching far into the jungle. Two monkeys were playing like puppies in a cleared spot. One jumped on Felicia's shoulder and she screamed.

"He's just being friendly," Dave assured her.

She tossed him toward Dave and the monkey landed on Dave's head. "He's more your type," she said.

The "entrance stairs" consisted of a log standing upright with notches cut for steps. The guide went up in a second. Felicia tried and kept slipping back down. Dave pushed her up by her derriere which brought a stream of cutting comment. He himself made it easily.

They stepped out on a bamboo boardwalk, 12 feet or so wide, that ran for a mile in front of the "condos," all on stilts. Each "condo" occupied about 10 or 12 feet of frontal space and they were all hooked together with a common roof of woven palm thatch and common walls of bamboo or tree bark. While the homes were narrow, they ran quite deep, like a railroad boxcar.

Above some of the doorways were "holes" about a foot square where the family placed rice to ward off evil spirits. Small children were playing on the boardwalk where colorful clothes were drying. Several women were squatting around big brown pots, using pestles to grind grain. They wore dark blue dresses pulled tight above the breasts, leaving their shoulders bare. Their faces had a look different from other Asians. These were the descendants of the Mongoloid hordes that had swept this land 10,000 to 20,000 years ago. This "village" had been in this one location for at least a century, and possibly many centuries.

The guide indicated the Headman's home. Both Felicia and Dave hesitated. This could be the showdown, the end of the hunt.

The Malays waited outside while the guide, Felicia and Dave entered. "Please remove your shoes," the guide said, and they took them off, mud and all.

Inside was an office with one wall plastered with movie posters and a Coca-Cola one, with a banged up desk, a chair literally on its last legs, and a mat neatly placed on the floor. In a dark corner sat a rocking chair that was being propelled by a giant of a man. He brought his rumpled 300 pounds to a standing position. He was bare to the waist, and a hairy belly protruded over a grimy belt that held up dark, baggy trousers. He gave them a handshake that threatened to topple them. He had a smile as big as his body. He was unlike any native Dave had ever met. And that included his English. He was a graduate of John Hopkins University, as attested to by a certificate on one wall.

"I doctor everyone," he said in a voice that befitted his image. "One hundred and twenty-eight patients with three more on the way. Better than your Medicare."

He felt the need to explain his background. "I traveled the world over after graduation. I was offered jobs by clinics and hospitals in some of your big cities. Then one day I realized that the paradise I was hunting was here among my own people, near my ancestors."

He got three small glasses from a shelf in the kitchen, which was one corner of the room. He rubbed the glasses thoroughly with a ragged, dirty looking towel, then filled them from a brownish, unmarked bottle. "To your health," he said.

Felicia eyed her drink suspiciously. "Tuak," he said. "Rice wine."

The guide whispered. "Drink it — or he'll be insulted."

Felicia downed hers in one quick gulp and so did Dave.

Dave explained their situation. "No problem," the Headman said. He sent a boy who had been peeking in the door at the "aliens" to summon two of his assistants. They were built about the Headman's size.

The Dayak guide said he had been instructed to deliver Felicia and Dave to the girl at the General Store. The Headman agreed. "Very fine young lady. A tribute to all of us. Beautiful, too."

Could Dave get him some magazines and books? He would pay. Dave agreed to send a shipment complimentary.

The General Store was tiny, not more than 10 by 8. Except for an old-fashioned, weak, yellow light bulb, it would have been totally dark. It offered Cola and other soft drinks, two local beers, and a few standards, such as rice, flour, etc. The girl was about 20 with fair skin, dark inquisitive eyes, and a lovely face that would have been the envy of a Hollywood actress. She was barefoot, in a simple cotton dress, and wore a small cross on a necklace. She was shy and directed her conversation at Felicia.

She said "someone" was waiting to meet them, and led the way to a small structure with a display window. Skulls lined the shelves. "Mementos," she said.

"I must apologize," she continued, "but I have instructions that only Mr. Anderson will be admitted to the Skull House."

Felicia drew in her breath. "You're not going in by yourself," she told Dave.

The girl overheard. "No, miss. It is not that. The Longhouse has a rule. We had to take a vote. No outsider has been in the Skull House as long as I have been here."

"Who is Mr. Anderson meeting?" Felicia asked.

"I was asked not to say."

"I'm going in with you," Felicia stated flatly. Dave's thoughts flashed back to the wharf at Kota Kinabalu. She will pull a gun — and use it if necessary.

The others sensed a problem if not trouble. The two assistants conferred in the Dayak language with the young lady. They talked rapidly, gesturing wildly.

The girl turned to Felicia. "There is no danger. The Headman would permit none. I swear on the Bible." She indicated the cross at her throat. "I am a Christian."

"That does it," Dave said, and before Felicia could protest, walked to the entrance, pulled aside a drape where the door should have been, and entered.

The single room was in semi-darkness, lighted only by a light bulb similar to the one at the General Store. He saw no one.

Then the voice that he would forever remember spoke. "Hi, Gringo. It's been a long time."

Chapter 39

Mac emerged from the shadows to envelop Dave in a bear hug. "God, it's good to see you. Never thought I would...but in this crazy world..."

For a scant moment, Dave stood stunned. "I knew you were around, Mac, when I read the story in the newspaper, even though your lawyer said you were dead."

Mac reached back into the dark for a couple of handmade wooden chairs. "Let's sit. We've got a lot to catch up on. Been how long...six, seven years?"

He couldn't hold back. "Dave, I've pulled off the biggest scam in history. I've got millions...I don't even know how many...and I've got them cached away where no one will ever find them. Plenty for both of us, old friend. I'll give you a little pocket money...a million...maybe two."

They sat facing each other, a few feet apart, with the light bulb swinging slightly in a breeze that was stirring through the open windows and the draped doorway. Skulls of all sizes, from those of children to adults, were everywhere, on shelves with nametags of the owners, hanging in clusters from the ceiling. Skulls whitened with age, stained with the marks of battle, perfect ones and cracked and splintered ones, long faces and short, squatty ones. And the musty smell of Death.

"When I was a kid, I would have loved this place. I never missed a horror movie. But now, well, nobody would think to find me here. These people love me and I love them. If I have to get out in a hurry, no problem. They've got an exit out of here you wouldn't believe. I'd just vanish."

Dave shifted uneasily. "Glad you had the young lady radio me."

"Been wanting to get in touch with you since you arrived in KK but wasn't about to play target for some bloody sharpshooter. Then when my mouthpiece told me you'd been in, I said okay, get the bastard up here — and be sure to send along a bottle of Johnny Walker."

He took a deep breath. "Just like old times, right, Dave?

Remember when we used to sit around Ed's hash house and talk about the bums we'd written up that day? Remember, Dave?"

Dave remembered. "Those were the days."

They had been rough days, hard days. Only in reminiscence did they seem good. Why was it that as one ages, the yesteryears take on a shine they never actually had? Is it because we want to believe that the experiences of our youth were so much more exciting than the experiences of age? They give a glow to a life we never had but wished we had had.

Mac was saying, "I didn't expect you to bring a delegation. But then you always were the cautious one. The woman, your girlfriend?"

Dave shook his head. "She's along for the ride. Represents Lloyd's of London." He might as well get it out.

Mac laughed. "My favoritest insurance company. Well, we've got a lot to talk about but first, tell me about Ming Toy."

He was the same old Mac, gregarious, outgoing, brash. Dave couldn't tell if he had aged. His full black beard covered most of his face and his bushy hair fell to his shoulders. His voice still had deep, full volume, filled with exuberance.

Mac knew the Triad had cut her up. "The bastards!" he said. "I was going to settle with them for fifty cents on the dollar — but not now."

Dave chose his words carefully. He wanted to get across to Mac precisely what the situation was. "I'm here, Mac, because of Ming Toy. The Triads are laying off her to see what I produce in the way of money. If I don't produce, they'll lean on her."

Mac said, "Simple. Sneak back into Hong Kong and get her and her mother on a plane to Australia."

"She won't go."

"Why not? I left her a box with $100,000 in it. American cash. That'll buy a few kangaroos."

He looked around. "This is a hell of a place to meet. Next time, the Waldorf Astoria."

He returned to Ming Toy. "She's a great gal. I loved her and she loved me. I never straddled her, not that I didn't want to, but she wouldn't have understood that way of life. I should have married her instead of Heather but in spite of all our talk about everybody being equal, we don't believe it. I couldn't have introduced her as my wife in Hong Kong and done business there. She would always have been a sampan woman. What about you, you got a girl...married?"

"Nothing serious."

"Marry Ming Toy. It's different in the States. Buy her some clothes, get somebody to make her over. They'd never know she'd been a sampan woman."

Dave smiled. "What about Heather? What became of her?"

Mac turned deadly serious. "I left her to wind up our business affairs. I got you in to look after Ming Toy and tell everyone I was dead. I went up to a little fishing village in China and paid a couple of ancient ones to say I'd died there if anyone came snooping around.

"So now, I've collected the money, and I'm dead, and I'm home free — except Heather tries to blackmail me."

He got up and walked about. The same Mac. Restless as a caged bear. "Look around you. All these heads cut off...loved ones left suffering, maybe dying of hunger...children who will never have a father. What's wrong with us? It doesn't matter whether we're natives out in the jungle or popping beer before a TV set. Kill. Kill. Kill."

Dave said, "Still the rebel?"

Mac sat back down. "You got it."

"You sent me $60,000. Five was for Laurie's foundation. That leaves 55."

"Yeah, figured if something went wrong, I'd come by to pick it up. Knew you'd have it. You wouldn't put a dollar in the church box unless you could write a check and take a tax deduction."

Dave laughed. "Same old Mac. I knew you weren't dead. Neither God nor the devil would have you."

"You got it. Now...some business. Tell your lady friend the ship sank with all the cargo and Lloyd's paid off. It's all legal. All over, Fini, kaboosh."

Dave said slowly, "Lloyd's thinks someone planted explosives aboard the Mintoro, and everyone took to a boat that was waiting, and someone blew up the ship by remote control."

"Prove it."

"They wonder why your solicitor ordered the payment of $30,000 from funds on deposit in KK to the ship's captain."

Mac's silence was loud. He had no idea anyone knew about the $30,000 withdrawal. "The Captain did everything possible to save the ship. He deserved a bonus — a big one."

"He says Heather fired him at Zamboanga. He wasn't on the ship when it went down."

Mac snorted. "He's protecting his ass." He added quickly, "Whose side are you on, Dave?"

"Yours. I was repeating what I heard. I need answers to report to my boss, Alfred Kwan."

"Give him my best. Great guy. What about Khun Sa?"

"I have no special interest there."

"Or Barney?"

"None."

"That about takes care of everything. No one gets anything."

"Hold it, Mac. There's still Ming Toy. We both love her. I think we run a risk getting her out of Hong Kong that may end up in the Triads torturing and murdering her."

"Make it L.A. Not Australia. She'll get used to American ways. All except burial. I've never met a Chinese who didn't want to be buried where he was born. Tell her we'll arrange that later."

Dave leaned forward. "You've got millions, old friend, and as one Gringo to another, why don't you get these tigers off your back, the Triads..."

Suddenly the silence was broken by a woman's scream — Felicia's — the shouting of men...and the Muslim woman stood in the doorway with a gun in her hand. Mac and Dave went for their weapons, pulling them in swift moves from their belts. But it was too late. The Muslim woman aimed three deadly shots at Mac. He twisted and fought to stand up, and fired wildly, and then dropped with blood spurting forth.

Another burst of gunfire exploded. The Muslim woman moaned and slumped to the floor. Felicia's shot was dead on target, the Muslim woman's gun hand.

Chapter 40

Shortly after nine o'clock the next morning, Mac died in the Kuching hospital. Dave had stayed with him from the time the Headman at the Longhouse had administered emergency treatment, and then during the long trip down the river to the dock where an ambulance met them, and all that night.

Twice Mac had come out of a coma and talked about old stories the two had worked together on *The Times* crime beat. Felicia had waited on a bench outside the room and was there when Dave came out on brief respites. She said little but the touch of her hand on his arm told him she felt for him. Once Joseph Kurup, the solicitor, came by and asked to speak in private with Mac.

Dave suffered guilt feelings. "I knew Heather was following us but I thought we were the target. I had no idea we were leading her to Mac."

The young woman at the General Store had accompanied Heather in a long boat. When the boat put to shore, Heather was arrested on a murder charge. She was under guard somewhere in the same hospital. Neither Dave or Felicia cared about her whereabouts, and when Heather asked to talk with Dave, he refused. "Why should I? She killed in cold blood the best friend I'll ever have."

Newspaper reporters besieged them and the authorities came in. By now, everyone knew that it was Mac who had given $50,000 M to the Land Dayak Children's Fund. In death, Mac was a celebrity. The press wanted to know who Mac was, what his business was, and primarily, what was Heather's motive. As best he could, Dave sidestepped the questions.

Already shattered by Mac's death, Dave grew increasingly nervous over the passage of time. By now the Hong Kong newspapers would have the story. The Triads would be calling Alfred Kwan. Had Dave found the money — or was Mac's death the end of the trail?

Rudely, Dave pushed his way through the reporters and with Felicia by the arm, hastened down a corridor, saw a sign in English indicating hospital supplies, and slipped inside. There was no light and both knocked cans and bottles to the floor where they rolled noisily. They settled down and leaned against a wall.

"Did Mac tell you what he did with the money?" she asked.

"He was dying. I couldn't ask him. You do believe me?"

She kissed him lightly.

His voice was husky. "I think I know where the money is — but don't ask me how I know or where it is. I can't get it now. It might take weeks, months. So Ming Toy is in immediate danger."

He paused, then continued, "I did a lot of thinking while I sat with Mac. Why do we pay the Triads? They will use the money to torture and murder. Or Khun Sa. He will market more opium, ruin more lives. If we all cleared out of Hong Kong, they couldn't get to us."

"What about Lloyd's?" she asked.

"That's different. We'll pay off the judgment, if they get one."

They decided to make phone calls, she to Alfred Kwan, to brief him, and Dave to Inspector Yeung.

They were outside the hospital, waiting for a taxi to take them to the hotel when a loud voice called from across the street. "Hey, you guys," Barney yelled and half ran.

He was puffing. "I came for my bank's money."

Dave said soberly, "Mr. Dunleavy died without making any financial arrangements — with you or anyone else."

Barney was furious. "Don't give me that. Don't try to hog it all. We won't stand for it. We've got killers for hire here who would take care of each of you for $100 a head. For a bonus they will plug you today...within the next hour. I'm warning you!" He ran out of breath.

Peripherally, Dave saw Felicia's hand slip into her purse. "Hold it," he whispered.

To Barney, he said, "Take it easy, Barney. If there's no money, there's no money. You can cut us down but you still won't get a dollar. We figure we've got a good lead — and we are working on it. Give us time."

Barney simmered down — but he was still mad. "You're giving me a runaround and I'm not going to —"

Felicia had palmed the gun as she withdrew it from the purse. Dave took note. "You should talk with Joseph Kurup. He's Mac's lawyer and he's got $340,000 in cash in a Kota Kinabalu bank."

Barney shook himself, as if to cast out his anger. "What's his name? Where do I find him?"

Dave told him.

Barney noticed the sun on Felicia's 9 mm. "You wouldn't," he said in alarm. "You wouldn't."

"I would," she answered quietly. "Please get out of my way." She elbowed him as she walked past.

Later Dave was to ask, "Did you ever play basketball?"

She was mystified. "Why?"

"Only a basketball player would know that elbow move."

Their phone calls produced alarming reactions. Alfred Kwan instructed Felicia to stay out of Hong Kong for at least a few weeks. Perhaps her mother should take a vacation.

The Inspector informed Dave that he — the Inspector — would place a plan into operation that the Inspector had been considering. "It will insure the safety of Ming Toy and her mother." He refused to discuss the plan. "I will inform you as soon as we have completed the operation."

Hours later, Joseph Kurup came by to report in a casual way — so casual that it had to be an act — that a few hours before Mac died, Mac had signed a check that would clear out the $340,000 deposit at the KK bank. The check was made out to the Land Dayak Children's Fund. "With that kind of money, they can gold plate all of their skulls," Dave said.

Kurup did not think the remark amusing. "As an American, you do not understand that the Skull House still stands as a place that once was a spiritual temple."

Dave approved of the contribution. If that was what Mac wanted, then Mac should have it. It was like Mac, even dying, to think of children, even though he never had had any. If he had married Ming Toy, then there would have been children, and his life, Dave was certain, would have taken a different course. Without knowing anything about ethics, Ming Toy sensed instinctively what was right and wrong. Her goodness and compassion would have carried him into a world he had never known.

Possibly she had loved him in her shy way. She had said repeatedly, "I loved Mister Mac." Possibly it was that kind of distant love some have, a love they think cannot be reciprocated since the two are of such separate worlds.

She had said, too, "I love you, Mister David." He wondered about that, if it were expressing a great fondness or a longing. The man who married her would find himself gliding slowly down a river into a happy world that few ever knew.

He was indulging in a kind of summer-day idling of the mind when he was called to the phone. Ming Toy was on the line. She was sobbing. He could scarcely make out what she was saying.

"Take it easy," he said. "I don't understand you."

"Mean police come. Bad men. Very bad men. Say will put me in jail for do good. If leave Hong Kong, no put me in jail."

"My heavens, where are you?"

"Tokyo."

"Tokyo! How did you get there?"

"Police get tickets. Put on plane. Say no come back. Say do good in Japan."

She was crying her heart out. This minute he could have killed the Inspector. How dare he?

"Where are you? I mean, at the airport, where?"

"Yes, airport with Mum. Sitting. No know where go. Night. Many people. What to do. Mum hungry."

"Listen carefully. I have a friend in Tokyo. I will phone him. Tell me exactly where you are. Look around for signs. And stay there until he comes."

He would call World Coverage's correspondent for Japan.

He hadn't known Felicia was nearby waiting for him. She said, "You love her, don't you?"

That infuriated him. "Just because I help a poor sampan woman doesn't mean I love her."

Felicia smiled knowingly. He had to fight to hold back words he would regret.

They agreed they should leave Borneo quickly. She phoned her mother and they decided to meet in Tokyo, as Dave suggested. He would have his correspondent in Japan meet them with tickets to Los Angeles. "You can rest there and decide where you want to settle down. You've been in L.A. before and it won't be like going into a big city where you don't know your way around."

He would follow shortly. He wanted to see Mac off. Although not a Christian, the Longhouse Headman would give Mac a Christian burial in the jungle. The shy girl in the little store would offer a prayer to "my dear Jesus." A few other Christians would gather, including surprisingly the guide. Several Muslims and a Christian or two would come from the Land Dayaks Children's Fund.

He phoned Marge and awakened her. "I'm getting married, Marge," he told her.

"You wake me up at three in the morning to tell me that?"

"I'm marrying a beautiful Chinese girl."

"You know how your dog feels about sharing."

He gave her the names of the four women arriving from Tokyo and the flight time. Would she help get them settled? He would arrive the next day.

"And Marge, will you call a boat company and have them build me a sampan?"

"A what?"

"You'd better call *The Times* morgue and —"

"The morgue?"

"The photo files. Get a picture of a sampan. I want the authentic article."

“Strange wedding gift.”

“Just do it, Marge. Don’t ask questions.”

“Do I decorate it, like a cake?”

He hung up. Good old Marge. He wouldn’t know what to do without her. As his mother would say, she was a blessing.

Chapter 41

FROM THE DIARY OF DAVID ANDERSON, NOVEMBER 18TH —

I know you would like her, Laurie. She's beautiful and stunning, brilliant, independent and gutsy. She's compassionate and honest and loving. She's also one of the most infuriating women I have ever met. But I love her madly. I know we will have a great life together. I almost didn't get her. She had this hang-up about not wanting children half Chinese and half Caucasian. She thought they would have miserable lives. No one would accept them. But the world is changing, and by the time they are teenagers, I hope to God we won't have all of this racial divisiveness. Anyway, we all carry around baggage. When we are in our teens, people think we don't know anything, then when we are 70 the kids think you don't know how to manage your lives and try to do it for you. I am not sure she is convinced but if not, we can adopt two Chinese children and two anglos or make it four all around. I don't care. I keep thinking of Mac and how he loved children and I think I will, too. We all need children to keep the child in us alive. We are going to be married tomorrow in Santa Monica. I think she will become a Christian one of these days but the important thing is to have faith and believe in something beyond ourselves...As for Heather, we've never heard or read anything about her — and hope we never do — although it's inevitable that some time we will learn she has been convicted of murder in far off Kuching.

FROM A STATEMENT WRITTEN BY DAVID ANDERSON:

My darling Felicia,

I am writing this so that if anything happens to me you will know where to find the millions that Mac hid away. I will put this in our safety deposit box. You may remember that bright, sunny day when the taxi driver at Kota Kinabalu drove us out to the beach and we talked with a scavenger who told us about a night when he saw and heard between eight and 10 men leave a speedboat anchored off the